IRA LEVIN

THE BOYS FROM BRAZIL

A NOVEL

Random House / New York

This book is a work of fiction. The events
described in it are imaginary, and the
characters—with the exception of persons of note
referred to by their true names—are also
imaginary and not intended to represent specific
living persons.

To

JED LEVIN
NICHOLAS LEVIN
ADAM LEVIN

And the Memory of

CHARLES LEVIN

The author is grateful for information given him by Dr. Maurice F. Goodbody, Jr., Mr. and Mrs. Samuel Halperin, Mr. Anthony Koestler, and Mr. Edmund C. Wall.

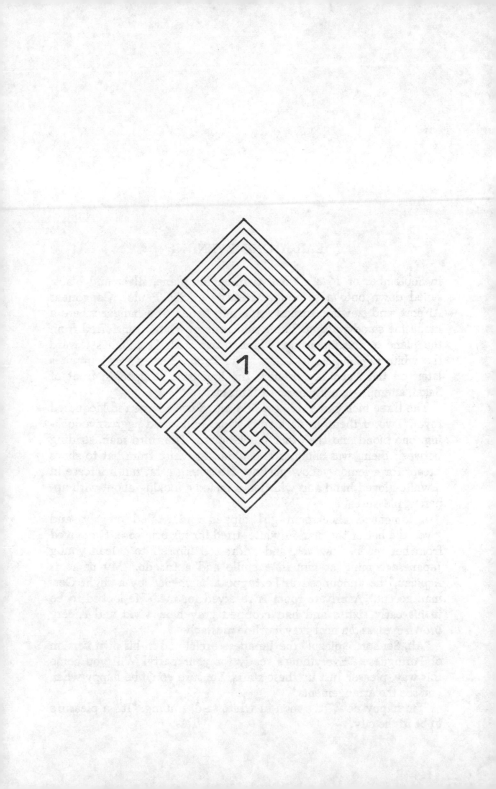

EARLY ONE EVENING

in September of 1974 a small twin-engine plane, silver and black,
sailed down onto a secondary runway at São Paulo's Congonhas
Airport, and slowing, turned aside and taxied to a hangar where a
limousine stood waiting. Three men, one in white, transferred from
the plane to the limousine, which drove from Congonhas toward
the white skyscrapers of central São Paulo. Some twenty minutes
later, on the Avenida Ipiranga, the limousine stopped in front of
Sakai, a temple-like Japanese restaurant.

The three men came side by side into Sakai's large red-lacquered
foyer. Two of them, in dark suits, were bulky and aggressive-look-
ing, one blond and the other black-haired. The third man, striding
between them, was slimmer and older, in white from hat to shoes
except for a lemon-yellow necktie. He swung a fat tan briefcase in
a white-gloved hand and whistled a melody, looking about with ap-
parent pleasure.

A kimonoed checkroom girl dipped and smiled prettily, and
given the hat of the man in white, tried for his briefcase. He moved
from her reach, however, and addressed himself to a lean young
Japanese coming at him in a smile and a tuxedo. "My name is
Aspiazu," he announced in Portuguese harshened by a slight German accent. "A private room is reserved for me." He looked to be
in his early sixties and had cropped gray hair, vivid and cheery
brown eyes, and a neat gray hairline mustache.

"Ah, Senhor Aspiazu!" the Japanese exclaimed in his own version
of Portuguese. "Everything's ready for your party! Will you come
this way, please? Just up these stairs. I'm sure you'll be happy when
you see the arrangements."

"I'm happy now," the man in white said, smiling. "It's a pleasure
to be in the city."

"You live in the country?"

The man in white, following the blond man up the stairs, nodded and sighed. "Yes," he said drily, "I live in the country." The black-haired man went after him, and the Japanese went last. "The first door on the right," he called ahead. "Will you remove your shoes before you go in, please?"

The blond man ducked to peer through an octagonal wall-opening, then braced a hand against a doorpost, raised his foot behind him, and pulled the shoe from it. The man in white put forward a white-shod foot on the hallway's carpet, and the black-haired man crouched down and unfastened a gold buckle at the side of it. The blond man, having set both his shoes aside, opened an intricately carved door and went into a pale-green room beyond. The Japanese toed himself nimbly out of pumps. "Our best room, Senhor Aspiazu," he said. "Very nice."

"I'm sure it is." The man in white pressed white-gloved fingertips against a doorpost as he watched the removal of his second shoe.

"And our Imperial Dinner for seven, with beer, not saki, and brandy and cigars after."

The blond man came to the doorway. Small white scars darned his face; one of his ears had no lobe. He nodded and stepped back. The man in white, shorter now by more than normal heel-height, went into the room. The Japanese followed him.

The room was cool and sweet-smelling, a placid oblong silk-walled in the hazy pale green of its tatami floormats. At its center, bamboo backrests with tan-and-white-patterned cushions faced three sides of a low black oblong table set with white plates and cups; three settings and backrests at each of the table's long sides and one at its right end. A shallow foot-well smaller than the table lay beneath it. At the room's right end another low black table stood against the wall, two electric burners set into its surface. The wall opposite was shoji screens of black-framed white paper. "Plenty of room for seven," the Japanese said, gesturing toward the central table. "And our best girls will be serving you. Prettiest too." He smiled and raised his eyebrows.

The man in white, pointing at the shoji screens, asked, "What's behind there?"

"Another private room, senhor."

"Is it being used tonight?"

"It hasn't been reserved, but a party might want it."

"I reserve it." The man in white gestured to the blond man to open the screens.

The Japanese looked at the blond man and at the man in white again. "It's a room for six," he said uncertainly. "Sometimes eight."

"Of course." The man in white strolled away toward the end of the room. "I'll pay for eight more dinners." He bent to study the burners in the table. His fat briefcase moved against his trouser leg.

The blond man was sliding the screens apart; the Japanese hurried to help him, or perhaps to prevent him from damaging the screens. The room beyond proved to be a mirror-image of the first room, except that its ceiling lighting panel was dark and the table beneath it was set for six, two at each side and one at each end. The man in white had turned to look; the Japanese smiled across the room at him uncomfortably. "I'll only charge you if someone asks for it," he said, "and then only the difference between what we charge downstairs and what we charge up here."

The man in white, looking surprised, said, "How nice! Thank you."

"Excuse me, please," the black-haired man said to the Japanese. He stood just within the room, his dark suit rumpled, his round swarthy face sheened with sweat. "Is there any way of closing this?" He pointed back toward the octagonal opening in the wall. His Portuguese was Brazil-accented.

"It's for the girls," the Japanese explained hopefully. "To see if you're ready for your next course."

"That's all right," the man in white told the black-haired man. "You'll be outside."

The black-haired man said, "I thought maybe he could . . ." and he shrugged apologetically.

"Everything is satisfactory," the man in white said to the Japanese. "My guests will arrive at eight o'clock and—"

"I'll show them up."

"No need; one of my men will be waiting below. And after we eat we'll have a conference here."

"You can stay till three if you like."

"No need for that either, I hope! An hour should be sufficient. And now would you bring me please a glass of Dubonnet, red, with ice and a twist of lemon peel."

"Yes, senhor." The Japanese bowed.

"And is it possible to have more light? I plan to read while I wait."

"I'm sorry, senhor, this is all there is."

"I'll manage. Thank you."

"Thank *you*, Senhor Aspiazu." The Japanese bowed again,

bowed less deeply to the blond man, bowed hardly at all to the black-haired man, and went quickly from the room.

The black-haired man closed the door, and facing it, raised his arms high, curved his fingers, and set the tips of them on top of the doorframe as if to play a key board. He moved his hands slowly apart.

The man in white went and stood with his back to the wall-opening while the blond man went to the backrest at the end of the table and crouched beside it. He pressed its tan-and-white cushions and lifted them from the bamboo frame and put them aside. He inspected the frame, turned it over to look at its bottom, and put it aside with the cushions. He felt the tatami matting all around the end of the table; with widespread hands he explored the plaited grass, gently pressing.

Getting down on his knees, he thrust his blond head in under the table and looked into the foot-well. He bent lower, turned his head, and looked up with one blue eye at the table's underside, scanning it slowly from end to end.

He backed from the table, took the bamboo frame, restored its two cushions, and placed the backrest at an accessible angle. Rising, he stood attentively behind it.

The man in white came, unbuttoning his jacket. He set his brief-case on the floor and turned and lowered himself carefully, finding the backrest's arms. He folded his legs in under the table, his feet toward the foot-well.

The blond man, bending, pushed at the backrest and squared it to the table.

"*Danke*," the man in white said.

"*Bitte*," the blond man said, and went and stood with his back against the wall-opening.

The man in white peeled at a glove, looking approvingly at the table before him. The black-haired man, arms high, side-stepped slowly across the opening between the two rooms, fingering along the top of a projecting black lintel.

A soft tapping sounded; the blond man moved to the door and the black-haired man turned, lowering his arms. The blond man listened, and opened the door to a pink-kimonoed waitress who came in with her head bowed, holding a tinkling glass and its tray. Her white-mittened feet whispered over the tatami.

"Ah!" the man in white exclaimed happily, folding his gloves. His enthusiastic expression faltered as the waitress, a flat-faced woman, crouched beside him and moved the napkin and chopsticks from his plate. "And what's your name, dear?" he asked with strained jollity.

"Tsuruko, senhor." The waitress put a paper coaster down.

"Tsuruko!" With wide eyes and pursed lips the man looked to the blond man and the black-haired man, as if marveling with them at an impressive revelation.

The waitress, having put the drink down, rose and backed away.

"Until my guests come, Tsuruko, I don't want to be disturbed."

"Yes, senhor." She turned and hurried close-kneed from the room.

The blond man closed the door and stepped back to his place before the wall-opening. The black-haired man turned and raised his hands to the lintel-top.

"Tsu, ru, ko," the man in white said, drawing his briefcase close to his side. In German he said, "If she's a pretty one what do the not-so-pretty ones look like?"

The blond man grunted a laugh.

The man in white finger-sprang the lockflap of his briefcase and opened it wide enough so that it stayed open. He tucked his folded gloves into an end of it, and leafing through the edges of papers and manila envelopes, drew from among them a thin magazine. He set it down—*Lancet*, the British medical journal—on the table beside his plate. Scanning its cover, he took from his breast pocket a frayed and faded petit-point eyeglass case, from which he drew a pair of black-framed glasses. Opening them, he put them on, pocketed the case and side-fingered his thin bristly mustache. His hands were small, pink, clean, young-looking. From inside his jacket he brought a gold cigarette case on which a lengthy handwritten inscription was engraved.

The blond man stood before the wall-opening. The black-haired man examined the walls, and the floor, and the serving table, and the backrests. He moved one of the middle table settings aside, spread his handkerchief in its place, and stepping up on it, opened with a screwdriver the chrome-bordered lighting panel.

The man in white read *Lancet*, sipping now and then at his Dubonnet, smoking a cigarette. He hissed air intently through a gap in his upper teeth. Occasionally he seemed surprised by what he read. Once he exclaimed in English, "Absolutely wrong, sir!"

The guests arrived within a period of four minutes, the first checking his hat but not his attaché case at three minutes of eight, the last at one minute after. When each made his way through waiting groups and couples to the tuxedoed Japanese, he was graciously directed to the blond man at the foot of the stairs; words were exchanged and the guest was shown upward, to the black-haired man pointing at the row of shoes beside the open door.

Six well-dressed businessmen in their middle fifties, fair-skinned, Nordic; sock-footed, they nodded politely to one another and bent to present themselves in Portuguese and Spanish to the man in white. "Ignacio Carreras, Doctor. An honor to meet you."

"Hello! How are you? I can't get up, I'm trapped here. This is José de Lima from Rio. Ignacio Carreras from Buenos Aires."

"Doctor? I'm Jorge Ramos."

"My friend! Your brother was like this right hand to me. Forgive me for sitting; I'm trapped. Ignacio Carreras from Buenos Aires, José de Lima from Rio. Jorge Ramos from right here in Paulo."

Two of the guests were old friends, happy to see each other. "In Santiago! Where have *you* been?" "In Rio!" Another introduced himself with a heel-click that failed: "Antônio Paz, Pôrto Alegre."

They lowered themselves in at the sides of the table, joking about their awkwardness, groaning; settled themselves with portfolios and attaché cases close beside; shook napkins open, named their drinks to a pretty young waitress gracefully crouching. Flat-faced Tsuruko set a steaming rolled-up washcloth before each man; the man in white and his guests scrubbed appreciatively at their hands, wiped at their mouths.

Wiping away, apparently, Portuguese and Spanish. German began to emerge; German names were exchanged.

"Ah, I know you. You served under Stangl, right? At Treblinka?"

"Did you say 'Farnbach'? My wife is a Farnbach, from Langen near Frankfurt."

The drinks were served, and small plates of appetizers—baby shrimp and balls of browned meat. The man in white demonstrated the use of chopsticks. The men who were adept gave guidance to those who weren't.

"A fork, for God's sake!"

"No, no!" the man in white laughed to the pretty young waitress. "We'll make him learn! He has to learn!"

Her name was Mori. The girl in the plain kimono, bringing plates and covered bowls to Tsuruko at the serving table, blushed and said, "Yoshiko, senhor."

The men ate and drank. They talked about an earthquake in Peru, and the new American president, Ford.

Bowls of clear soup were served, and more plates of food, fried and raw; tea was poured.

The men talked about the oil situation and its probable lessening of the West's sympathy for Israel.

More food was served—strips of cooked meat, chunks of lobster— and Japanese beer.

The men talked about Japanese women. Kleist-Carreras, a thin man with a glass eye that moved badly, told a wonderfully funny story about a friend's misadventure in a Tokyo brothel.

The tuxedoed Japanese came in and asked how everything was. "First rate!" the man in white assured him. "Excellent!" The other men agreed, in Portuguese-Spanish-German.

Melon was served. More tea.

The men talked about fishing, and different ways of cooking fish.

The man in white asked Mori to marry him; she smiled and pleaded a husband and two children.

The men climbed up from creaking backrests, stretched their arms and stood on tiptoe, patted their stomachs. A few, the man in white among them, went out into the hallway to find the men's room. The others talked about the man in white: how charming he was, and how lively and youthful for—was it sixty-three? Sixty-four?

The first group came back; the others went.

The table was clean black, set with brandy snifters, ashtrays, and a box of glass-tubed cigars. Mori went around crouching with a bottle, feeding each snifter a bottomful of dark amber. Tsuruko and Yoshiko whispered at the serving table, disagreeing about the clearing up. "Out, girls," the man in white said, going to his place. "We wish to speak in private."

Tsuruko shooed Yoshiko before her; apologized passing the man: "We'll clear up later." Mori gave the last snifter its brandy, set the bottle on the table's unoccupied end, and scurried toward the door, standing aside with her head bowed as the rest of the men came in.

The man in white lowered himself into his backrest. Farnbach-Paz helped him position it.

The black-haired man looked in at the door, counted the men, and drew the door closed.

The men lowered themselves into their places, gravely this time, not joking. The cigar box was passed.

The wall-opening was blocked on the other side by dark-gray suiting.

The man in white took a cigarette from his gold case, closed it, looked at it, and offered it to Farnbach on his right, who shook his bald-shaven head; but realizing he was being invited to read, not smoke, he took the case and held it out to focus on it. His blue eyes widened in recognition. "Ohhh!" He sucked air in through thick puckered lips as he read. Smiling excitedly at the man in white, he said, "How marvelous! Even better than a medal. May I?" He gestured with the case toward Kleist beside him.

The man in white nodded, smiling and pink-cheeked, and turned to put his cigarette to the flame of a lighter held waiting at his left. Squinting against smoke, he drew his briefcase nearer his side and opened it wide again. "Wonderful!" Kleist said. "Look, Schwimmer." The man in white found and pulled from his briefcase a sheaf of papers, which he set before him, moving his brandy aside. He put his cigarette into the notch of a white ashtray. Watching handsome young-looking Schwimmer pass the case across the table toward Mundt, he took his eyeglass case from his breast pocket, the glasses from the case. He smiled at admiring smiles from Schwimmer and Kleist, pocketed the eyeglass case, shook the glasses open and slid them on. A whistle from Mundt, long and low. The man in white took up his cigarette, drew on it savoringly, and set it in the ashtray again. He squared the papers before him and studied the topmost one, reaching for his brandy. "Mm, mm, mm!"—from Traunsteiner. The man in white sipped brandy, thumbed the bottom of the sheaf of papers.

The cigarette case came back to him, from silver-haired Hessen, blue eyes bright in his gaunt face. "What a wonderful thing to possess!"

"Yes," the man in white agreed, nodding, "I'm enormously proud of it." He put the case down beside the papers.

"Who wouldn't be?" Farnbach asked.

The man in white put his snifter aside and said, "Let's get down to business now, boys." Tipping his cropped gray head, he pushed his glasses lower on his nose and looked at the men over them. They faced him attentively, cigars poised. Silence took the room; only a low whine of air conditioning persisted against it.

"You know what you're going out to do," the man in white said, "and you know it's a long job. I'll fill you in on the details now." He leaned his head forward, looking down through his glasses. "Ninety-four men have to die on or near certain dates in the next two and a half years," he said, reading. "Sixteen of them are in West Germany, fourteen in Sweden, thirteen in England, twelve in the United States, ten in Norway, nine in Austria, eight in Holland, and six each in Denmark and Canada. Total, ninety-four. The first is to die on or near October sixteenth; the last, on or near the twenty-third of April, 1977."

He sat back and looked at the men again. "*Why* must these men die? And why on or near their particular dates?" He shook his head. "Not now; later you can be told that. But this I *can* tell you now: their deaths are the final step in an operation to which I and the leaders of the Organization have devoted many years, enormous effort, and a large part of the Organization's fortune. It's the most important operation the Organization has ever undertaken, and 'important' is a thousand times too weak a word to describe it. *The hope and the destiny of the Aryan race lie in the balance.* No exaggeration here, my friends; literal truth: the destiny of the Aryan people—to hold sway over the Slavs and the Semites, the Black and the Yellow—will be fulfilled if the operation succeeds, will not be fulfilled if the operation fails. So 'important' isn't a strong enough word, is it? 'Holy,' maybe? Yes, that's closer. It's a *holy* operation you're taking part in."

He picked up his cigarette, tapped ash away, and carried its shortness carefully to his lips.

The men looked at one another silently, awed. They reminded themselves to draw at cigars, to sip brandy. They looked at the man in white again; he ground his cigarette in the ashtray, looked up at them.

"You'll be leaving Brazil with new identities," he said, and touched the briefcase at his side. "Everything's here. Genuine stuff, not forgeries. And you'll have ample funds for the two and a half years. In diamonds"—he smiled—"which I'm afraid you'll have to take through customs in the uncomfortable way."

The men smiled and shrugged.

"You'll each be responsible for the men in one or a pair of countries. You have from thirteen to eighteen assignments each, but a few of the men will already have died of natural causes. They're sixty-five years old. Not too many of them will have died, though, as they were in excellent health as of their fifty-second year, with no signs of incipient disorder."

"All the men are sixty-five?" Hessen asked, looking puzzled.

"Almost all," the man in white said. "That is, they will be when their dates come around. A few will be a year or two younger or older." He lifted aside the paper from which he had read the countries and numbers, and picked up the other nine or ten sheets. "The addresses," he told the men, "are their addresses in 1961 and '62, but you shouldn't have any trouble locating them today. Most are probably still where they were. They're family men, stable; civil servants mostly—tax examiners, principals of schools, and so on; men of minor authority."

"They have that in common too?" Schwimmer asked.

The man in white nodded.

Hessen said, "A remarkably homogeneous group. The members of another organization, opposed to ours?"

"They don't even know one another, or us," the man in white said. "At least I hope they don't."

"They'll be retired now, won't they?" Kleist asked. "If they're sixty-five?" His glass eye looked elsewhere.

"Yes, most of them will probably be retired," the man in white agreed. "But if they've moved, you can be sure they'll have taken care to leave proper forwarding addresses. Schwimmer, you get England. Thirteen, the smallest number." He handed a typewritten sheet to Kleist to pass on to Schwimmer. "No reflection on your abilities," he smiled at Schwimmer. "On the contrary, a recognition of them. I hear you can turn yourself into an Englishman of whom the Queen herself wouldn't be suspicious."

"You do know how to flatter one, old man," Schwimmer drawled in Oxonian English, fingering his sandy mustache as he glanced at the sheet. "Actually, the old girl's not all that bright, y' know."

The man in white smiled. "That talent might very well prove useful," he said, "though your new identity, like all the others', is that of a German national. You're traveling salesmen, boys; maybe between assignments you'll have time to discover a few farmers' daughters." He looked at his next sheet. "Farnbach, you'll be traveling in Sweden." He handed the sheet to his right. "With fourteen customers for your fine imported merchandise."

Farnbach, taking the sheet, leaned forward, his hairless browridge creased by a frown. "All of them elderly civil servants," he said, "and by killing them we fulfill the destiny of the Aryan race?"

The man in white looked at him for a moment. "Was that a question or a statement, Farnbach?" he asked. "It sounded a little like a question there at the end, and if so, I'm surprised. Because you, and all of you, were chosen for this operation on the basis of your unquestioning obedience as well as your other attributes and talents."

Farnbach sat back, his thick lips closed and his nostrils flaring, his face flushed.

The man in white looked at his next clipped-together sheets. "No, Farnbach, I'm sure it was a statement," he said, "and in that case I have to correct it slightly: by killing them you *prepare the way* for the fulfillment of the destiny, et cetera. It will come; not in April 1977, when the ninety-fourth man dies, but in time. Only obey your order. Traunsteiner, you've got Norway and Denmark." He handed the sheets away. "Ten in one, six in the other."

Traunsteiner took the sheets, his square red face set in a grim demonstration: Unquestioning Obedience.

"Holland and the upper part of Germany," the man in white said, "are for Sergeant Kleist. Sixteen again, eight and eight."

"Thank you, Herr Doktor."

"The eight in lower Germany and nine in Austria—make seventeen for Sergeant Mundt."

Mundt—round-faced, crop-headed, eyeglassed—grinned as he waited for the sheets to reach him. "When I'm in Austria," he said, "I'll take care of Yakov Liebermann while I'm at it!" Traunsteiner, passing the sheets to him, smiled with gold-filled teeth.

"Yakov Liebermann," the man in white said, "has already been taken care of, by time, and ill health, and the failure of the bank where he kept his Jewish money. He's hunting for lecture-bookings now, not for us. Forget about him."

"Of course," Mundt said. "I was only joking."

"And I'm not. To the police and the press he's a boring old nuisance with a file cabinet full of ghosts; kill him and you're liable to turn him into a neglected hero with living enemies still to be caught."

"I never heard of the Jew-bastard."

"I wish I could say the same."

The men laughed.

The man in white handed his last pair of sheets to Hessen. "And for you, eighteen," he said, smiling. "Twelve in the United States and six in Canada. I count on your being your brother's brother."

"I am," Hessen said, lifting his silver head, the sharp-planed face proud. "You'll see I am."

The man in white looked around at the men. "I told you," he said, "that the men are to be killed on or near the date given with each one's name. 'On' is of course better than 'near,' but only microscopically so. A week one way or the other will make no real difference, and even a month will be acceptable if you have reason to think it will make an assignment less risky. As for methods: whichever you choose, provided only that they vary and that there's never any suggestion of premeditation. The authorities in no country must suspect that an operation is under way. It shouldn't be difficult for you. Bear in mind that these are sixty-five-year-old men: their eyes are failing; they have slow reflexes, diminished strength. They're likely to drive poorly and cross streets carelessly, to suffer falls, to be knifed and robbed by hoodlums. There are dozens of ways in which such men can be killed without attracting high-level attention." He smiled. "I trust you to find them."

Kleist said, "Can we hire someone else to take an assignment or to help with it? If that seems the best way of bringing it off?"

The man in white turned his hands out in wondering surprise. "You're sensible men with good judgment," he reminded Kleist; "that's why we chose you. However you think the job should be done, that's the way to do it. As long as the men die at the right time and the authorities don't suspect it's an operation, you have a completely free hand." He raised a finger. "No, not completely; I'm sorry. One proviso, and it's a very important one. We don't want the men's families involved, either as co-victims in any sort of accident or—in the case, say, of younger wives who might be open to romantic overtures—as accomplices. I repeat: the families aren't to be involved in any way, and only outsiders used as accomplices."

"Why should we need accomplices?" Traunsteiner asked, and Kleist said, "You never know what you're liable to run up against."

"I've been all over Austria," Mundt said, looking at one of his sheets, "and there are places here I've never heard of."

"Yes," Farnbach groused, looking at his single sheet, "I know Sweden but I certainly never heard of any 'Rasbo.'"

"It's a small town about fifteen kilometers northeast of Uppsala," the man in white said. "That's Bertil Hedin, isn't it? He's the postmaster there."

Farnbach looked at him, his brow uplifted.

The man in white met his gaze, and smiled patiently. "And killing Postmaster Hedin," he said, "is every bit as important—correction, as holy—as I said it was. Come on now, Farnbach, be the fine soldier you've always been."

Farnbach shrugged and looked at his sheet again. "You're . . . the doctor," he said drily.

"So I am," the man in white said, still smiling as he turned to his briefcase.

Hessen, looking at his sheets, said, "Here's a good one: 'Kankakee.'"

"Right outside Chicago," the man in white said, bringing up a stack of manila envelopes between spread-open hands. He spilled them onto the table—half a dozen large swollen envelopes, each lettered at a corner with a name: *Cabral, Carreras, de Lima*—a snifter was snatched from the sliding rush of them.

"Sorry," the man in white said, sitting back. He gestured for the envelopes to be distributed, and took his glasses off. "Don't open them here," he said, pinching his nose, rubbing it. "I checked everything myself this morning. German passports with Brazilian entrance stamps and the right visas, working permits, driver's licenses, business cards and papers; everything's there. When you get back to your rooms, practice your new signatures and sign whatever needs signing. Your plane tickets are in there too, and some currency of the destination countries, a few thousand cruzeiros' worth."

"The diamonds?" Kleist asked, holding his *Carreras* envelope in both hands before him.

"Are in the safe at headquarters." The man in white homed his eyeglasses in their petit-point case. "You'll pick them up on your way to the airport—you leave tomorrow—and you'll give Ostreicher your present passports and personal papers to hold for your return."

Mundt said, "And I just got used to 'Gómez,'" and grinned. The others laughed.

"What are we getting?" Schwimmer asked, zipping his portfolio. "In diamonds, I mean."

"About forty carats each."

"Ouch," Farnbach said.

"No, the tubes are quite small. A dozen or so three-carat stones, that's all. They're each worth about seventy thousand cruzeiros in today's market, and more in tomorrow's, with inflation. So you'll have the equivalent of at least nine-hundred-thousand-odd cruzeiros for the two and a half years. You'll live very nicely, in the manner befitting salesmen for large German firms, and you'll have more than enough money for any equipment you need. Incidentally, be sure not to take any weapons with you on the plane; they're searching *everybody* these days. Leave anything you've got with Ostreicher. You'll have no trouble selling the diamonds. In fact, you'll probably have to drive buyers away. Does that cover everything?"

"Checking in?" Hessen asked, putting his attaché case by his side.

"Didn't I mention that? The first of each month, by phone to your company's Brazilian branch—headquarters, of course. Keep it businesslike. You in particular, Hessen; I'm sure nine out of ten phones in the States are tapped."

Traunsteiner said, "I haven't spoken Norwegian since the war."

"Study." The man in white smiled. "Anything else? No? Well then, let's have some more brandy and I'll think of an appropriate toast to speed you on your way." He picked up his cigarette case, opened it, and took out a cigarette. He closed the case and looked at it—and bringing his white sleeve to its inscribed face, briskly polished it.

Tsuruko bowed and thanked the senhor. Tucking the folded bills down into the waist of her kimono, she slipped past him and hurried to the serving table, where Yoshiko was nesting together small bowls of drying leftovers. "He gave me twenty-five!" Yoshiko whispered excitedly. "What did you get?"

"I don't know," Tsuruko whispered, crouching low, putting the leaning cover onto a rice bowl beneath the table. "I didn't look yet." With both hands she brought out the wide flat red-lacquered bowl.

"Fifty, I'll bet!"

"I hope so." Rising, Tsuruko hurried with the bowl past the senhor and one of his guests joking with Mori, and out into the hallway. She zigzagged her way through the other guests—handing shoehorns to one another, bending, crouching—and shouldered a swing-door open.

She carried the bowl down a narrow flight of stairs lit by wire-strung bare bulbs, and along an equally narrow corridor with walls of plastered lath.

The corridor opened into a steamy jangling kitchen where antique ceiling fans slowly turned their blades over a hubbub of waitresses, cooks, and helpers. Tsuruko in her pink kimono carried the wide red bowl among them; she passed a helper quick-chopping vegetables, and another who glanced up at her as he hauled a tray of dishes from a dripping glass-walled washer.

She set the bowl on a table where boxes of mushrooms stood stacked, and turning, took from a canvas hamper of linens a used napkin, which she shook out and spread beside the bowl on the metal tabletop. She lifted the bowl's cover and put it aside. Within the red bowl a black-and-chrome tape recorder lay, a Panasonic with English-marked controls, the sprockets of the cassette in its windowed compartment smoothly turning. Tsuruko hovered a hand above the buttons, then lifted the recorder from the bowl and set it on the napkin. She folded the napkin-sides up around it.

Holding the wrapped recorder to her bosom, she went to a glass-paned door and took hold of its knob. A man sitting close by sewing at an apron looked up at her.

"Leftovers," she said, flashing the napkined shape at him. "An old woman comes by."

The man looked at her with tired eyes in a pinched yellow face; he looked down at his sewing hands.

She opened the door and went out into an areaway. A cat sprang from garbage cans and fled toward a far-off passage end of streetlights and neon.

Tsuruko closed the door behind her and leaned into darkness. "Hey, are you there?" she called softly in Portuguese. "Senhor Hunter?"

A figure hurried from the side of the passage, a tall lean man with a shoulderbag. "You do it?"

"Yes," she said, unwrapping the recorder. "It's still going. I couldn't think which button turns it off."

"Good, good, no difference." He was a young man; his fine-featured face and crinkly brown hair caught the door's light. "Where you put that?" he asked.

"In a rice bowl under the serving table." She gave the recorder to him. "With the cover leaning against it so they wouldn't see."

He tilted the recorder toward the door and pressed one of its buttons and another; a high-pitched twittering sang. Tsuruko, watching, moved aside to allow him more light. "Near of where they sit?" he asked her. His Portuguese was bad.

"From here to there." She gestured from herself to the nearest garbage can.

"Good, good." The young man pressed a button, stopping the twittering, and pressed another: the voice of the man in white spoke in German, distantly, an echo surrounding it. "Very good," the young man said, and stopped the voice with another button. He pointed to the recorder. "When you begin this?"

"After they finished eating, just before he sent us out. They talked for almost an hour."

"They leave?"

"They were going when I came down."

"Good, good." The young man tugged at the zipper of his blue-and-white airline bag. He was wearing a short blue denim jacket and blue jeans; he looked to be about twenty-three, North American. "You are a big helper to me," he told Tsuruko, fitting the recorder into the bag. "My magazine is very happy when I bring home a story about Senhor Aspiazu. He is the most famous maker of the cinema." Reaching to his hip, he brought out a wallet and opened it toward the light.

Tsuruko watched, holding the balled napkin. "A North American magazine?" she asked.

"Yes," the young man said, separating bills. "*Movie Story*. A very important magazine of the cinema." He smiled brightly at Tsuruko and gave bills to her. "One hundred and fifty cruzeiros. Many thanks. You are a big helper to me."

"Thank you." She glanced at the bills and smiled at him, bobbed her head.

"Your restaurant smells like a good one," he said, pocketing his wallet. "I am in much hunger while I wait."

"Would you like me to get something for you?" She tucked the bills into her kimono. "I could—"

"No, no." He touched her hand. "I eat at my hotel. Thanks. Many thanks." He gave her hand a squeeze, and turned and went long-legging into the passage.

"You're welcome, Senhor Hunter," she called after him. She watched for a moment, then turned and opened the door and went in.

■

They had a round of complimentary drinks at the bar, persuaded to do so less by the pleadings of the tuxedoed Japanese—who introduced himself as Hiroo Kuwayama, one of Sakai's three owners—than by the presence there of a novel electronic ping-pong game; and this proved so engaging that another round was ordered and drunk, and still another debated upon but decided against.

At about eleven-thirty they went en masse to the checkroom to collect their hats. The kimonoed girl, giving Hessen his, smiled and said, "A friend of yours came in after you, but he didn't want to go upstairs uninvited."

Hessen looked at her for a moment. "Oh?" he said.

She nodded. "A young man. A North American, I think."

"Oh," Hessen said. "Of course. Yes. I know who you mean. Came in after me, you say."

"Yes, senhor. While you were going up the stairs."

"He asked where I was going, of course."

She nodded.

"You told him?"

"A private party. He thought he knew who was giving it, but he was wrong. I told him it was Senhor Aspiazu. He knows him too."

"Yes, I know," Hessen said. "We're all good friends. He should have come up."

"He said it was probably a business meeting and he didn't want to break in. Besides, he wasn't dressed right." She gestured down her sides, regretfully. "Jeans." She fluttered slim fingers at her throat. "No tie."

"Oh," Hessen said. "Well, it's a shame he didn't come up anyway, just to say hello. He went right out again?"

She nodded.

"Oh well," Hessen said, and smiled and gave her a cruzeiro.

He went and spoke to the man in white. The other men, holding hats and attaché cases, gathered around them.

The blond man and the black-haired man went quickly toward the carved entrance doors; Traunsteiner hurried into the bar and came out a moment later with Hiroo Kuwayama.

The man in white put a white-gloved hand on Kuwayama's black shoulder and talked earnestly to him. Kuwayama listened, and drew in breath, bit his lip, wagged his head.

He spoke and gestured reassuringly and hurried off toward the rear of the restaurant.

The man in white waved the other men sharply away from him. He moved to the side of the foyer and put his hat and his briefcase, less fat now, on a black lamp table. He stood looking toward the rear of the restaurant, frowning and rubbing his white-gloved hands together. He looked down at them, and put them at his sides.

From the rear of the restaurant Tsuruko and Mori came, in colorful slacks and blouses, and Yoshiko, still in her kimono. Kuwayama hustled them forward. They looked confused and worried. Diners glanced at them.

The man in white curved his mouth into a friendly smile.

Kuwayama delivered the three women to the man in white, nodded to him, and moved aside to watch with folded arms.

The man in white smiled and shook his head sorrowfully, ran a gloved hand back over his cropped gray hair. "Girls," he said, "a really bad thing has come up. Bad for *me*, I mean, not for you. *Fine* for you. I'll explain." He took a breath. "I'm a manufacturer of farm machinery," he said, "one of the biggest in South America. The men who are with me tonight"—he gestured back over his shoulder —"are my salesmen. We got together here so I could tell them about some new machines we're putting into production, give them all the details and specifications; you know. Everything top secret. Now I've found out that a *spy for a rival North American concern* learned about our meeting just before it started, and knowing the way these people work, I'm willing to bet he went back to the kitchen and got hold of one of you, or even all of you, and asked you to eavesdrop on our conversation from some . . . secret hiding place, or maybe take pictures of us." He raised a finger. "You see," he explained, "some of my salesmen formerly worked for this rival concern, and they don't know—the concern doesn't know—who's with me now, so pictures of us would be useful to them too." He nodded, smiling ruefully. "It's a very competitive business," he said. "Dog eat dog."

Tsuruko and Mori and Yoshiko looked blankly at him, shaking their heads slightly, slowly.

Kuwayama, who had moved around beside and behind the man in white, said sternly, "If any of you did what the senhor—"

"Let me!" The man in white threw an open hand back but didn't turn. "Please." He lowered the hand, smiled, and took half a step forward. "This man," he said good-naturedly, "a young North American, would have offered you some money, of course, and he would have told you some kind of story about it being a practical joke or something, a harmless little trick he was playing on us. Now, I can fully understand how girls who are not, I'm sure, being vastly overpaid—You aren't, are you? Is my friend here vastly over-paying any of you?" His brown eyes twinkled at them, waiting for an answer.

Yoshiko, giggling, shook her head vehemently.

The man in white laughed with her, and reached toward her shoulder but withdrew his hand short of touching her. "I didn't think so!" he said. "No, I was pretty damn sure he isn't!" He smiled at Mori and Tsuruko; they smiled uncertainly back at him. "Now, I can fully understand," he said, getting serious again, "how girls in your situation, hard-working girls with family responsibilities—you with your two children, Mori—I can fully understand how you could go along with such an offer. In fact, I can't understand how you *couldn't* go along with it; you'd be stupid not to! A harmless lit-tle joke, a few extra cruzeiros. Things are expensive these days; I know. That's why I gave you nice tips upstairs. So if the offer was made, and if you accepted it, believe me, girls: there's no anger on my part, there's no resentment; there's only understanding, and a *need to know.*"

"Senhor," Mori protested, "I give you my word, nobody offered me anything or asked me to do anything."

"Nobody," Tsuruko said, shaking her head; and Yoshiko, shaking hers, said, "Honestly, senhor."

"As proof of my understanding," the man in white said, holding his jacket-front from him and reaching into it, "I'll give you twice what *he* gave you, or twice what he only offered." He brought out a thick black crocodile billfold, split it open, and showed the inside edges of two sheaves of bills. "This is what I meant before," he said, "about it being a bad thing for me but a good thing for you." He looked from one woman to another. "Twice what he gave you," he said. "For you, and the same amount also for Senhor . . ." He jerked his head back toward Kuwayama, who said, "Kuwayama." "So he won't be angry with you either. Girls? Please?" The man in white showed his money to Yoshiko. "*Years* have been spent on this —on these new machines," he told her. "Millions of cruzeiros!" He showed his money to Mori. "If I know how much my rival knows, then I can take steps to protect myself!" He showed his money to Tsuruko. "I can speed up production, or maybe find this young man and . . . get him onto my side, give money to *him* as well as to you and Senhor—"

"Kuwayama. Come on, girls, don't be afraid! Tell Senhor Aspiazu! I won't be angry with you."

"You see?" the man in white urged. "Only good can come! For everyone!"

"There's nothing to *tell*," Mori insisted, and Yoshiko, looking at the bent-open billfold with its sheaves of bills, said sadly, "Nothing. Honestly." She looked up. "I *would* tell, gladly, senhor. But there's really nothing."

Tsuruko looked at the billfold.

The man in white watched her.

She looked up at him, and hesitantly, with embarrassment, nodded.

He let his breath out, looking intently at her.

"It was just the way you said," she admitted. "I was in the kitchen, when we were getting ready to serve you, and one of the boys came to me and said there was a man outside who wanted to speak to someone serving your party. Very important. So I went out, and he was there, the North American. He gave me two hundred cruzeiros, fifty before and a hundred and fifty after. He said he was a reporter for a magazine, and you made films and never gave interviews."

The man in white, looking at her, said, "Go on."

"He said it would be a good story for him if he found out what new films you were planning. I told him you were going to talk with your guests later on—Senhor K. told us you were—and he—"

"Asked you to hide and listen."

"No, senhor, he gave me a tape recorder, and I brought it in, and brought it out to him when you were done talking."

"A . . . tape recorder?"

Tsuruko nodded. "He showed me how to work it. Two buttons at once." With both her forefingers she pressed air before her.

The man in white closed his eyes and stood motionless except for a slight side-to-side swaying. He opened his eyes and looked at Tsuruko and smiled faintly. "A tape recorder was in operation throughout our conference?" he asked.

"Yes, senhor," she said. "In a rice bowl under the serving table. It worked very well. The man tried it before he paid me, and he was very happy."

The man in white took in air through his mouth, licked his upper lip, allowed the air out, and closed his mouth and swallowed. He put a white-gloved hand to his forehead and wiped it slowly.

"Two hundred cruzeiros altogether," Tsuruko said.

The man in white looked at her, moved closer to her, and drew in a deep breath. He smiled down at her; she was half a head shorter than he. "Dear," he said softly, "I want you to tell me everything you can about the man. He was young—how young? What did he look like?"

Tsuruko, uneasy in their closeness, said, "He was twenty-two or -three, I think. I couldn't see him clearly. Very tall. Nice-looking, friendly. He had brown hair in close little curls."

"That's good," the man in white said, "that's a good description. He was wearing jeans . . ."

"Yes. And a jacket the same—you know, short blue. And he had a bag from an airline, on a strap." She gestured at her shoulder. "That's where he had the recorder."

"Very good. You're very observant, Tsuruko. What airline?"

She looked chagrined. "I didn't notice. It was blue and white."

"A blue-and-white airline bag. Good enough. What else?"

She frowned and shook her head, and remembered happily: "His name is Hunter, senhor!"

"Hunter?"

"Yes, senhor! Hunter. He said it very plainly."

The man in white smiled wryly. "I'm sure he did. Go on. What else?"

"His Portuguese was bad. He said I was a 'big helper' to him; all kinds of mistakes like that. And his pronunciation was wrong."

"So he hasn't been here very long, has he? You're being a 'big helper' to *me*, Tsuruko. Keep going."

She frowned, and gave an impotent shrug. "That's all, senhor."

He said, "Please try to think of something else, Tsuruko. You have *no idea* how important this is to me."

She bit at a knuckle of her fisted hand, and looking at him, shook her head.

"He didn't tell you how to get in touch with him in case I should arrange another party?"

"No, senhor! No! Nothing like that. Nothing. I would tell you."

"Keep thinking."

Her distressed face suddenly brightened. "He's at a hotel. Does that help you?"

The brown eyes looked questioningly at her.

"He said he would eat at his hotel. I asked him if he wanted some food—he got hungry waiting—and that's what he said, he would eat at his hotel."

The man in white looked at Tsuruko and said, "You see? There *was* something else." He stepped back, and looking down, opened his billfold. He drew out four hundred-cruzeiro bills and gave them to her.

"Thank you, senhor!"

Kuwayama came closer, smiling.

The man in white gave him four bills, and one each to Mori and Yoshiko. Putting his billfold inside his jacket, he smiled at Tsuruko and reprimanded her: "You're a good girl, but in the future you should give a little more thought to your patrons' interests."

"I will, senhor! I promise!"

To Kuwayama he said, "Don't be hard on her. Really."

"Oh no, not now!" Kuwayama grinned, withdrawing his hand from his pocket.

The man in white took his hat and his briefcase from the lamp table, and smiling at the bowing women and Kuwayama, turned from them and went toward the men who stood waiting, watching him.

His smile died; his eyes narrowed. Reaching the men, he whispered in German, "Fucking cock-sucking yellow bitch, I would cut her teats off!"

He told the men about the tape recorder.

The blond man said, "We checked the street and all the cars; no young North American in jeans."

"We'll find him," the man in white said. "He's a loner; the groups that are still active are all Rio and Buenos Aires men. And he's an amateur, not only by reason of his age—twenty-two or -three—but also because he gives the name 'Hunter,' which is English for *Jäger;* no one with experience would bother with such jokes. And he's stupid, or he wouldn't have let the bitch know he's at a hotel."

"Unless," Schwimmer said, "he isn't at one."

"In which case he's smart," the man in white said, "and I hang myself in the morning. Let's find out. Hessen, our *Paulista* who allows himself to be followed by an amateur 'hunter,' will now make amends by giving each of you the name of a hotel." He looked at Hessen, who looked up from an examination of his hat. "A hotel good enough to serve food at late hours," the man in white told him, "but not so good as to discourage the wearing of jeans. Put yourself in his place: you're a boy from the States who's come down to Paulo to hunt for Horst Hessen or maybe even Mengele; which hotel would you stay at? You've got money enough to overbribe waitresses—I don't *think* the bitch lied about the amount —but you're romantic; you want to feel you're a new Yakov Liebermann, not a comfortable tourist. Five hotels, please, Hessen, in order of likelihood."

He looked at the others. "When Hessen names your hotel," he said, "you'll take a box of matches from that bowl there and go outside and repeat the name to a taxi driver. When you reach the hotel you'll find out whether or not they have there a *tall young North American with brown hair in close curls,* who recently came in wearing blue jeans, a short blue denim jacket, and a blue-and-white airline shoulderbag. You'll then phone the number on the matchbox. I'll be here. If the answer is yes, Rudi and Tin-tin and I will be right over; if the answer is no, Hessen will give you the name of another hotel. Everything clear? Good. We'll have him in half an hour and he won't even be through *listening* to his damned tape. Hessen?"

Hessen said to Mundt, "The Nacional," and Mundt said, "The Nacional" and went to get a matchbox.

Hessen said to Schwimmer, "The Del Rey."

And to Traunsteiner, "The Marabá."

To Farnbach, "The Comodora."

To Kleist, "The Savoy."

He listened for about five minutes, then he stopped, rewound, and started again from where they finished admiring whatever the hell they were admiring and "Aspiazu" said *"Lasst uns jetzt Geschäft reden, meine Jungens"* and sure enough got down to business. Business! Jesus!

He listened to the whole thing through this time—saying "Jesus!" and *"God* almighty!" now and then, and "Ooh you *fuck*, you!—and after the *clonk* and the long silence that had to be the waitress bringing the bowl downstairs he stopped and rewound partway and replayed a few bits and pieces, just to make sure it was really there and he wasn't spaced out from hunger or something.

Then he paced as much as the room allowed, shaking his head and scratching the back of it, trying to figure out what the fuck to *do* in this hotbed of who-knows-who-isn't-one-of-them-or-at-least-being-paid-by-them.

There was only *one* thing to do, he finally decided, and the sooner the better, never mind the time-difference. He brought the recorder over to the night table and put it by the phone; got his wallet out and sat down on the bed. He found the card with the name and number on it, tucked it under the foot of the phone, and picked up the handset, pocketing his wallet. He asked for the long-distance operator.

She sounded cute and sexy. "I'll call you when I get it."

"I stay on the telephone," he said, not trusting her not to go out and samba someplace. "Hurry, please."

"It's going to take five or ten minutes, senhor."

He listened to her giving the number to an overseas operator and rehearsed in his head what he would say. Assuming, of course, that Liebermann was there and not off speaking somewhere or running down a lead. Be home, please, Mr. Liebermann!

A light rap sounded at the door.

"It's about time," he said in English, and hanging on to the phone, got up, reached, and just managed to give the doorknob the turn that unlocked it. The door opened against his hand, and the waiter with the droopy mustache came in with a napkin-covered plate and the bottle of Brahma but no glass on the tray. "Sorry it took so long," he said. "Eleven o'clock they all run. I had to make it myself."

"That is all right," he said in Portuguese. "Put the tray on the bed, please."

"I forgot the glass."

"That is all right. I need no glass. Give me the check and the pencil, please."

He signed the check against the wall, holding it there with his phone-hand; added a tip beyond the service charge.

The waiter went out without thanking him and belched as he closed the door.

He never should have left the Del Rey.

He sat back down on the bed, the phone whistling hollowly in his ear. He turned to steady the tray, and looked with misgiving at the yellow napkin with *Miramar* stamped big and black and burglar-proof in a corner of it. He took hold of it, and what the hell, whipped it away: the sandwich was thick and beautiful, all chicken, no lettuce or crap whatsoever. Forgiving the waiter, he gathered up a half of it, bent his head to meet it, and took a big delicious middle bite. God, he was starving!

"*Ich möchte Wien*," an operator said. "*Wien!*"

He thought of the tape and what he would say to Yakov Liebermann, and his mouth was full of cardboard; he chewed and chewed and somehow got it down. He put the sandwich down and picked up the beer. It was one of the really great beers and it tasted lousy.

"Not much longer," Cute Sexy Operator said.

"I hope. Thank you."

"Here you are, senhor."

A phone rang.

He grabbed another swallow and put the bottle down, wiped his hand on a jeaned knee, turned more toward the phone.

The other phone rang, and rang, and was picked up: "*Ja?*"—as clear as around the corner.

"Mr. Liebermann?"

"*Ja. Wer'st da?*"

"It's Barry Koehler. Remember, Mr. Liebermann? I came to see you early in August, wanted to work for you? Barry Koehler from Evanston, Illinois?"

Silence.

"Mr. Liebermann?"

"Barry Koehler, I don't know what time it is in Illinoise, but in Vienna it's so dark I can't see the clock."

"I'm not in Illinois, I'm in São Paulo, Brazil."

"That doesn't make it lighter in Vienna."

"I'm sorry, Mr. Liebermann, but I've got a good reason for calling. Wait till you hear."

"Don't tell me, I'll guess: you saw Martin Bormann. In a bus station."

"No, not Bormann. Mengele. And I didn't see him, but I've got a tape of him talking. In a restaurant."

Silence.

"Dr. Mengele?" he prompted. "The man who ran Auschwitz? The Angel of Death?"

"Thank you. I thought you meant a whole other Mengele. The Angel of Life."

Barry said, "I'm sorry. You were so—"

"I drove him into the jungle; I know Josef Mengele."

"You were so quiet, I had to say *something*. He's out of the jungle, Mr. Liebermann. He was in a Japanese restaurant tonight. Doesn't he use the name 'Aspiazu'?"

"He uses lots of names: Gregory, Fischer, Breitenbach, Rindon—"

"And Aspiazu, right?"

Silence. "*Ja*. But I think maybe it's also used by people it belongs to."

"It's *him*," Barry insisted. "He had half the SS there. And he's sending them out to kill ninety-four men. Hessen was there, and Kleist. Traunsteiner. Mundt."

"Listen, I'm not sure I'm awake. Are you? Do you know what you're talking about?"

"Yes! I'll play you the tape! It's sitting right here!"

"Just a minute. Begin at the beginning."

"All right." He picked up the bottle and drank some beer; let *him* listen to silence for a change.

"Barry?"

Ho-*ho!* "I'm here. I was just drinking some beer."

"Oh."

"A *sip*, Mr. Liebermann; I'm dying of thirst. I haven't had dinner yet and I'm so sick from this tape, I can't eat. I've got a gorgeous chicken sandwich here and I can't even swallow it."

"What are you doing in São Paulo?"

"You wouldn't take me on, so I figured I'd come down here on my own. I'm more highly motivated than you think I am."

"It's a question of *my* finances, not *your* motivation."

"I *said* I'd work for free; who's paying me now? Look, let's skip that. I came down, and nosed around, and finally I figured that the best thing to do was hang out around the Volkswagen plant, the one Stangl worked at. So I did. And a couple of days ago I spotted Horst Hessen; at least I thought I did, I wasn't sure. His hair is sort of silvery now, and he must have had some plastic surgery. But anyway, I thought it was him and began tailing him. He went home early today—he lives in the cutest little house you ever saw, with a knockout wife and two daughters—and at seven-thirty he comes out again and takes a bus downtown. I follow him into this fancy Japanese restaurant and he goes upstairs to a private party. There's a Nazi guarding the stairs, and the party is being given by 'Senhor Aspiazu.' Of the Auschwitz Aspiazus."

Silence. "Go ahead."

"So I went around back and got to one of the waitresses. Two hundred cruzeiros later she gave me a whole cassette of Mengele Dispatching the Troops. Mengele is crystal-clear; the troops range from fairly clear to mumble-mumble. Mr. Liebermann, they're going out tomorrow—to Germany, England, the States, Scandinavia, all over the place! It's a *Kameradenwerk* operation, and it's big and it's crazy and I'm really sorry I got into this whole thing, it's supposed to—"

"Barry."

"—fulfill the destiny of the Aryan race, for God's sake!"

"Barry!"

"*What?*"

"Calm yourself."

"I *am* calm. No I'm not. All right. *Now* I'm calm. Really. I'm going to rewind the tape and play it for you. Press the button. See?"

"Who's going out, Barry? How many?"

"Six. Hessen, Traunsteiner, Kleist, Mundt—and two others, uh, Schwimmer and Farnbach. You heard of them?"

"Not Schwimmer and Farnbach and Mundt."

"Mundt? You haven't heard of Mundt? He's in your book, Mr. Liebermann! That's where *I* heard about him."

"A Mundt, in *my book?* No."

"Yes! In the chapter on Treblinka. I've got it in my suitcase; you want me to give you the page number?"

"I never *heard* of a Mundt, Barry; this is a mistake on your part."

"Oh Jesus. All right, forget it. Anyway, there are six of them, and they're going out for two and a half years, and they've got certain dates when they're supposed to kill certain men, and here comes the crazy part. Are you ready, Mr. Liebermann? These men they're going to kill, there are *ninety-four of them*, and they're *all sixty-five-year-old civil servants*. How do you like *them* apples?"

Silence. "Apples?"

He sighed. "It's an expression."

"Barry, let me ask you something. This tape is in German, yes? Are you—"

"I understand it perfectly! I don't *spreche* too well but I understand it *perfectly*. My grandmother speaks nothing but, and my parents use it for secrets. It didn't even work when I was a kid."

"The *Kameradenwerk* and Josef Mengele are sending men out—"

"To kill sixty-five-year-old civil servants. A few of them are sixty-four and sixty-six. The tape's rewound now and I'm going to play it, and then you're going to tell me who I should take it to, someone high-up and reliable. And you'll call him and tell him I'm coming, so he'll see me, and see me quickly. They've got to be stopped before they leave. The first killing is slated for October sixteenth. Wait now, I've got to find the right place; there's a lot of sitting down and admiring something first."

"Barry, it's ridiculous. Something is wrong with your tape recorder. Or else—or else they're not the men you think they are."

A triple-knock at the door. "Go way!" he shouted at it, covering the mouthpiece; remembered Portuguese: "I talk the long distance."

"They're someone else," the phone said. "They're playing a joke on you."

"*Mr. Liebermann, will you just listen to the tape?*"

Louder knocking, a nonstop barrage.

"Shit. Hold on." Putting the phone on the bed, he got up and stepped to the racketing door, held its knob. "What is?"

Portuguese raced, a man's voice.

"Slow! Slow!"

"Senhor, there's a Japanese lady here, looking for someone who looks like you. She says she has to warn you about something a man is—" He turned the knob and in the door burst a dark bull of a man that slammed him backward; he was grabbed and turned, his mouth crushed, his arm wrenched back breakingly; the Nazi of the stairs lunged with a knife six inches shiny-sharp. His head was yanked back; the ceiling slid, stained with pale-brown watermarks; his arm hurt, and his stomach deep inside.

The man in white came into the room, wearing his hat and holding his briefcase. He closed the door, and standing before it, watched the blond man stab and stab the young American. Stab, twist, pull out; stab, twist, pull out; overhand now, the red-streaked knife into white snug-shirted ribs.

The blond man, panting, stopped stabbing, and the black-haired man lowered the surprised-eyed young man gently to the floor, laid him down there half on gray rug and half on varnished wood. The blond man held his bloody knife-hand over the young man and said to the black-haired man, "A towel."

The man in white looked toward the bed, moved to it, and set his briefcase down on the floor. "Barry?" the phone on the bed asked.

The man in white looked at the tape recorder on the night table; pressed a white fingertip to its end button. The window sprang; the cassette jumped free. The man in white picked it up, looked at it, and slipped it into his jacket pocket. He glanced at the card under the foot of the phone, took it, and looked at the black handset lying on the bed. "Barry!" it called. "Are you there?"

The man in white reached out slowly and picked the handset up; raised it, brought it to his ear. Listened with brown eyes narrowed, vein-threaded nostrils quivering. His lips opened to the mouthpiece, stayed open. And closed and clenched firmly, mustache bristling.

He put the handset into its cradle, drew his fingers away, stared at the phone. He turned and said, "I almost spoke to him. I was longing to."

The blond man, toweling red from his knife, looked curiously at him.

The man in white said, "Hating each other so long. And he was *here*, in my hand! To finally speak to him!" He turned to the phone again, shook his head regretfully. Softly he said, "Liebermann, you bastard Jew. Your stooge is dead. How much did he tell you? It makes no difference; no one here will listen to you, not without proof. And the proof is in my pocket. The men will fly tomorrow. The Fourth Reich is coming. Good-by, Liebermann. See you at the door of the gas chamber." He shook his head, smiling, and turned, putting the card in his pocket. "It would have been foolish, though," he said. "I might have been making another tape."

The black-haired man, by an open closet, pointed at a suitcase in it and asked in Portuguese, "Should I pack his things, Doctor?"

"Rudi will. You go downstairs to Traunsteiner. Find a back door you can open and get the car to it. Then one of you come up and help us down. And *don't tell him the boy was on the phone*. Say he was listening to the tape."

The black-haired man nodded and went out.

The blond man said in German, "Won't they get caught? The men, I mean."

"The job has to be done," the man in white said, taking out his eyeglass case. "As much of it as possible, at any cost. With luck they'll do it all. Will anyone listen to Liebermann? *He* didn't believe; you heard how the boy was arguing with him. God will help us; enough of the ninety-four will die." He put on his glasses, and taking a matchbox from his pocket, turned to the phone. He lifted the handset and read the operator a number.

"Hello, my friend," he said cheerfully. "Senhor Hessen, please." He glanced away, white-gloved fingers covering the phone's mouthpiece. "Empty his pockets, Rudi. And there's a sneaker under the bureau there. Hessen? Dr. Mengele. Everything's fine, there's nothing to worry about. Exactly the amateur I expected. I don't think he even understood German. Send the boys home to practice their signatures; it was just an excitement to round off the evening. No, not till 1977, I'm afraid; I fly back to the compound as soon as we clean up. So go with God, Horst. And say it for me to the others: 'Go with God.'" He hung up and said, "Heil Hitler."

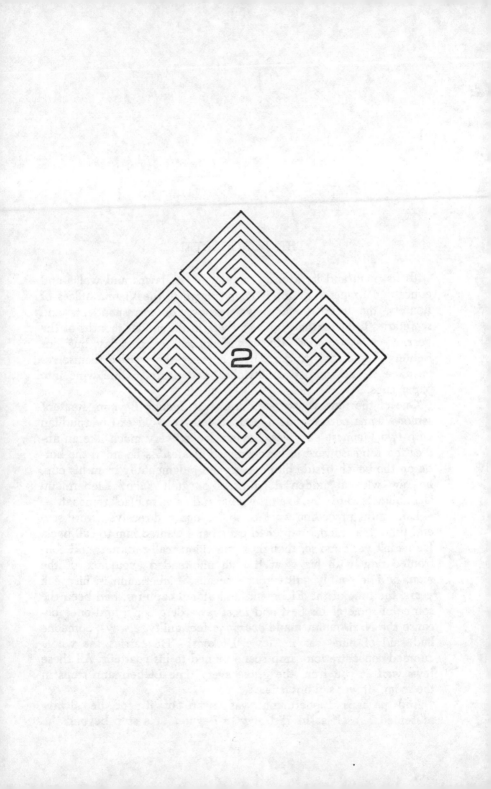

THE BURGGARTEN,

with its pond and its Mozart monument, its lawns and walks and equestrian Emperor Franz, is near enough to the Vienna offices of Reuters, the international news agency, for correspondents and secretaries to bring their lunches there in the milder months of the year. Monday, October 14th, was a cool and overcast day, but four Reuters people came to the Garten anyway; they settled themselves on a bench, unwrapped sandwiches, and poured white wine into paper cups.

One of the four, the wine-pourer, was Sydney Beynon, Reuters' senior Vienna correspondent. A forty-four-year-old ex-Liverpudlian with two Viennese ex-wives, Beynon looked very much like an abdicating King Edward in horn-rimmed glasses. As he stood the bottle on the bench beside him and sipped judgmentally from his cup, he saw with a sudden down-press of guilt Yakov Liebermann shambling toward him, in a brown hat and an open black raincoat.

During the preceding week or so, Beynon had received word several times that Liebermann had called and wanted him to call back. He hadn't yet done so, though a punctilious call-returner; and confronted now with his clear though unintended avoidance of the man, he felt doubly guilty: once because Liebermann in his peak years, the time of the Eichmann and Stangl captures, had been the source of some of his best and most rewarding copy; and once because the Nazi-hunter made *everyone* feel guilty, always. Someone had said of him—was it Stevie Dickens?—"He carries the whole damned concentration-camp scene pinned to his coattails. All those Jews wail at you from the grave every time Liebermann steps in the room." It was sad but true.

And perhaps Liebermann was aware of it, for he always presented himself as he did now to Beynon, at a step beyond the ordinary social distance, with a slight air of apology; rather, Beynon thought, like a considerate bear with something contagious. "Hello, Sydney," Liebermann-bear said, touching his hat-brim. "Please. Don't get up."

Beynon's guilt was more bothersome than his lapful of sandwich, so he made the effort anyway, half rising. "Hello, Yakov! It's good to see you." He put out his hand and Liebermann leaned and reached forward and wrapped it pressurelessly in the warmth of his bigger one. "Sorry I haven't called you yet," Beynon apologized; "I was in and out of Linz all last week." He sat back down and sketched introductions with his cup-hand: "Freya Neustadt, Paul Higbee, Dermot Brody. This is Yakov Liebermann.

"Oh my." Freya wiped a bony hand along her skirt and extended it, smiling vivaciously. "How are you? What a great pleasure." She looked guilty.

Watching Liebermann nodding and shaking hands down the line, Beynon was dismayed to see how much the man had aged and diminished since their last meeting some two years before. He was still a presence, but no longer as massive or implicit with bearish strength as he had been then; the broad shoulders seemed pulled down now by the raincoat's scant weight, and the then-powerful face was lined and gray-jowled, the eyes weary under drooping lids. The nose at least was unchanged—that thrusting Semitic hook —but the mustache was streaked with gray and wanted trimming. The poor chap had lost his wife and a kidney or such, and the funds of his War Crimes Information Center; the losses were recorded all over him—the crushed and finger-marked old hat, the darkened tie knot—and Beynon, reading the record, realized why his inner self had blocked that return call. His guilt swelled, but he quashed it, telling himself that to avoid losers was a natural and healthy instinct, even—or perhaps especially—to avoid losers who had once been winners.

Though one wanted to be kind, of course. "Sit down, Yakov," he invited heartily, gesturing at the bench-end beside him and drawing the wine bottle closer.

"I don't want to disturb your lunch," Liebermann said in his heavily accented English. "If we could talk later?"

"Sit down," Beynon said. "I get enough of these chaps at the office." He put his back toward Freya and pushed a bit; she ceded a few inches and turned the other way. Beynon gave the added space to the bench-end, and smiling at Liebermann, gestured at it.

Liebermann sat down and sighed. Holding his knees with big

hands, he scowled down between them, rocking his feet. "New shoes," he said. "Killing me."

"How are you otherwise?" Beynon asked. "And how's your daughter?"

"I'm all right. She's fine. She has three children now, two girls and a boy."

"Oh, that's nice." Beynon touched the neck of the bottle between them. "I'm afraid we don't have another cup."

"No, no. I'm not allowed anyway. No alcohol."

"I heard you were in hospital . . ."

"In, out, in, out." Liebermann shrugged, and turned his weary brown eyes on Beynon. "I had a very crazy phone call," he said. "A few weeks ago. Middle of the night. This boy from the States, from Illinoise, calls me from São Paulo. He has a tape of Mengele. You know who Mengele is, don't you?"

"One of your wanted Nazis, isn't he?"

"One of everybody's," Liebermann said, "not only mine. The German government still offers sixty thousand marks for him. He was the chief doctor at Auschwitz. 'The Angel of Death,' he was called. Two degrees, an M.D. and a Ph.D., and he did thousands of experiments on *children*, twins, trying to make good Aryans, to change brown eyes into blue eyes with chemicals, through the genes. A man with two degrees! He killed them: thousands of twins from all over Europe, Jewish and non-Jewish. It's all in my book."

Beynon picked up half his egg-salad sandwich and bit into it determinedly.

"He went home to Germany after the war," Liebermann went on. "His family is rich there, in Günzburg; farm machinery. But his name began to come up in the trials, so ODESSA got him out and into South America. We found him there and chased him from city to city: Buenos Aires, Bariloche, Asunción. Since '59 he lives in the jungle, in a settlement by a river on the Brazil and Paraguay border. He has an army of bodyguards, and Paraguayan citizenship, so he can't be extradited. But he has to lay low anyway because groups of young Jews down there still try to get him. Some of them are found floating down the river, the Paraná, with their throats cut."

Liebermann paused. Freya tapped Beynon's arm and asked for the wine; he passed the bottle to her.

"So the boy has a tape," Liebermann said, looking straight ahead, his hands on his knees. "Mengele in a restaurant sending out former SS men to Germany, England, Scandinavia, and the States. To

kill a bunch of sixty-five-year-old men." He turned and smiled at
Beynon. "Crazy, yes? And it's a very important operation. The
Kameradenwerk is involved too, not only Mengele. The Comrades
Organization, that keeps them safe and with jobs down there. Do
you like the apples, as they say?"

Beynon blinked at him and smiled. "No, I'm afraid I don't," he
said. "Did you actually hear this tape?"

Liebermann shook his head. "No. Just when he's ready to play it
for me, there's a knock at the door, his door, and he goes to answer
it. Bumping and thumping, and a little later the phone is hung up."

"Perfect timing," Beynon said. "It smells rather like a hoax, don't
you think? Who is he?"

Liebermann shrugged. "A boy who heard me speak two years
ago, at his university, Princeton. He came to me in August and said
he wanted to work for me. Do I need new workers? I'm only using
a handful of the old ones. You know, I'm assuming, that all my
money, all the Center's money, was in the Allgemeine Wirtschafts-
bank."

Beynon nodded.

"The Center is in my apartment now—all the files, a few desks,
and me and my bed. The ceiling downstairs is cracking. The landlord sues me. The only new workers I need are fund-raisers, which
isn't the boy's field of interest. So he went down to São Paulo, his
own boss."

"Not exactly someone I'd put much faith in."

"That's just what I think while he talks to me. And he doesn't
have all his facts right either. One of the SS men is named Mundt,
he says, and he knows about this Mundt from *my book*. Now, in my
book I know there's no Mundt. I never *heard* of a Mundt. So this
doesn't increase my confidence. But still . . . after the bumping and
thumping, while I'm calling to him to come back to the phone,
there's a certain sound, not very loud but very clear, and it's one
thing and nothing else: it's the sound of a cassette being dejected
from a tape recorder."

"Ejected," Beynon said.

"Not *dejected*? Pushed out?"

"That's *ejected*. *De*jected is sad, pushed *down*."

"Ah." Liebermann nodded. "Thank you. Being *e*jected from a
tape recorder. And one thing more. It was quiet then, for a long
time, and I was quiet too, putting the bumping and thumping together with the cassette sound; and in that long quiet"—he looked
forebodingly at Beynon—"hate came over the phone, Sydney." He

nodded. "Hate like I never felt before, not even when Stangl looked at me in the courtroom. It came to me as plain as the boy's voice, and maybe it was because of what he said, but I was absolutely certain the hate came from Mengele. And when the phone was hung up I was absolutely certain that Mengele hung it." He looked away and leaned forward, his elbows on his knees, a hand gripping his other hand's fist.

Beynon watched him, skeptical but moved. "What did you do?" he asked.

Liebermann sat up straight, rubbed his hands, looked at Beynon and shrugged. "What *could* I do, in Vienna at four in the morning? I wrote down what the boy said, all I could remember, and read it, and told myself that *he* was crazy and *I* was crazy. Only who . . . ejected the cassette and hung up the phone? Maybe it wasn't Mengele, but it was somebody. Later, when it was morning there, I called Martin McCarthy at the U.S. Embassy in Brasília; he called the police in São Paulo, and they called the phone company and found out where the call to me came from. A hotel. The boy disappeared from it during the night. I called Pacher here and asked him if he could get Brazil to watch for the SS men—the boy said they were leaving that day—and Pacher didn't exactly laugh at me but he said no, not without something concrete. A boy disappearing from a hotel room without paying his bill isn't concrete. And neither is me saying SS men are leaving because the boy told me so. I tried to get the German prosecutor in charge of the Mengele case but he was out. If it was still Fritz Bauer, he would be in for me, but the new one was out." He shrugged again, rubbed at the lobe of his ear. "So the men left Brazil, if the boy was right, and he hasn't been found yet. His father is down there pushing the police; a well-to-do man, I understand. But he has a dead son."

Beynon said apologetically, "I can't very well file a story in Vienna about a—"

"No, no, no," Liebermann interrupted, a quelling hand on Beynon's knee. "I don't want you to file a story. What I want you to do is this, Sydney; I'm sure it's possible and I hope it isn't too much trouble. The boy said the first killing will happen the day after tomorrow, October sixteenth. But he didn't say where. Will you have your main office in London send you clippings or reports from their other offices? Of men sixty-four to sixty-six years old, murdered or dying in accidents? Anything except natural deaths, from Wednesday on. Only men sixty-four to sixty-six."

Beynon frowned, poked at his glasses, and looked his doubts at Liebermann.

"It wasn't a hoax, Sydney. He wasn't a boy who would do that. He's been missing three weeks, and he wrote home regularly, called even when he changed hotels."

"Granted he's probably dead," Beynon said. "But mightn't he have been killed simply for snooping around where he wasn't welcome, another young fellow out after Mengele? Or even have been robbed and done away with by an ordinary thief? His death in no way proves that a . . . Nazi plot is under way to kill men of a particular age."

"He had it on tape. Why would he lie to me?"

"Perhaps he didn't. The tape might have been a hoax on *him*. Or maybe he was misinterpreting it."

Liebermann drew a breath, let it out, and nodded. "I know," he said. "That's possible. That's what I thought myself at first. And still think sometimes. But somebody has to check a little, and if I don't, who will? If he was wrong, he was wrong; I waste some time and bother Sydney Beynon for nothing. But if he was right—then it's something very big, and Mengele has a reason for doing it. And I have to find something *concrete*, so prosecutors will be in, not out, and stop it before it's finished. I'll tell you something, Sydney. You know what?"

"What."

"There's a Mundt in my book." He nodded somberly. "Right where he said there was, in a list of guards at Treblinka who committed atrocities. SS Hauptscharführer Alfried Mundt. I forgot him; who can remember all of them? He's a very thin folder: a woman in Riga saw him break the neck of a fourteen-year-old girl; a man in Florida was castrated by him and wants to come testify if I catch him. Alfried Mundt. So the boy was right *once*, maybe he was right *twice*. Will you get the clippings for me, please? I'd appreciate it."

Beynon pulled in breath, and yielded. "I'll see what I can do." He tucked his cup down beside him and got his notebook and pen from his jacket. "Which countries did you say?"

"Well, the boy mentioned Germany, and England, and Scandinavia—Norway, Sweden, Denmark—and the States. But the way he said it made it sound like there was other places besides that he was leaving out. So you should ask also for France and Holland."

Beynon glanced at him, and jotted shorthand.

"Thank you, Sydney," Liebermann said. "I'm really grateful.

Anything I turn up, you're the first to know. Not only in this, in everything."

Beynon said, "Do you have any idea how many men in their mid-sixties die every day?"

"By murder? Or in accidents that *could* be murder?" Liebermann shook his head. "No, not too many. I hope not. And some I'll be able to eliminate by their professions."

"What do you mean?"

Liebermann wiped a hand down over his mustache and held his chin, a finger crossing his lips. After a moment he lowered his hand and shrugged. "Nothing," he said. "Some other details the boy gave. Listen"—he pointed at Beynon's notebook—"be sure to put down there 'between sixty-four and sixty-six.'"

"I did," Beynon said, looking at him. "What other details?"

"Nothing important." Liebermann reached into his coat. "I fly to Hamburg at four-thirty," he said. "I'm speaking in Germany till November third." He brought out a wallet, a thick worn brown one. "So whatever you get, please mail it to my apartment so I'll have it when I get back." He gave a card to Beynon.

"And if you find what looks like a Nazi killing?"

"Who knows?" Liebermann put his wallet back in his coat. "I only walk one step at a time." He smiled at Beynon. "Especially in these shoes." He braced his hands on his thighs and stood up, looked about and shook his head disapprovingly. "Mm. A gloomy day." He turned and rebuked them all: "Why do you eat outside on such a day?"

"We're the Monday Mozart Club," Beynon said, smiling and cocking a thumb back toward the monument.

Liebermann held out his hand; Beynon took it. Liebermann smiled at the others and said, "I apologize for taking away from you this charming man."

"You can have him," Dermot Brody said.

Liebermann said to Beynon, "Thank you, Sydney. I knew I could depend on you. Oh, and listen." He bent and spoke lower, holding Beynon's hand. "Ask them please from Wednesday on. To continue, I mean. Because the boy said six men was going, and would Mengele send them all at once if some will do nothing for a long time? So there should be two more killings not long after the first one—that's if they're working in two-man teams—or five more, God forbid, if they're working separately. And if, of course, the boy was right. Will you do that?"

Beynon nodded. "How many killings are there to be altogether?" he asked.

Liebermann looked at him. "A lot," he said. He let go of Beynon's hand, straightened up, and nodded good-bys to the others. Thrusting his hands into his coat pockets, he turned and set off quickly toward the bustle and traffic of the Ring.

The four on the bench watched him go.

"Oh Lord," Beynon said, and Freya Neustadt shook her head sadly.

Dermot Brody leaned forward and said, "What was that last bit, Syd?"

"Would I ask them to *continue* pulling clips." Beynon put his notebook and pen inside his jacket. "There are going to be three or six killings, not merely one. And more besides."

Paul Higbee took his pipe from his mouth and said, "Funny thought: he's absolutely right."

"Oh, come off it," Freya said. "Nazis hating him over the telephone?"

Beynon picked up his cup and grappled at a sandwich-half. "The past two years have been awfully rough on him," he said.

"How old is he?" Freya asked pointedly.

"I'm not sure," Beynon said. "Oh, yes, I see. Just around sixty-five, I should think."

"You see?" Freya said to Paul. "So Nazis are killing sixty-five-year-old men. It's a nicely worked-out paranoid fantasy. In a month he'll be saying they're coming for *him*."

Dermot Brody, leaning forward again, asked Beynon, "Are you really going to get the clips?"

"Of course not," Freya said, and turned to Beynon. "You aren't, are you?"

Beynon sipped wine, held his sandwich. "Well I did say I'd try," he said. "And if I don't, he'll only come pestering me when he gets back. Besides, London will think I'm working on something." He smiled at Freya. "It never hurts to give that impression."

Unlike most men his age, sixty-five-year-old Emil Döring, once second administrative assistant to the head of the Essen Public Transport Commission, had not allowed himself to become a creature of habit. Retired now and living in Gladbeck, a town north of the city, he took especial care to vary his daily routine. He went for the morning papers at no regular hour, visited his sister in

Oberhausen on no particular afternoon, and passed the evenings—when he didn't decide at the last moment to stay home—at no one favorite neighborhood bar. He had three favorite bars rather, and chose among them only when he left the apartment. Sometimes he was back in an hour or two, sometimes not until after midnight.

All his life Döring had been aware of enemies lying in wait for him, and had protected himself not only by going armed, when he was old enough, but also by keeping his movements as unpredictable as possible. First there had been the big brothers of small schoolmates who had unjustly accused him of bullying. Then there had been his fellow soldiers, dullards all, who had resented his knack for ingratiating himself with officers and getting easy and safe assignments. Then there had been his rivals at the Transport Commission, some of whom could have given lessons in treachery to Machiavelli. Could Döring tell you stories about the Transport Commission!

And now, in what should have been his golden years, when he had thought he could finally lower his guard and relax, stow the old Mauser in the night-table drawer—now more than ever he knew himself to be in real danger of attack.

His second wife Klara, who was, as she never tired of reminding him in subtle ways, twenty-three years younger than he, was having, he was positive, an affair with their son's former clarinet teacher, a despicable near-faggot named Wilhelm Springer who was even younger than she—thirty-eight!—and at least half Jewish. Döring had no doubts whatsoever that Klara and her faggot-Jew Springer would be delighted to get him out of the way; not only would she be a widow, but a rich one. He had over three hundred thousand marks (that *she* knew about, plus five hundred thousand that *nobody* knew about, buried in two steel boxes in his sister's backyard). It was the money that kept Klara from divorcing him. She was waiting, and had been since the day they married, the bitch.

Well, she would go right *on* waiting; he was in fine health and ready for a dozen Springers to spring at him from alleyways. He went to the gym twice a week—not on regular afternoons—and sixty-five or no, was still damn good at man-to-man wrestling even if he wasn't so great any more at the man-to-woman kind. *He* was still damn good and his *Mauser* was still damn good; he liked to tell himself that, smiling as he patted the nice big hardness through the underarm of his coat.

He had told it to Reichmeider too, the surgical-equipment salesman he had met here at the Lorelei-Bar last night. What a pleasant fellow that Reichmeider was! He had really been interested in Döring's Transport Commission stories—had almost fallen off his stool laughing at the outcome of the '58 appropriation business. Talking to him had been a bit awkward at first because of the erratic way one of his eyes moved—it was obviously artificial—but Döring had soon got used to it and told him not only about the appropriation business but about the state investigation of '64 and the Zellermann scandal too. Then they had got to a more personal level —five or six beers had gone down the hatch—and Döring had opened up about Klara and Springer. That was when he had patted the Mauser and said what he said about himself and it. Reichmeider couldn't believe he was actually sixty-five. "I'd have sworn you were no more than fifty-seven, tops!" he had insisted. What a nice chap! It was a shame he was only going to be in the area for a few days; lucky, though, that he was staying in Gladbeck rather than in Essen proper.

It was to meet Reichmeider again, and tell him about the rise and fall of Oskar Know-It-All Vowinckel, that Döring had come back to the Lorelie-Bar tonight. But nine o'clock had long since passed and no Reichmeider, despite their clear understanding of the night before. There were a lot of noisy young men and pretty girls, one with her teats half out, and only a few old regulars—Fürst, Apfel, what's-his-name—none of them good listeners. It was more like a Friday or Saturday than a Wednesday. A soccer game tided back and forth on the television; Döring watched it, drank slowly, and looked through the mirror at those gorgeous young teats. Now and then he leaned back on his stool and tried to catch a glimpse of newcomers by the door, still hoping Reichmeider would make his promised appearance.

And make it he did, but most strangely and suddenly, a hand gripping Döring's shoulder, a skew-eyed urgency of whispering: "Döring, come outside quickly! There's something I have to tell you!" And he was gone again.

Confused and puzzled, Döring flagged for Franz's attention, threw a ten down, and pushed his way out. Reichmeider beckoned intently, withdrawing a ways down Kirchengasse. A handkerchief was wrapped around his left hand as if he had injured it; chalky dust streaked the legs and shoulders of his expensive-looking gray suit.

Hurrying to him, Döring said, "What's up? What happened to you?"

"It's *you* things are liable to happen to, not me!" Reichmeider said excitedly. "I've been stumbling through that building they're demolishing, down the street in the next block. Listen, what's-his-*name*, that fellow you told me about, the one who's fooling around with your wife!"

"Springer," Döring said, thoroughly puzzled but catching Reichmeider's excitement. "Wilhelm Springer!"

"I *knew* that was it!" Reichmeider exclaimed. "I *knew* I wasn't mistaken! What luck that I just happened to—Listen, I'll explain everything. I was coming along this street here, heading this way, and I had to take a leak, simply couldn't hold it in. So when I came to the building, the one they're demolishing, I went into the alley beside it; but it was too light there, so I found an opening in the doors they've got walling the place and slipped inside. I did what I had to, and just as I'm ready to come out again, two men come and stop right at the place where I came in. One calls the other one Springer"—he nodded his head slowly, affirmingly, as Döring drew breath—"and that one says to the first one things like, 'He's in the Lorelei right now, the old bastard.' And, 'We'll beat the shit out of that fat prick.' I *knew* Springer was the name you'd mentioned! That *is* your way home, isn't it?"

Döring, his eyes shut, breathed deeply and swallowed a portion of his fury. "Sometimes," he whispered, and opened his eyes. "I go different ways."

"Well, they're expecting you to go that way tonight. They're waiting there, both of them, with sticks of some kind, caps pulled down over their eyes, collars turned up; exactly as you said last night, Springer planning to spring from an alley! I went through the building and found a way out on this side."

Döring pulled in another deep breath and clapped a hand gratefully to Reichmeider's dusty shoulder. "Thank you," he said. "Thank you."

Smiling, Reichmeider said, "I'm sure you could lick both of them with one hand tied behind your back—the other fellow's a skinny little nothing—but the wisest thing, of course, is simply to go home another way. I'll go with you if you'd like. Unless, that is, you'd rather get rid of this Springer once and for all."

Questioningly, Döring looked at him.

"It's a golden opportunity, really," Reichmeider pointed out, "and he'll only come at you another night if you don't. It's quite simple; you walk down there, they attack"—he glanced down at Döring's coat and smiled skew-eyed at him—"and you let them have it. I'll be a few steps behind, to serve as your witness, and in the unlikely event that they give you any real trouble"—he leaned close and pulled his lapel out to show a holstered gun-butt—*"I'll* take care of them and *you'll* be *my* witness. Either way you'll be rid of him, and the most you'll have to pay is getting hit with a stick once or twice."

Döring stared at Reichmeider. He put his hand to his coat, pressed the hardness within. "My God," he said wonderingly, "to actually use this thing!"

Reichmeider unwrapped the handkerchief from his hand and blew at a bloody scrape on the back of it. "It'll give that wife of yours something to think about," he remarked.

"My God," Döring exulted, "I hadn't even thought of that! She'll faint at my feet! 'Oh say, Klara, do you remember Wilhelm Springer, Erich's clarinet teacher? He jumped me in the street tonight—I can't imagine why—and I killed him.'" He clutched his cheeks delightedly and whistled. "My God, it'll kill *her too!*"

"Come on, let's do it!" Reichmeider urged. "Before they lose their nerve and run away!"

They hurried down Kirchengasse's dark decline. Bright headlights swept up and raced past them.

"Who says there's no justice, eh?"

"'Fat prick'? Oh, you shitty little faggot, I'm going to get you right through the heart!"

They crossed deserted Lindenstrasse; walked slowly now and quietly, close against shuttered storefronts. And came to four stories of stonework building, dark and broken-topped against moonlit sky, footed at front and side with rough-built passages of lumber and painted doors. Reichmeider drew Döring into the side passage's blackness. "You stay here," he whispered; "I'll go through and make sure he didn't have ten others joining them."

"Yes, you'd better!" Döring got out the gun.

"I know the way now and I have a penlight; I won't be long. Stay right here."

"Don't let them see you!"

Away already, Reichmeider whispered, "Don't worry." The passage appeared, plank-roofed and door-walled in bobbing dim light. Reichmeider's tall thin silhouette strode into it, and turned to the inner wall and was gone, leaving blackness.

Alert and excited—and needing to pee—Döring held the wonderfully weighty Mauser, so many years carried and now to be used! He brought it closer to the passage's opening and inspected it in faint light from Lindenstrasse; caressed a hand along its smooth barrel, carefully pushed its safety catch down into the *ready* position.

He moved back against the wall where Reichmeider had put him. What a friend! What a real man! He would take him to dinner tomorrow night, at the Kaiserhof. And buy him something too, something gold. Cuff links maybe.

He stood in the now-growing-visible passage with the gun big in his hand; thought about shooting its death-bullets into Wilhelm Springer.

And—after police business—going home and telling Klara. Die, bitch.

There would even be stories in the papers! *Retired Transport Commission Administrator Slays Attackers.* A picture of him too. Television interviews?

He *really* had to pee. The beer. He pushed the safety catch back up and returned the gun to its neatly receiving holster. He turned to the wall, unzipped his fly, drew himself out; spread his feet wide and let go. What relief!

"Are you there, Döring?" Reichmeider called softly from above.

"Yes!" he answered, looking up at planks. "What are you doing up *there?*"

"It's easier to get across on this level. There's all kinds of crap down below. I'll be with you in a minute. Stay there. The light's gone out and I won't be able to find you if you move around."

"Did you see them?"

No answer. He peed on, looking at a crack between pale doors. Would Reichmeider be able to get down all right without the light? And had he seen Springer and the other, or was he still on the way? Hurry, Reichmeider!

A pattering above; he looked up again. Gravel or something falling on the planks. They burst in at him with thunder behind them; and wondering, hurting, he died quickly.

■

The last time he had spoken at Heidelberg—in 1970, that was—the auditorium had been a splendid old cathedral of blackened oak, crowded even beyond its thousand-seat capacity. This time it was a new sand-colored oyster shell for five hundred, very modern and well designed, with the last two rows empty. The speaking was much easier, of course, like talking in someone's large living room.

Real eye-to-eye contact with all these bright young kids. But still . . .

Well. It was going along nicely, as it had every night so far. German audiences, young ones, were always the best; really caring, attending, concerned about the past. They made *him* be his best, finding genuine feeling again where American and English audiences, less involved, allowed him to lapse into mechanical delivery of memorized lines. Speaking German made a difference too, of course—the freedom to use natural words rather than cope with "was" and "were" (and "*de*jected" and "*e*jected"; are you getting the clippings for me, Sydney?).

He snapped himself back into it. "In the beginning I only wanted vengeance," he told an intently watching young woman in the second row. "Vengeance for the deaths of my parents and sisters, vengeance for my own years in the concentration camps"— he spoke to the farther rows—"vengeance for *all* the deaths, for *everyone's* years. Why had I been spared if not to exact vengeance?" He waited. "Vienna certainly didn't need another composer." The usual small uplift of relieved laughter came; he smiled with it and chose a brown-haired young man on the far right (he looked a little like Barry Koehler). "But the trouble with vengeance," he told him, trying not to think about Barry, "is that, one, you can't get it, not really"—he looked away from the Barry-like young man, to the whole audience—"and two, even if you could, would it be of much use?" He shook his head. "No. So now I want something better than vengeance, and something almost as hard to get." He told it to the young woman in the second row: "I want remembrance." He told it to all of them: "Remembrance. It's hard to get because life goes on; every year we have new horrors—a Vietnam, terrorist activities in the Middle East and Ireland, assassinations"—(ninety-four sixty-five-year-old men?)—"and every year," he drove himself on, "the horror of horrors, the Holocaust, becomes farther away, a little less horrible. But philosophers have warned us: *if we forget the past, we are doomed to repeat it.* And *that* is why it's important to capture an Eichmann and a Mengele; so that they can—" He heard what he had said, was lost. "A Stangl, I mean," he fumbled. "Excuse me, I was indulging in some wishful thinking there."

They laughed a little, but it was no good, it had broken the build; he tried to restore it: "And that's why it's important to capture an Eichmann and a *Stangl*," he said. "So that they can be made to stand trial—not necessarily to convict them, no—but so that *witnesses can be brought forward*, to remind the world, and especially to remind *you*, who weren't even born yet when these things happened, that men no different on the outside from you and me can commit under certain circumstances the most barbarous and inhuman atrocities. So that you"—he pointed—"and you—and you—and you—will take care to see that those circumstances *shall never again be permitted to arise.*"

The End. He bent his head; applause flooded at him and he withdrew a step from the lectern, keeping title to it with a hand touching a rounded corner. He waited, breathing hard, then stepped forward, grasped the lectern again with both hands, and faced the applause into spattering near-silence. "Thank you," he said. "If you have questions now, I'll do my best to answer them." He looked around, chose and pointed.

Traunsteiner, leaning forward over a tightly held steering wheel, fired his car full-speed at the back of a gray-haired man walking on the road's shoulder. Swelling close in the headlight's explosive radiance, the man turned, raised a folded magazine above his eyes, back-stepped. The car's fender bowled him up and away. Fighting a smile, Traunsteiner swerved the car back full onto pavement, barely missing a white-on-blue intersection warning. Braking, and braking more, he swung the car screechingly left into a wider road posted *Esbjerg—14 Km.*

"Mainly by contributions," Liebermann said, "from Jews and other concerned people all over the world. And also by my income from writing and from engagements such as this." He pointed to a hand in the back row. A young woman stood up, pink-faced and plump; she began asking what he saw was going to be the Frieda Maloney question.

"I can see," the young woman said, "that it's important to get the key people put on trial, the ones who held high positions. But aren't you still motivated by vengeance in a case like Frieda Maloney, a rank-and-file guard who gets dragged back here after being an American citizen for so many years? Whatever she did during the war, hasn't she made up for it by what she's done since? She was a very useful citizen there. Teaching and so on." The young woman sat down.

He nodded and stayed silent for a moment, smoothing his mustache down thoughtfully—as if he had never been asked the question before. Then he said, "I gather from your question that you're aware that a woman who has been a nursery-school teacher, and a finder of homes for homeless babies, and a good housewife, kind to stray dogs, can also have been—the self-same woman!—a 'rank-and-file' concentration-camp guard, guilty, perhaps—her trial, when it finally takes place, will tell us—of mass murder. I ask you now: would you be aware of this somewhat surprising possibility if Frieda Altschul Maloney hadn't been found and extradited? I don't think so, and I don't think it's an unimportant possibility for you to be aware of. Neither does your government."

He looked around—at hands springing up, including the hand of the Barry-like young man. He looked away from him (not now, Barry, I'm busy) and pointed at a shrewd-looking blond young man at dead center. ("There are *ninety-four of them*," Barry's telephone voice insisted, "and they're *all sixty-five-year-old civil servants*. How do you like *them* apples?")

A new question was coming at him. "But Frieda Maloney hasn't even been indicted yet," the blond young man was saying. "Is our government really so interested in pursuing Nazi criminals? Is any government in the world today, even the Israeli? Hasn't there been a decline of interest, and isn't that one of the reasons why you haven't been able to reopen your Information Center?"

So who tells you to pick the shrewd-looking ones? "First of all," he said, "the Center is temporarily in smaller quarters, but it's still open. People are working; letters come in, advisories go out. As I said before, we're funded by private individuals and in no way dependent on any government. Secondly, though it's true that both German and Austrian prosecutors are no longer as . . . responsive as they once were, and Israel has other more pressing problems, the cause of justice hasn't yet been deserted. I have it on good authority that Frieda Maloney will be indicted sometime in January or February, and brought to trial soon after. The witnesses have been found, a difficult and time-consuming job in which the Center played a part." He looked at raised hands again, bright young faces —and suddenly realized exactly what he was looking at. A gold mine, for God's sake! Right in front of him!

Here in this luminous oyster shell were nearly five hundred of the smartest young people in Germany, the cream of their generation, and he was trying to figure the thing out alone, one old fool with one tired brain. Dear God!

Ask *them?* Crazy!

He must have pointed at someone; the neo-Nazism question had been asked. "Two factors are necessary for a resurgence of Nazism," he recited quickly, "a worsening of social conditions till they approximate those of the early thirties and the emergence of a Hitler-like leader. Should both these factors come into being, neo-Nazi groups around the world would of course become a focus of danger, but at the present time, no, I'm not particularly alarmed." Hands sprang up, but he raised his hand against them. "Just a minute, please," he said. "I'd like to interrupt the questions for a moment—and ask one instead of answering."

The hands fell away. The bright young faces looked at him expectantly.

Crazy! But how could he *not* try to make use of such brainpower?

He gripped the lectern with both hands, took a breath, thought. "I want," he said to the oyster shell full of such excellent pearls, "to borrow your brains to solve a problem. A *hypothetical* problem that a young friend presented to me. I'm very anxious to solve it, so much so that I'm willing to cheat a little and get help." Small laugh. "And who could help me better than students of this great university and their friends?"

He let go of the lectern and stood straight, looked at them casually—a man offering a hypothetical problem, not a real one.

"I've told you about the Comrades Organization in South America," he said, "and about Dr. Mengele. Here's the problem my friend presented. The Organization and Dr. Mengele decide that they want to kill a large number of men in different countries of Europe and North America. Ninety-four men, to be exact, and they're *all sixty-five years old and civil servants*. The killings are to take place over a two-and-a-half-year period, and there's a political motivation for them, a Nazi motivation. What is it? Can you find an answer for me? Who are these men? Why are their deaths desirable to the Comrades Organization and Dr. Mengele?"

The audience of young people sat uncertainly. A hum of whispering grew among them. A cough broke out: another cough echoed it.

He took the lectern—casually. "I'm not joking with you," he said. "This problem was put to me. As an exercise in logic. Can you help me?"

They leaned to one another, and the hum of whispering intensified, became the buzz of ideas being hazarded.

"Ninety-four men," he said slowly, guidingly. "Sixty-five years old. Civil servants. In various countries. Two and a half years."

A hand came up, and another.

Hoping, he took the first; a few rows back, left of center. "Yes?"

A young man in a blue sweater stood up. "The men hold positions of responsibility," he said in an unexpectedly high-pitched voice. "Their deaths will directly or indirectly bring about the worsening of social conditions you just referred to, creating a more suitable climate for a rebirth of Nazism."

He shook his head. "No, I don't think so," he said. "Could the killing of highly placed men go on for months, let alone two and a half years, without attracting attention and causing investigation? No, the men must be *low*-echelon civil servants. And at sixty-five they'll more than likely be retiring anyway, so removing them from their jobs can't possibly be the object of killing them."

"Why kill them at all?" a voice called from the right rear. "They'll soon die naturally!"

He nodded. "That's right," he said. "They'll soon die naturally. So why kill them at all? That's what I'm asking you." He pointed at the second hand that had come up, at the rear center; other hands were up now.

A tall young man stood and said, "They're Nazi sympathizers without families, who've left their life savings to Nazi groups. It's murder for money. There's some reason why they need funds now rather than five or ten years from now."

"That's possible," he said, "though it seems unlikely. As I mentioned before, the Comrades Organization has enormous wealth that it smuggled from Europe before the war's end." He pulled his pen free of his breast pocket and clicked its top. "Still, it's a possibility." He turned over one of his note cards on the lectern, and on the back of it wrote: *Money?* He raised the pen and pointed with it to the right.

A young woman with glasses and long brown hair stood up. "It seems much more likely to me," she said, "that the men are anti-Nazi rather than pro-Nazi, and obviously there's a connection of some kind between them. Could they be members of an international Jewish group that threatens the Comrades Organization in some way?"

"I think I would know of such a group," he said, "and I've never heard of *any* group of *any* kind whose members are all sixty-five."

The young woman stayed standing. "Maybe their being sixty-five now isn't what's important," she said. "The . . . connection might have been established when they were younger, when they were all *thirty*-five or *twenty*-five. Maybe they were all involved in a certain military action in the war, and killing them is an act of revenge."

"Some are German," he said, "and some are English and American, and some are Swedes, who were neutral. But—"

"A U.N. patrol!" someone called.

"They'd have been too old," he answered, and looked again to the long-haired young woman, who had sat down. "But that's an interesting point," he said, "about sixty-five not being the significant age, for of course they've all been the same ages all their lives, so that opens the door to other possibilities. Thank you."

He wrote: *Link at earlier age?*—and someone called out, "Are they natives of those countries or only living there?"

He looked up. "Another good point," he said. "I don't know. Perhaps they *were* one nationality originally." *Where born?* he wrote. "This is good, keep it up!" He pointed.

A young man sitting cross-legged in the front row said, "They're people who help *you*, your major contributors."

"You flatter me. I'm not that important and I also don't *have* ninety-four major contributors. Of any age." He pointed elsewhere.

The Barry-like young man: "When does the two-and-a-half-year period begin, sir?"

"Two days ago."

"Then it ends in the spring of 1977. Is there an important political event scheduled to take place then? Maybe the killings are going to be announced, as a show of strength, or a warning."

"But why these particular men? Yet again an interesting point. Does anyone know of an important event, political or otherwise, scheduled for the spring of 1977?" He looked around.

Silence, and heads shaking. "My graduation!" someone called. Laughter and applause.

Spring '77? he wrote, and smiling, pointed.

The young man in the blue sweater again, with his high-pitched voice: "The men aren't highly placed themselves, but their sons, who are in their forties, are. And the men are to be killed so that their sons will have to neglect important work to attend their funerals."

Derision. Booing and hoots of scorn.

"That's slightly far-fetched," he said, "but still, there's the germ of something to think about. *Are* the men related to important people, or associated with them somehow?" He wrote: *Relations? Friends?* —and pointed.

The shrewd-looking blond young man stood up. Smiling, he said, "Herr Liebermann, is this really only a hypothetical problem?"

Never pick this boy again. A stillness expanded through the auditorium. "Of course it is," he said.

"Then you must ask your friend to give you some more information," the shrewd-looking young man said. "Not even the great brains of Heidelberg can solve his problem without at least one more relevant fact about the ninety-four men. Given the information we have now, we can only speculate blindly."

"You're right," he said, "more information is needed. But the speculation helps; it suggests possibilities." He looked around. "Does anyone have any more speculation?"

A hand came up at the left rear; he pointed at it.

An elderly man stood up, white-haired and frail-looking—a faculty member or perhaps a student's grandfather. Leaning on the back of the seat before him, he said in a firm and contemptuous voice, "Not one of the suggestions made so far has recognized *Dr. Mengele's* presence in the problem. Why is he introduced if the killings are only political killings of the conventional kind, which the Comrades Organization could engineer without him? He is introduced, obviously, because of his *medical background*, and I therefore suggest a medical aspect to the killings. They might, for instance, constitute the covert testing of a new *means* of killing, and the men would therefore have been chosen precisely *because* they're old, unimportant, and no menace to Nazism. A testing program would also explain the lengthy time-span. In the spring of 1977 the real killings would begin." He sat down.

Liebermann stood looking at him for a moment, and then he said, "Thank you, sir." To the whole audience he said, "I hope for your sake this gentleman is one of your professors."

"He is," several voices assured him bitterly, and the name Geirasch was spoken.

WHY M.??? he wrote—and looked up again in the man's direction. "I don't think a testing program would be limited to civil servants," he said, "or even carried out in this part of the world rather than in South America, but you're surely right about there being a specific reason for Dr. Mengele's involvement. Can anyone think of one?" He looked around.

The young people sat silently.

"A medical aspect to the ninety-four killings?" He looked to the long-haired young woman; she shook her head.

The Barry-like young man shook his, and so did the young man in the blue sweater.

He hesitated—and looked to the shrewd-looking blond young man, who smiled at him and shook his head.

He looked at his card on the lectern:

> *Money?*
> *Link at earlier age?*
> *Where born?*
> *Spring '77?*
> *Relations? Friends?*
> *WHY M.???*

He looked at the audience. "Thank you," he said. "You haven't solved the problem, but you've given me suggestions that may lead to the solution, so I'm grateful to you. We'll go back now to *your* questions."

Hands sprang up. He pointed.

A young woman next to the Barry-like young man stood up and said, "Herr Liebermann, what's your opinion of Moshe Gorin and the Jewish Defenders?"

"I've never met Rabbi Gorin, so I have no opinion of him personally," he said automatically. "As for his Young Jewish Defenders; if they're defending, fine. But if, as is sometimes reported, they're attacking, then not so fine. Brown shirts are never good, no matter who's wearing them."

And silver-haired Horst Hessen, sweating in bright sunlight, raised large binoculars to his blue eyes and watched a bare-chested man in a white sun hat riding a power mower slowly across a vivid green lawn. A flagpole flew an American flag; the house beyond was a neat one-story box of glass and redwood. A black cloud shot with leaping orange replaced the man and the mower, and a thud of explosion came bluntly through distance.

the Führer's portrait and all the smaller photos and mementos of him over to the west wall above the sofa—which had meant moving his own degrees and commendations and family photos to whatever spaces he could find for them between the two outside windows in the south wall and around the laboratory observation window and the doorway in the east wall. He had then had the cleared north wall fitted with a waist-level three-inch wood molding, above which the pale-gray wallpaper had been stripped away. Two coats of white paint had been laid on, the first flat and the second semi-glossy. The molding had been painted pale gray. When all the paint was thoroughly dry he had had a sign-painter flown down from Rio.

The sign-painter made beautifully straight thin black lines and lettered handsomely, but in his first light pencilings he showed an inclination to miscopy and/or misplace unfamiliar marks of pronunciation, and to go his own Brazilian way in the matter of spelling. For four days, therefore, Mengele had sat behind his desk, watching, instructing, warning. He had come to dislike the sign-painter, and by the second day was glad the dolt was going to be thrown from the plane.

When the job was done, and the long table with its neat stacks of journals in place against the wall, Mengele could lean back in his steel-and-leather chair and admire the very chart he had envisioned. The ninety-four names, each with its country, date, and square box as if for balloting, were set out in three columns, the middle one of necessity a name longer than the two outer ones (a small annoyance, but what could be done at this late date?). There they all were, from 1. *Döring—Deutschland—16/10/74* ☐ to *94. Ahearn—Kanada—23/4/77* ☐. How he looked forward to filling in each of those boxes! He would do *that* himself, of course, with either red or black paint, he hadn't yet decided which. Perhaps he would try making checks, and if the first few didn't turn out uniformly, *then* fill in the boxes.

He swung in his chair and smiled at the Führer. *You don't mind being moved to the side for this, do you, my Führer? Of course not; how could you?*

Then, alas, there had been nothing to do but wait—till the first of November, when the calls would come in to headquarters.

He had busied himself in the laboratory, where he was trying, not very enthusiastically, to transplant chromosomes in frog-cell nuclei.

He flew into Asunción one day; visited his barber and a prostitute, bought a digital clock, had a good steak at La Calandria with Franz Schiff.

And now, at last, the day had come—a fine one, so blinding-bright that he had drawn the study curtains. The radio was on and tuned to the headquarters frequency, with the earphones lying ready beside a memo pad and pen. On a corner of the desk's glass top a white linen towel was laid out; on it, in surgical line-up, were a small unopened can of red enamel, a screwdriver, a new thin short-bristled paintbrush, a coverless petri dish, and a screw-top can of turpentine. The left end of the long table had been drawn from the wall; a stepladder waited before the first column of names and countries.

He had decided to try the checks.

Shortly before noon, when he was beginning to get quite impatient, the drone of a plane came with increasing loudness through the curtains. The drone of the *headquarters* plane—which meant either very good or very bad news. He hurried from the study, through the hall, and out onto the porch, where a few servants' children sat breaking up a flat cake of some kind. He stepped over them and went around the side of the house to the back and down the few steps. The plane was just dropping behind treetops. Shielding his eyes, he hurried across the yard—a servant stopped leaning, started hoeing—and past the servants' house and the barracks and the generator shed. Jogging, he entered the greened-over pathway cut through thick jungle foliage. He could hear the plane landing. He slowed to a fast walk, tucked the back of his shirt down into his trousers, got out his handkerchief and wiped his brow and cheeks. Why the plane, why not the radio? Something had gone wrong; he was sure of it. Liebermann? Had that *filth* somehow managed to end everything? If he had, he himself would personally go to Vienna and find and kill him. What else would he have left to live for?

He came out onto the side of the grass airstrip in time to see the red-and-white twin-engine plane rolling slowly toward his own smaller silver-and-black one. Two of the guards were lounging there with the pilot, who waved at him. He nodded. Another guard was across the strip at the chain-link fence, holding something through it, trying to lure an animal. Against rules, but he didn't call out to him; he watched the door of the red-and-white plane, stopped now, propellers dying. Silently prayed.

The door swung down, and one of the guards trotted over to help a tall man in a light-blue suit down the steps.

Colonel Seibert! It *had* to be bad news.

He started forward slowly.

The colonel saw him, waved—cheerfully enough—and came toward him. He was carrying a red shopping bag.

Mengele walked faster. "News?" he called.

The colonel nodded, smiling. "Yes, *good* news!"

Thank God! He speeded. "I was worried!"

They shook hands. The colonel, handsome with his strong Nordic face and white-blond hair, smiled and said, "All the 'salesmen' checked in. The October 'customers' have all been seen; four on the exact dates, two a day early, and one a day late."

Mengele pressed his chest and breathed. "Praise God! I was worried, the plane coming."

"I felt like taking a flight," the colonel said. "It's such a beautiful day."

They walked together toward the pathway.

"*All seven?*"

"All seven. Without a hitch." The colonel offered the shopping bag. "This is for you. A mystery package from Ostreicher."

"Oh," Mengele said, and took it. "Thanks. It's no mystery. I asked him to get me some silk; one of my housemaids is going to make shirts for me. Will you stay for lunch?"

"I can't," the colonel said. "I have a rehearsal for my granddaughter's wedding at three o'clock. Did you know she's marrying Ernst Roebling's grandson? Tomorrow. I'll have some coffee and talk awhile, though."

"Wait till you see my chart."

"Chart?"

"You'll see."

The colonel saw, and was enthusiastic. "Beautiful! An absolute work of art! You didn't do this yourself, did you?"

Putting the shopping bag by the desk, Mengele said happily, "God no, I'm not even sure I can make the checks decently! I had a man flown down from Rio."

The colonel turned and looked at him, surprised and questioning.

"Don't worry," Mengele said, raising a reassuring hand, "he had an accident on his way home."

"A bad one, I hope," the colonel said.

"Very."

Their coffee was brought. The colonel examined some of the Führer's photos and then they sat on the sofa and sipped at small gold-and-white cups of steaming blackness. "They've all settled themselves in apartments," the colonel said, "except Hessen, who's bought a camping truck. I told him to call in once a week, since we won't be able to reach *him* if we want to. He's only going to use it till the bad weather sets in."

Mengele said, "I need to have the dates the men were killed. For my records."

"Of course." The colonel put his cup and saucer on the coffee table. "I've had it all typed up." He reached inside his jacket.

Mengele put his cup and saucer down and took the folded sheet of flimsy the colonel offered. He opened it, held it away, squinted at typing. Smiling, he shook his head. "Four out of seven on the exact dates!" he marveled. "Isn't that something?"

"They're good men," the colonel said. "Schwimmer and Mundt have their next ones set up already. Farnbach needed some talking to; he's a bit of a questioner."

"I know," Mengele said. "He gave me trouble when I briefed them."

"I don't think he'll give any more of it," the colonel said. "I chewed him out good and proper."

"Good for you." Mengele refolded the pleasingly crackly paper and put it on the coffee table's corner, set it flush with the edges. He looked at the chart and imagined the seven red checks he would paint when the colonel left. He lifted his cup, hoping to set an example.

"Colonel Rudel called me yesterday morning," the colonel said. "He's on the Costa Brava."

"Oh?" Mengele saw at once that the pleasure of flying wasn't the reason the colonel had come. What was? "How is he?" he asked, and sipped his coffee.

"Fine," the colonel said. "But a little concerned. He had a letter from Günter Wenzler, warning him that Yakov Liebermann may be on to an operation of ours. Liebermann spoke at Heidelberg two weeks ago. He asked the audience a rather unusual 'hypothetical question.' A friend of Wenzler's, whose daughter was there, told him to pass the word, just in case."

"What exactly did Liebermann ask?"

The colonel looked at Mengele for a moment, and said, "Why we —you and us—would want to kill ninety-four sixty-five-year-old civil servants. A 'hypothetical question.'"

Mengele shrugged. "So obviously he doesn't know," he said. "I'm sure no one came up with the right answer."

"Rudel is sure too," the colonel said, "but he'd like to know how Liebermann came up with the right question. It doesn't seem to surprise *you* very much."

Mengele sipped his coffee and spoke casually. "The American wasn't listening to the tape when we found him. He was talking to Liebermann." He put his cup down and smiled at the colonel. "As I'm sure you found out from the telephone company yesterday afternoon."

The colonel sighed and leaned toward Mengele. "Why didn't you tell us?" he asked.

"Frankly," Mengele said, "I was afraid you would want to postpone, in case Liebermann got an investigation going."

"You were right, that's *exactly* what we would have wanted," the colonel said. "Three or four months—would it have been so terrible?"

"It might have changed the results completely. Believe me, that's true, Colonel. Ask any psychologist."

"Then we could have skipped those men and picked up on schedule with the others."

"Reducing the outcome by twenty percent? There are eighteen men in the first four months."

"And don't you think you've reduced the outcome more this way?" the colonel demanded. "Is Liebermann only talking to students? The men, *our* men, could be arrested tomorrow! And the outcome reduced by *ninety-five* percent!"

"Colonel, please," Mengele placated.

"Assuming, of course, that there *is* an outcome. So far we have only your word for that, you know!"

Mengele sat silently, inhaled deeply. The colonel lifted his cup, glared at it, set it down again.

Mengele let his breath out. "There will be exactly the outcome I promised," he said. "Colonel, stop and think a moment. Would Liebermann bother with questions to students if anyone else was listening to him? The men are out, aren't they? Doing their jobs? Of course Liebermann talked to others—maybe to every prosecutor and policeman in Europe!—but obviously they ignored him. What else would they do?—an old Naziphobe like him coming to them with a story that must sound *insane* when he can't give the reason behind it. That's what I counted on when I *made* the decision."

"*It wasn't your decision to make,*" the colonel said. "You put six of our men into much more danger than we bargained for."

"And by doing so preserved your very large investment, not to mention the destiny of the race." Mengele got up and went to the desk, took a cigarette from a brass cup of them. "Anyway, it's water over the dam," he said.

The colonel sipped coffee, looking at Mengele's back. He lowered his cup and said, "Rudel wanted me to call the men in today."

Mengele turned, took the lighted cigarette from his lips. "I don't believe that," he said.

The colonel nodded. "He takes his responsibilities as an officer very seriously."

"He has responsibilities as an Aryan!"

"True, but he's never been as sure as the rest of us that the project will work; you know that, Josef. Good Lord, the selling job we had to do!"

Mengele stood silently—hostile, waiting.

"I told him pretty much what you just told me," the colonel said. "If the men check in and everything's all right, then Liebermann hasn't been able to stir anything up, so why not leave them out? He finally agreed. But Liebermann's going to be watched from now on—Mundt's taking care of it—and if there's any sign that he *is* stirring anything up, then a decision will have to be made: either to kill him, which might only stir things up further, or to bring the men in."

Mengele said, "Do that and you throw everything down the drain. Everything I achieved. All the money you spent on staff and equipment and arranging the placements. How can he even think of it? I'd send out six *more* men if these were caught. And six *more*. And six *more!*"

"I agree, Josef, I agree," the colonel soothed. "And I'd like very much for you to have a voice in the decision if it ever actually has to be made. A strong voice. But if Rudel learns now that you let the men leave knowing Liebermann was alerted—he'll cut you out of the operation completely. You won't even get the monthly reports. So I'd rather not tell him. But before I can do that I have to have an assurance from you that you won't . . . make any more solo decisions."

"About what? There are no more decisions to be made, except to keep the men out and working."

The colonel smiled. "I wouldn't put it past you to hop on a plane and go after Liebermann yourself."

Mengele drew at his cigarette. "Don't be ridiculous," he said. "You know I wouldn't dare go to Europe." He turned to the desk and tapped ash into a tray.

"Do I have your assurance," the colonel asked, "that you won't do *anything* affecting the operation without checking with the Organization?"

"Of course you do," Mengele said. "Absolutely."

"Then I'll tell Rudel it's a mystery how Liebermann got wind of things."

Mengele shook his head incredulously. "I cannot believe," he said, "that that old fool—Rudel, I mean, not Liebermann—would write off so much money, and the Aryan destiny along with it, out of concern for the safety of six ordinary men."

"The money was only a fraction of what we have," the colonel said. "We exaggerated its importance to keep you cost-conscious. As for the Aryan destiny, well, as I said, he's never fully believed the project will work. I think it smacks a little of magic or witchcraft to him; he's hardly a scientific-minded man."

"You'd be insane to let him have the final say."

"We'll cross that bridge when we come to it," the colonel said. "*If* we come to it. Let's hope Liebermann stops talking even to students, and you get to make ninety-four checks on this beautiful chart." He stood up. "Walk me to the plane." He thrust out a robot-stiff leg and stumped in slow motion, singing: "'Here comes the bride'—step!—'All dressed in white'—step! What a nuisance! I'm for simple weddings, aren't you? But try telling that to a woman."

Mengele walked him to the plane, waved him into the sky, and went back into the house. His lunch was waiting in the dining room, so he ate it, and then scrubbed his hands at the lab sink and went into the study. He gave the can of enamel a good shaking and used the screwdriver to pry its lid off. He put on his glasses, and holding the can of bright red and the new thin brush, mounted the stepladder.

He dipped the bristles, pared them against the can's rim, took a steadying breath, and brought the red-tipped brush to the box next to *Döring—Deutschland—16/10/74*.

The check came out quite nicely: gleaming red on white, straight-edged and jaunty-looking.

He touched it up a bit and painted a similar check in the box of *Horve—Dänemark—18/10/74*.

And *Guthrie—V.St.A.—19/10/74*.

He got down off the stepladder, backed away, and studied the three checks over his glasses.

Yes, they would do.

He climbed back up on the stepladder and painted checks in the boxes of *Runsten—Schweden—22/10/74*, and *Rausenberger—Deutschland—22/10/74*, and *Goodwood—England—24/10/74*, and *Oste—Holland—27/10/74*.

He got back down and took another look.

Very nice. Seven red checks.

But hardly any pleasure at all.

Damn Rudel! Damn Seibert! Damn Liebermann! Damn *everybody!*

■

Pandemonium, that was what he came back to. Glanzer the landlord, who would have made a marvelous anti-Semite if not for the fact that he was Jewish, shouted accusations at a trembling little Esther while Max and a gawky young woman Liebermann had never seen before pushed at Lili's desk, forcing it toward the corner by the bedroom door. A musical pinging and plopping came from pots and bowls that sat everywhere catching water-drops that fell from dark wetnesses all over the ceiling. A piece of crockery smashed in the kitchen—"Oh *rats!*" (that was Lili in there)—and the phone rang. "Aha!" Glanzer cried, turning, pointing. "Now comes the big world figure who doesn't care about the average man's property. Don't put that suitcase down, *the floor won't take it!*"

"Welcome home," Max said, hauling at an end of the desk.

Liebermann put his suitcase down, and his briefcase. He had expected, because it was Sunday morning, a quiet, empty apartment. "What happened?" he asked.

"What happened?" Glanzer squeezed toward him between the backs of two desks, his bulbous face fire-red. "I'll tell you what happened! We had a flood upstairs, that's what happened! You overload the floor, you put strain on the pipes! So they break! You think they can take this load you've got here?"

"The pipes *upstairs* break and I'm to blame?"

"Everything's connected!" Glanzer shouted. "Strain is transmitted! The whole *house*'ll come down because of the overloading you've got here!"

"Yakov?" Esther held out the phone with a hand on its mouthpiece. "A man named von Palmen, in Mannheim. He called last week." A wisp of gray hair stuck out from under the side of her red-brown wig.

"Get the number, I'll call him back."

"I just broke the pink bowl," Lili said, standing mournfully in the kitchen doorway. "Hannah's favorite."

"Out!" Glanzer shouted, on top of Liebermann, spewing bad breath. "All these desks go out! This is an apartment house not an office building! And the file cabinets too, out!"

"*You* go out!" Liebermann shouted just as loud—the best way to deal with Glanzer, he had found. "Go fix your rotten plumbing! This is my furniture, desks and file cabinets! Does it say in the lease only tables and chairs?"

"You'll find out in court what it says in the lease!"

"*You'll* find out what you pay for this water damage! Get *out!*" Liebermann thrust a finger toward the door.

Glanzer blinked. He looked at the floor beside him as if hearing something, looked at Liebermann worriedly, nodded. "You bet I'm getting out," he whispered. "Before it happens." He tiptoed his bulk toward the open door. "My life is more precious to me than my property." He tiptoed out, and drew the door cautiously closed.

Liebermann stamped on the floor and called, "I'm stamping on the floor, Glanzer!"

From a distance came "Fall through!"

"Yakov, don't," Max said, touching Liebermann's arm. "We're liable to."

Liebermann turned. He looked around, and up, and let out a woeful "Ei, yei, *yei*" and bit his lower lip.

Esther, stretching to wipe at the top of a file cabinet, said, "We caught it early, it's not that bad. Thank God I baked this morning. I brought over a nut cake. When I saw what was doing I called Max and Lili. It's just in here and the kitchen, not the other rooms."

Max introduced the gawky young woman, who had beautiful large gray eyes; she was his and Lili's niece Alix from Brighton, England, staying with them on her vacation. Liebermann shook her hand and thanked her for helping, and took his coat off and joined in the work.

They wiped the desks and furniture, replaced full pots and bowls with emptied ones, held towel-covered brooms to the wet places in the ceiling.

Then, sitting at desks and the accessible half of the sofa, they had coffee and cake. The leaks had dwindled to half a dozen slow trickles. Liebermann talked about the trip a little, about old friends he had visited, changes he had seen. Alix, in halting German, answered questions from Esther about her work as a textile designer.

"A lot of contributions, Yakov," Max reported, nodding his gray head solemnly.

Lili said, "Always after the Holy Days."

"But more this year than last, darling," Max said, and to Liebermann: "People know about the bank."

Liebermann nodded and looked to Esther. "Did anything come for me from Reuters? Reports? Clippings?"

"There's a Reuters envelope," Esther said, "a big one. But it says Personal."

"Reports?" Max asked.

"I spoke to Sydney Beynon before I left. About the Koehler boy's story. There wasn't anything about *him*, was there?"

They shook their heads.

Esther, rising with her cup and saucer on her plate, said, "It can't be true, it's too crazy." She moved to Max's desk. Lili rose, gathering her plates, but Esther said, "Leave everything, I'll clean up. You go show Alix the sights."

Liebermann thanked Max and Lili and Alix as they put on their coats. He kissed Lili, shook hands with Alix and wished her a happy vacation, patted Max on the back. When he had closed the door after them, he picked up his suitcase and carried it into the bedroom.

He went to the bathroom, took his twelve-o'clock pills, hung his other suit in the closet, and exchanged his jacket for his sweater and his shoes for his slippers. With his glasses in his hand he went back into the living room, picked up his briefcase, and went around and between desks toward the French doors to the dining room.

Esther said from the kitchen doorway, "I'll stick around and keep an eye on the dripping. Do you want me to get that man in Mannheim?"

"Later," Liebermann said, and went into the dining room—his office now.

The desk was heaped with magazines and stacks of opened letters. He put the briefcase down, switched the lamp on, put on his glasses; moved a stack of letters from several large envelopes beneath. He found the gray Reuters envelope, hand-addressed, bulkily full. So many?

Sitting, he cleared everything else out of the way, pushed piles of mail to the sides and back of the desk. Hannah's picture turned; magazines slapped the floor.

He unwound the envelope's string fastener and tore the taped flap open. Tilting the envelope to green blotter, he shook out, pulled out, a mass of newspaper clippings and teletype tear-offs. Twenty, thirty, more, some of them photocopies, most quick-scissored patches of newsprint. *Mann getötet in Autounfall; Priest Slain by Robbers; Eldsvåda dödar man, 64.* Blue and yellow labels with dates and the names of newspapers were pasted to some of the clippings. A good forty items altogether.

He looked into the envelope and found two more small clippings and a sheet of white paper that had been folded around the whole bundle.

Keep me posted, it said in small neat handwriting at its center. S.B. Dated *30 Oct.*

He put it aside along with the envelope, and spreading the clippings and tear-offs with both hands, opened them out to greater visibility, a layered patchwork of French, German, English—and Swedish, Dutch, others, indecipherable except for a word here and there. *Död* was surely *tot* and *dead.* "Esther!" he called.

"Yes?"

"The dictionaries for translating, Swedish and Dutch. And Danish and Norwegian." He picked up a German clipping: an explosion in a chemical plant in Solingen had killed a night watchman, August Mohr, sixty-five. No. He put it aside.

And took it back. Mightn't a civil servant, a low-level one, have a second job at night? Unlikely for a sixty-five-year-old, but possible. The explosion had happened at one in the morning on the day before the story appeared, making it October 20th.

The overhead light went on, and Esther, crossing the room, said, "They must be in here." She went to the dining table against the wall and read the sides of the cartons on it. "We don't have a Danish one," she said. "Max uses the Norwegian."

Liebermann got a pad from the drawer. "You'd better give me the French too."

"First let me find."

He reached for his pen standing up among the mail. Glancing again at the clipping, he wrote on the large yellow pad—after a scribble at the top to get the pen going: *20; Mohr, August Solingen,* and put a question mark after it.

"Dictionaries," Esther announced, and opened the flaps of a carton. "Norwegian, Swedish, French?"

"And Dutch, please." He put the clipping to the left, where he would keep the possibles. He looked for the one in English about the priest, found it, skimmed it, and—"Ei"—put it to the right.

Esther came, unsteadily carrying four thick blue-bound volumes. He pulled mail in from the side of the desk to make room for them. "Everything was organized," she complained, setting them down.

"I'll *re*organize. Thanks."

She tucked hair in under the side of her wig. "You should have kept Max here if you wanted translations."

"I didn't think."

"Should I try to find him?"

He shook his head, picked up another clipping in English: *Dispute Ends in Fatal Knifing.*

Esther, looking troubledly at the spread of clippings, said, "So many men murdered?"

"Not all," he said, putting the clipping to his right. "Some are accidents."

"How will you know which ones the Nazis killed?"

"I won't," he said. "I'll have to go look." He picked up a German clipping.

"Look?"

"And see if I can find a reason."

She scowled at him. "Because a boy calls up and disappears?"

"Good-by, Esther dear."

She went from the desk. "*I* would be writing articles and making some money."

"Write them, I'll sign them."

"Do you want something to eat?"

He shook his head.

A few of the items reported the same deaths as others; a few of the dead men were outside the age-range. Many were tradesmen, farmers, retired industrial workers, vagrants; many had been killed by neighbors, relations, bands of young hoodlums. He searched the bilingual dictionaries with his magnifying glass; a *makelaar in onroerende goederen* was a real-estate broker, a *tulltjänsteman* a customs officer. He put the can't-bes to his right, the possibles to his left. Most of the words in the Danish clippings were in the Norwegian-German dictionary.

Late in the afternoon he put the final clipping with the can't-bes. There were eleven possibles.

He tore the list of them from the pad and started a fresh list, setting them down neatly according to the dates of death.

Three had died on October 16th: Chambon, Hilaire, in Bordeaux; Döring, Emil, in Gladbeck, a town in the Essen area; and Persson, Lars, in Fagersta, Sweden.

The phone rang; he let Esther take it.

Two on the 18th: Guthrie, Malcolm, in Tucson—

"Yakov? It's Mannheim again."

He picked up the phone. "Liebermann speaking."

"Hello, Herr Liebermann," a man's voice said. "How was your trip? And did you find the reason for the ninety-four killings?"

He sat still, looking at the pen in his hand. He had heard the voice before but couldn't place it. "Who is this, please?" he asked.

"My name is Klaus von Palmen. I heard you speak at Heidelberg. Maybe you remember me. I asked you if the problem was really hypothetical."

Of course. The shrewd-looking blond young man. "Yes, I remember you."

"Did any of your audiences do better than we did?"

"I didn't ask the question again."

"And it *wasn't* hypothetical, was it."

He wanted to say it was, or to hang up—but a stronger impulse took hold of him: to talk openly with someone who was willing to believe, even this antagonistic young Aryan. "I don't know," he admitted. "The person who told me about it . . . has disappeared. Maybe he was right and maybe he was wrong."

"I suspected as much. Would it interest you to know that in Pforzheim, on October twenty-fourth, a man fell from a bridge and drowned? He was sixty-five years old, and about to retire from the postal service."

"Müller, Adolf," Liebermann said, looking at his list of possibles. "I know already, and about ten others besides: in Solingen, Gladbeck, Birmingham, Tucson, Bordeaux, Fagersta . . ."

"Oh."

Liebermann smiled at the pen and said, "I have a source at Reuters."

"That's very good! And have you taken steps to find out whether it's statistically normal for eleven civil servants, age sixty-five, to die violently in—what is it, a three-week period?"

"There were others," Liebermann said, "who were killed by relations. And still others, I'm sure, that Reuters missed. And out of all of them, I think only six at the most could be . . . the ones I'm afraid of. Would six over normal prove anything? And besides, who keeps such statistics? Violent deaths on two continents, by age and occupation. God, maybe, would know what's 'statistically normal.' Or a dozen insurance companies put together. I wouldn't waste the time writing them."

"Have you spoken to the authorities?"

"It was you, wasn't it, who pointed out that they're not so interested in Nazi-hunting these days? I spoke, but they didn't listen. Can you blame them, really, when all I could say was, 'Maybe men will be killed, I don't know why'?"

"Then we must *find out* why, and the way to do it is to look into some of these cases. We have to investigate the circumstances of the deaths, and more important, the men's characters and backgrounds."

"Thank you," Liebermann said. "I figured that out for myself, back when I was an 'I' not a 'we.'"

"Pforzheim is less than an hour's drive from here, Herr Liebermann. And I'm a law student, the third highest in my class, quite capable of making observations and asking pertinent questions."

"I know about the pertinent questions, but this really isn't your business, young fellow."

"Oh? And why is that? Have you somehow secured the exclusive right to oppose Nazism? In *my* country?"

"Herr von Palmen—"

"You presented the problem in public; you should have informed us it was your exclusive property."

"Listen to me." Liebermann shook his head: what a German! "Herr von Palmen," he said, "the person who presented the problem to *me* was a young man like you. More pleasant and respectful, but otherwise not so different. And he's almost certainly been murdered. *That's* why it isn't your business; because it's a business for professionals, not amateurs. And also because you might muddy things up so that when *I* get to Pforzheim the job will be harder."

"I won't muddy things up and I'll try to avoid getting murdered. Do you want me to call and tell you what I find out or shall I keep the information to myself?"

Liebermann glared, trying to think of a way to stop him; but of course there wasn't any. "Do you at least know what information to look for?" he asked.

"Certainly I do. Who Müller left his money to, who he was related to, what his political and military activities were—"

"Where he was born—"

"I *know*. All the points that were suggested that evening."

"And whether he could have had any contact with Mengele, either during the war or immediately after. Where did he serve? Was he ever in Günzburg?"

"Günzburg?"

"Where Mengele lived. And try not to act like a prosecutor; it's easier to catch flies with honey than vinegar."

"I can be charming when I want to, Herr Liebermann."

"I can't wait for a demonstration. Give me your address, please; I'll send you pictures of three of the men who are supposed to be doing the killings. They're old pictures from thirty years ago and at least one of the men has had plastic surgery, but they might come in handy anyway, in case anyone saw strangers around. I'll also send you a letter saying you're working on my behalf. Or would you rather send *me* one saying I'm working on yours?"

"Herr Liebermann, I have the utmost admiration and respect for you. Believe me, I'm truly proud to be able to be of some help to you."

"All right, all right."

"Wasn't that charming? You see?"

Liebermann took von Palmen's address and phone number, gave him a few more pointers, and hung up.

A "we." But maybe the boy would manage; he was bright enough surely.

He finished making the second list, studied it a few minutes, and then opened the desk's left-hand bottom drawer and got out the folder of photos he had pulled from the files. He took out one each of Hessen, Kleist, and Traunsteiner—young men in SS uniforms, smiling or stern in coarse-grained enlarged snapshots; next to useless but the best there were. "Esther!" he called, putting them on the desk. Hessen smiled up at him, dark-haired and wolfish, hugging his beaming parents. Liebermann turned the photo over, and below the mimeographed history taped to its back, wrote: *Hair silvery now. Has had plastic surgery.*

"Esther?"

He picked up the photos, got up from the chair, and went to the door.

Esther sat sleeping at her desk, her head on her folded arms. A bowl of still water sat by her elbow.

He tiptoed over, put the photos on the desk's corner, and tiptoed on through the living room and into the bedroom.

"So where are you going?" Esther called.

Surprised that she was up and should ask, he called back, "To the bathroom."

"I mean where are you *going*. To look."

"Oh," he said. "To a place near Essen—Gladbeck. And to Solingen. It's all right with you?"

Farnbach paused outside the hotel. Admiring the luminous blue-violet twilight, which the clerk had assured him would stay as it was for hours, he pulled his gloves on, turned up his fur collar, and snugged his cap down more warmly over his ears and the back of his head. Storlien wasn't as cold as he had feared, but it was cold enough. Thank God this was his northernmost assignment; Brazil had made an orchid of him. "Sir?" His shoulder was tapped. He turned, and a black-hatted man taller than he offered an identity card on his palm. "Detective Inspector Löfquist. May I have a word with you, please?"

Farnbach took the card in its leather-and-plastic holder. He pretended to have more difficulty reading it in the twilight than he in fact had, so as to give himself at least that moment to think. He handed the card back to Detective Inspector Lars Lennart Löfquist, and putting a pleasant smile (he hoped) in front of the alarm and confusion inside him, said, "Yes, of course, Inspector. I've only been here since noon; I'm sure I haven't broken any laws yet."

Smiling too, Löfquist said, "I'm sure you haven't." He put the card-holder away inside his black leather coat. "We can walk while we talk, if you'd like."

"Fine," Farnbach said. "I'm going to take a look at the waterfall. That seems to be all one can do around here."

"Yes, at this time of year." They started across the hotel's cobbled forecourt. "Things are a little livelier in June and July," Löfquist said. "We have sun all night then, and quite a few tourists. By the end of August, though, even the center of town is dead after seven or eight, and out here it's practically a graveyard. You're German, aren't you?"

"Yes," Farnbach said. "My name is Busch. Wilhelm Busch. I'm a salesman. There's nothing wrong, is there, Inspector?"

"No, not at all." They passed through an arched gateway. "You can relax," Löfquist said. "This is entirely unofficial."

They turned toward the right, and walked side by side along the shoulder of the crushed-stone road. Farnbach smiled and said, "Even an innocent man feels guilty when he's tapped on the shoulder by a detective inspector."

"I guess that's so," Löfquist said. "I'm sorry if I worried you. No, I just like to keep an eye out for foreigners. Germans in particular. I find them . . . enlightening to talk with. What do you sell, Herr Busch?"

"Mining equipment."

"Oh?"

"I'm the Swedish representative of Orenstein and Koppel, of Lübeck."

"I can't say I've heard of them."

"They're fairly big in the field," Farnbach said. "I've been with them fourteen years." He looked at the detective walking along at his left. The man's upturned nose and pointy chin reminded him of a captain he had served under in the SS, one who had begun interrogations with exactly this disarming bullshit of "nothing to worry about, it's entirely unofficial." Later had come the accusations, the demands, the torture.

"And is that where you come from?" Löfquist asked. "Lübeck?"

"No, I'm from Dortmund originally, and I live now in Reinfeld, which is *near* Lübeck. When I'm not in Sweden, that is. I have an apartment in Stockholm." How much, Farnbach wondered, did the son of a bitch know, and how in God's name had he found it out? Had the whole operation been blown? Were Hessen and Kleist and the others facing the same situation right now, or was this his own private failure?

"Turn in here," Löfquist said, pointing toward a footpath into the woods at their right. "It leads to a better vantage point."

They entered the narrow path and followed its near-night darkness uphill. Farnbach unbuttoned the breast of his coat, concerned about getting his gun out quickly if worse came to worst.

"I've spent some time in Germany myself," Löfquist said. "Took ship from Lübeck once, as a matter of fact."

He had switched to German, and fairly good German. Farnbach, disconcerted, wondered whether there might really *be* nothing to worry about; was it possible that Lars Lennart Löfquist wanted only a chance to use his German? It seemed too much to hope for. In German too, he said, "Your German's very good. Is that why you like speaking with us, to get a chance to use it?"

"I don't speak to *all* Germans," Löfquist said, his voice charged with suppressed merriment. "Only former corporals who've put on weight and call themselves 'Busch' instead of Farnstein!"

Farnbach stopped and stared at him.

Smiling, Löfquist took his hat off; looked up and moved aside into better light; and laughing now, faced Farnbach and gave himself the substitute mustache of an extended finger.

Farnbach was astonished. "Oh my God!" he gasped. "I thought of you just a second ago! I guess I—My *God!* Captain Hartung!"

The two shook hands enthusiastically, and the captain, laughing, embraced Farnbach and clapped him on the back; then jammed his hat back on and grasped Farnbach's shoulders with both hands and grinned at him. "What joy to see one of the old faces again!" he exclaimed. "I'm liable to cry, God damn it!"

"But . . . how can this be?" Farnbach asked, thoroughly confused now. "I'm . . . astounded!"

The captain laughed. "You can be Busch," he said; "why can't I be Löfquist? My God, I've got an accent! Listen to me; I'm really a fucking Swede now!"

"And you *are* a detective?"

"That I am."

"Christ, you threw a scare into me, sir."

The captain nodded regretfully, patting Farnbach's shoulder. "Yes, we still worry that the ax might fall, eh, Farnstein? Even after all these years. That's why I keep an eye out for foreigners. I still dream once in a while that I'm hauled up on trial!"

"I can't believe it's you!" Farnbach said, not yet composed. "I don't think I've ever been so surprised!"

They walked on up the path.

"I never forget a face, I never forget a name." The captain laid an arm over Farnbach's shoulders. "I spotted you standing by your car, at the gas station on Krondikesvägen. 'That's Corporal Farnstein in that elegant coat,' I said; 'I'll bet a hundred kronor.'"

"It's Farn*bach*, sir, not 'stein.'"

"Oh? Well, 'stein' is close enough, isn't it, after thirty years? With all the men I commanded? Of course, I had to be absolutely certain before I could speak. It was your voice that clinched it; it hasn't changed at all. And drop the 'sir,' will you? Though I have to admit it's nice hearing it again."

"How in the world did you wind up here?" Farnbach asked. "And a detective, of all things!"

"It's no great story," the captain said, taking his arm from Farnbach's shoulders. "I had a sister who was married to a Swede, on a farm down in Skåne. After I was captured I escaped from the internment camp and got over by ship—Lübeck to Trelleborg; that was the sailing I mentioned—and hid out with them. He wasn't too keen on it. Lars Löfquist. A real s.o.b.; he mistreated poor Eri something awful. After a year or so he and I had a big row and I accidentally finished him. Well, I simply buried him good and deep and took his place! We were the same type physically, so his papers suited me, and Eri was glad to be rid of him. When someone who knew him came by I bandaged my face and she told them a lamp had exploded and I couldn't talk too much. After a couple of months we sold the farm and came up north here. To Sundsvall first, where we worked in a cannery, which was awful; and three years later, here to Storlien, where there were openings on the force and jobs for Eri in shops. And that's it. I liked police work, and what better way to get wind if anyone was looking for me? That roaring you hear is the fall; it's just around the bend. Now what about you, Farnstein? Farn*bach!* How did you become Herr Busch the affluent salesman? That coat must have cost you more than I make in a year!"

"I'm not 'Herr Busch,'" Farnbach said sourly. "I'm 'Senhor Paz' of Pôrto Alegre, Brazil. Busch is a cover. I'm up here on a job for the Comrades Organization, and a damned crazy job it is too."

Now it was the captain's turn to stop and stare, astonished. "You mean . . . it's real? The Organization exists? It's not just . . . newspaper stories?"

"It's real, all right," Farnbach said. "They helped me get settled there, found me a good job . . ."

"And they're *here* now? In Sweden?"

"*I'm* here now; *they're* still down there, working with Dr. Mengele to 'fulfill the Aryan destiny.' At least that's what they tell me."

"But . . . this is marvelous, Farnstein! My God, it's the most exciting news I've— We aren't done! We *won't* be beaten! What's going on? Can you tell me? Would it violate orders to tell an SS officer?"

"*Fuck* orders, I'm *sick* of orders," Farnbach said. He looked for a moment at the startled captain, then said, "I'm here in Storlien to kill a schoolteacher. An old man who's not our enemy and who can't possibly affect the course of history by so much as a hair. But killing him, and a lot of others, is a 'holy operation' that's going to bring us back to power somehow. So says Dr. Mengele." He turned and strode away up the path.

The captain, confused, watched him go, then hurried angrily after him. "Damn it, what's the idea?" he demanded. "If you can't tell me, say so! Don't give me— Was it *all* shit? That's a lousy trick to pull on me, Farn*BACH!*"

Farnbach, breathing hard through his nostrils, came out onto a small balcony of jutting rock, and grasping its iron railing with both hands, gazed bitterly at a broad sheet of shining water that sheared down torrentially at his left. He followed the gleaming water-sheet down and down into its thundering foaming basin, and spat at it.

The captain yanked him around. "That's a *lousy* trick to pull," he cried, close and loud against the fall's thunder. "I really believed you!"

"It wasn't a trick," Farnbach insisted. "It's the truth, every word of it! I killed a man in Göteborg two weeks ago—a teacher too, Anders Runsten. Did you ever hear of him? Neither did I. Neither did anyone. A complete nonentity, retired, sixty-five. A *beer-bottle* collector, for God's sake! *Bragged* to me about his eight hundred and thirty *beer bottles!* I . . . shot him in the head and emptied his wallet."

"Göteborg," the captain said. "Yes, I remember the report!"

Farnbach turned to the railing, held it, and stared at rock wall across the thundering twilit chasm. "And Saturday, I'm to do another one," he said. "It's senseless! Insane! How could it possibly . . . accomplish anything?"

"There's a definite date?"

"Everything is extremely precise!"

The captain stepped close to Farnbach's side. "And your orders were given to you by a ranking officer?"

"By Mengele, with the Organization's endorsement. Colonel Seibert shook our hands the morning we left Brazil."

"It's not only you?"

"There are other men, in other countries."

Grasping Farnbach's arm, the captain said angrily, "Then don't let me hear you say again 'Fuck orders'! You're a corporal who's been assigned a *duty,* and if your superiors have chosen not to tell you the reason for it, then they have a reason for *that* too. Good Christ, you're an SS man; behave like one! 'My Honor Is Loyalty.' Those words were supposed to be engraved on your soul!"

Turning, facing the captain, Farnbach said, "The war is *over*, sir."

"No!" the captain cried. "Not if the Organization is real and working! Don't you think your colonel knows what he's doing? My God, man, if there's a chance in a hundred of the Reich being restored, how can you *not* do everything in your power to help make it happen? Think of it, Farnbach! The Reich restored! We could go home again! As heroes! To a Germany of order and discipline in this fucked-up undisciplined world!"

"But how can the killing of harmless old men—"

"Who is this teacher? I'll bet he's not as harmless as you think! Who is he? Lundberg? Olafsson? Who?"

"Lundberg."

The captain was silent for a moment. "Well, I'll admit he *seems* harmless," he said, "but how do we know what he's really up to, eh? And how do we know what your colonel knows? And the doctor! Come on, man; stiffen your spine and do your duty! 'An order is an order.'"

"Even when it makes no sense?"

The captain closed his eyes, breathed deeply; opened his eyes, glared at Farnbach. "Yes," he said. "Even when it makes no sense. It makes sense to your superiors or they wouldn't have given it to you. My God, there's hope again, Farnbach; will it come to nothing because of your weakness?"

Frowning uneasily, Farnbach moved to the captain's side.

The captain turned to stay facing him. "You won't have any trouble at all," he said. "I'll point Lundberg out to you. I can even tell you his habits. My son had him for two years; I know him very well."

Farnbach snugged his cap down. He smiled quizzically and said, "The Löfquists . . . have a son?"

"Yes, why not?" The captain looked at him, and flushed. "Oh," he said; and coldly: "My sister died in '57. And then I married. You have a dirty mind."

"Forgive me," Farnbach said. "I'm sorry."

The captain thrust his hands into his pockets. "Well!" he said, still flushed. "I hope I've managed to put some starch back into you."

Farnbach nodded. "'The Reich restored,'" he said; "that's what I have to keep thinking of."

"And your officers and fellow soldiers," the captain said. "They're depending on you to do your job; you're not going to leave them out on a limb, are you? I'll give you a hand with Lund-berg. I'm on duty Saturday but I'll switch with one of the other men; no problem."

Farnbach shook his head. "It isn't Lundberg," he said. He lunged; gloved hands pushed black-leathered chest.

The captain, one eye gaping from under his hat, fell backward over the railing, pulled his hands free of his coat and scooped arm-fuls of air. Turning feet-over-head, he dropped away toward the foaming basin far below.

Farnbach leaned over the railing and looked down unhappily. "And it doesn't have to be Saturday," he said.

Getting off the Frankfurt-to-Essen plane at the Essen-Mülheim Airport, Liebermann was surprised to find that he felt pretty good. Not great, no, but not rotten either, and rotten was the way he had felt the other two times he had set foot in the Ruhr. This was where everything had come from: the guns, the tanks, the planes, the sub-marines. Hitler's armory this place had been, and its pall of smog had seemed to Liebermann (in '59 and again in '66) like a mark, not of peacetime industry but of wartime guilt; a sun-blocking shroud laid down from above rather than raised up from below. Going into it he had felt depressed and disheartened, reached for by the past. Rotten.

He had braced himself for the same reaction this time, but no, he felt pretty good; the smog was only smog, no different from Manchester's or Pittsburgh's, and nothing was reaching for him. On the contrary, it was he—in a smooth-speeding new Mercedes taxi—who was doing the reaching. And about time. Almost two months ago he had listened to Barry Koehler's wild story from São Paulo and felt Mengele's hatred assailing him; and now, finally, he was taking action, was going into Gladbeck to ask questions about Emil Döring, sixty-five, "until recently on the staff of the Essen Public Transport Commission." Had he been murdered? Was he linked in any way to men in other countries? Was there a reason why Men-gele and the Comrades Organization should have wanted him dead? If ninety-four men really were to die, there was a one-in-three chance that Döring had been the first of them. By tonight he might *know*.

But ei . . . what if Reuters had missed some of the October 16th possibles? The chance might really be one in four or five. Or six. Or ten. Don't think about it; stay feeling good.

"He went into the passageway to relieve himself," Chief Inspector Haas said in his guttural North German accent. "Bad luck; the wrong place at the wrong time." He was a hard-looking man in his late forties, his face ruddy and pitted with pockmarks, his blue eyes close-set, his fair hair almost gone. His clothes were neat, his desk was neat, his office was neat. His manner to Liebermann was courteous. "It was a whole section of third-floor wall that came down on him. The foreman of the job said later that someone must have worked at it with a crowbar, but of course he *would* say that, wouldn't he? It couldn't be proved, because the first thing we did, naturally, after getting Döring out from under the rubble, was to use crowbars ourselves, to knock down everything that still threatened to fall. We felt we were dealing with a straightforward accident. Which we were; that's what it's been declared. The wrecker's insurers have already reached an agreement with the widow; if there were any suspicion of murder, you can be sure they wouldn't have been in such a hurry."

"But still," Liebermann said, "it *could* have been murder, conceivably."

"It depends what kind you mean," Haas said. "Some tramps or hoodlums might have been scavenging around in the building, yes. They see a man go into the passageway and decide to have themselves some sick excitement. Yes, that's conceivable. Slightly. But murder with a more normal motive, aimed specifically at Herr Döring? No, that's *not* conceivable. How could anyone who was following him have got up to the third floor and pried loose a whole section of wall in the short time he was in the passage way? He was in the act of urinating when he died, and he'd had *two* beers, not two hundred." Haas smiled.

Liebermann said, "The prying could have been done in advance. One man is waiting, ready to give the final shove, and another, *with* Döring, induces him somehow to . . . go to the right place."

"How? 'Why don't you stop and piss, my friend? Right over there on that X someone's painted'? And he left the bar alone. No, Herr Liebermann"—Haas spoke with finality—"I've been through this before; you can be sure it was an accident. Murderers don't go to such lengths. They choose the simple ways: shoot, stab, strike. You know that."

Thoughtfully Liebermann said, "Unless they have *many* murders to do, and want them all . . . not to be similar . . ."

Haas squinted his close-set eyes at him. "Many murders?" he asked.

Liebermann said, "What did you mean just now, you've 'been through this before'?"

"Döring's sister was in here the next day, screaming at me to arrest Frau Döring and a man named Springer. Is this . . . someone you're interested in? Wilhelm Springer?"

"Possibly," Liebermann said. "Who is he?"

"A musician. Frau Döring's lover, according to the sister. The Frau is much younger than Döring was. Good-looking too."

"How old is Springer?"

"Thirty-eight, thirty-nine. The night of the accident he was filling in with the orchestra at the Essen opera. I think that lets him out, don't you?"

"Can you tell me anything about Döring?" Liebermann asked. "Who his friends were? What organizations he belonged to?"

Haas shook his head. "I only have the vital statistics." He turned a paper in the folder lying open before him. "I saw him a few times but I never met him; they moved here just a year ago. Here we are: sixty-five years old, one hundred and seventy centimeters, eighty-six kilos . . ." He looked at Liebermann. "Oh, one thing that might interest you; he was carrying a gun."

"He was?"

Haas smiled. "A museum piece, a Mauser 'Bolo.' It hadn't been fired, or cleaned and oiled, in God knows how many years."

"Was it loaded?"

"Yes, but he probably would have blown his hand off if he'd fired it."

Liebermann said, "Could you give me Frau Döring's address and phone number? And the sister's? And the address of the bar? Then I'll be on my way." He sat forward and put a hand down to his briefcase.

Haas wrote on a memo pad, copying from a typed form in the folder. "May I ask," he said, "how you come to be interested in this? Döring wasn't a 'war criminal,' was he?"

Liebermann looked at Haas busily writing, and after a moment said, "No, as far as I know he wasn't a war criminal. He may have had contact with one. I'm checking a rumor. Probably there's nothing in it."

To the bartender in the Lorelei-Bar he said, "I'm looking into it for a friend of his, who thinks the collapse may not have been an accident."

The bartender's eyes widened. "You don't say! You mean someone purposely . . . ? Oh my." He was a small bald man with a mustache with waxed tips. A yellow smile-face button smiled on his red lapel. He didn't ask Liebermann's name and Liebermann didn't offer it.

"Was he a regular customer?"

The bartender frowned and stroked his mustache. "Mmm, so-so. Not every night, but once or twice a week. An afternoon sometimes."

"I understand he left here alone that night."

"That's right."

"Was he with anyone *before* he left?"

"He was alone, right where you are now. One seat over maybe. And he left in a hurry."

"Oh?"

"He had change coming, eight and a half marks on a one-fifty bill, and he didn't wait for it. He was a good tipper, but not like that. I meant to give it to him the next time he came in."

"Did he say anything to you while he was drinking?"

The bartender shook his head. "It wasn't a night I could stand around and talk. They had a dance at the business school"—he pointed over Liebermann's shoulder—"and we were packed solid from eight o'clock on."

"He was waiting for someone," a man at the end of the bar said, a round-faced old man in a derby hat and a shabby overcoat buttoned up tightly to the collar. "He kept looking at the door, watching for someone to come in."

Liebermann said, "You knew Herr Döring?"

"Very well," the old man said. "I went to the funeral. Such a small turn-out! I was surprised." To the bartender he said, "You know who wasn't there? Ochsenwalder. That surprised me. What did he have to do that was so important?" He picked up his stein with both hands and drank from it.

"Excuse me," the bartender said to Liebermann, and went away toward the other end of the bar, where a few men sat.

Liebermann got up, and with his tomato juice and his briefcase, went over and sat down near the old man, around the bar's corner from him.

"Usually he sat here with us," the old man said—he wiped his mouth with the back of his hand—"but that night he sat alone, in the middle there, and kept watching the door. Waiting for someone, looking at the time. Apfel said it was probably the salesman from the night before. He was some talker, Döring. To be honest, we weren't sorry he was there not here. But he could have come over and said hello, couldn't he? Now don't get me wrong; we liked him, and not just because he picked up the tab sometimes. But he told the same stories over and over again. Good stories, but how many times can you listen? Over and over, the same stories; how he'd been smarter than different people."

"He was telling them to a salesman the night before?" Liebermann asked.

The old man nodded. "In medicine. First he was talking to all of us, asking about the town, and then it was him and Döring, Döring talking and him laughing. The first time you heard them they were good stories."

"That's right, I forgot," the bartender said, back with them. "Döring was here the night before the accident. That was unusual for him, two nights in a row."

"You know how old his wife is?" the old man asked. "I thought it was a daughter, but it was the wife, the widow."

Liebermann said to the bartender, "Do you remember the salesman he was talking to?"

"I don't know if he was a salesman," the bartender said, "but I remember. A glass eye, and a way of snapping his fingers that annoyed the hell out of me; as if I should have been there ten minutes ago."

"How old was he?"

The bartender stroked his mustache and sharpened a tip of it. "In his fifties, I'd say," he said. "Fifty-five maybe." He looked at the old man. "Wouldn't you say that?"

The old man nodded. "Around there."

Liebermann, unstrapping his briefcase on his lap, said, "I have some pictures. They were taken a long time ago, but would you look at them and tell me if one of the men in them might have been the salesman?"

"Glad to," the bartender said, coming closer. The old man shifted around.

Getting the photos out, Liebermann said to the old man, "Did he give his name?"

"I don't think so. If he did I don't remember it. But I'm good with faces."

Liebermann moved his tomato juice aside, and turning the photos around, put them on the bar and separated the three of them. He pushed them closer to the old man and the bartender.

They bent over the glossy photos, the old man putting a hand to his derby.

"Add thirty years," Liebermann told them, watching. "Thirty-five."

They raised their heads, looking at him warily, resentfully. The old man turned away. "I don't know," he said. He picked up his stein.

The bartender, looking at Liebermann, said, "You can't show us pictures of . . . young soldiers and expect us to recognize a fifty-five-year-old man we saw over a month ago."

Liebermann said, "Three weeks ago."

"Still."

The old man drank.

Liebermann said to them, "These men are criminals. They're wanted by your government."

"*Our* government," the old man said, setting his stein down onto its wet print. "Not yours."

"That's true," Liebermann said. "I'm Austrian."

The bartender went away. The round-faced old man watched him go.

Liebermann, putting spread hands on the photos, leaned forward and said, "This salesman may have killed your friend Döring."

The old man looked at his stein, his lips pursed. He turned the stein's handle around toward him.

Liebermann looked bitterly at him, and gathered the photos and put them back in his briefcase. He closed the briefcase, strapped it, and stood up.

The bartender, coming back, said, "Two marks."

Liebermann put a five-mark note on the bar and said, "Some coins for the phone, please."

He went into the booth and dialed Frau Döring's number. The line was busy.

He tried Döring's sister, in Oberhausen. No answer.

He stood crated in the phone booth with his briefcase between his feet, tugging at his ear and thinking of what to say to Frau Döring. She might very well be hostile to Yakov Liebermann, Nazi-hunter; and even if she weren't, after her sister-in-law's accusations she probably wouldn't want to discuss Döring and his death with any stranger. But what could he tell her except the truth? How else gain a meeting with her? It struck him that Klaus von Palmen, in Pforzheim, might be getting better results than he. That would be all he'd need, to be outdone by von Palmen.

He tried Frau Döring again, following Chief Inspector Haas's neatly penned digits. The phone at the other end rang.

"Yes?" A woman; quick, annoyed.

"Is this Frau Klara Döring?"

"Yes, who's this?"

"My name is Yakov Liebermann. From Vienna."

Silence. "Yakov Liebermann? The man who . . . finds the Nazis?"—surprised and puzzled, but not hostile.

"Looks for them," Liebermann said, "only sometimes finds. I'm here in Gladbeck, Frau Döring, and I wonder if you'd be kind enough to let me have a little of your time, only half an hour or so. I'd like to talk with you about your late husband. I think he may have been involved—entirely innocently and without knowing about it—in the affairs of certain persons I'm interested in. May I come talk with you? Whenever it's convenient for you?"

A clarinet piped faintly. Mozart? "Emil was involved . . . ?"

"Maybe. Without his knowing it. I'm in your neighborhood now. May I come over? Or would you prefer to come out and meet me somewhere?"

"No. I can't see you."

"Frau Döring, please, it's very important."

"I can't possibly. Not now. It's the worst possible day."

"Tomorrow, then? I've come to Gladbeck for the sole purpose of speaking to you." The clarinet stopped, then piped again, repeating its last phrase, definitely Mozart. Played by the lover Springer? Which was why it was such a bad day to see *him?* "Frau Döring?"

"All right. I work until three. You can come over tomorrow at four."

"That's Frankenstrasse Twelve?"

"Yes. Apartment thirty-three."

"Thank you. At four tomorrow. Thank you, Frau Döring."

He freed himself from the phone booth and asked the bartender for directions to the building where Döring had died.

"It's gone."

"Which way *was* it, then?"

The bartender, bending, washing glasses, pointed a dripping finger. "Down there."

Liebermann went down a narrow street and across a busy wider one. Gladbeck, or this part of it at least, was urban, gray, charmless. The smog didn't help.

He stood looking at a rubbled lot flanked by masonry walls of old factory buildings. Three children piled broken stones, making an angled barrier. One of them wore a military knapsack.

He walked on. The next cross-street was Frankenstrasse; he followed it to Number 12, a soot-streaked buff apartment house, conventionally modern, behind a narrow well-kept lawn. From its rooftop a finger of black smoke rose up to join the smog-shroud.

He watched a woman struggle a baby carriage through the glass entrance door, and went on in the direction of his hotel, the Schultenhof.

In his clean stark German room he tried again to reach Döring's sister. "God bless you whoever you are," a woman greeted him. "We just this second stepped in. You're our very first call."

Fine. He could guess. "Is Frau Toppat there?"

"Oh poo. No, I'm sorry, she's gone. She's in California, or on the way. We bought the house from her the day before yesterday. *It's for Frau Toppat!* She's gone to live with her daughter. Do you want the address? I've got it here somewhere."

"No, thanks," Liebermann said. "Don't bother."

"Everything's ours now: the furniture, the goldfish—we even have vegetables growing! Do you know the house?"

"No."

"It's awful, but it's perfect for us. Well, the God-bless still goes. Are you sure you don't want her address? I can find it."

"Positive. Thank you. Good luck."

"We've got it already, but thanks, we can always use a little more."

He hung up, sighed, nodded. Me too, lady.

After he had washed up and taken his late-afternoon pills, he sat down at the much-too-small writing table, opened his briefcase, and got out the draft of an article he was writing about the extradition of Frieda Maloney.

The door opened to the extent of its short tight chain and a boy looked out, pushing dark hair aside from his forehead. He was thirteen or so, gaunt and sharp-nosed.

Liebermann, wondering if he had got the number wrong, said, "Is this Frau Döring's apartment?"

"Are you Herr Liebermann?"

"Yes."

The door closed partway; metal scraped.

The boy was a grandson, Liebermann supposed, or maybe—since Frau Döring was much younger than Döring had been—a son. Or maybe only a neighbor invited over so she wouldn't be alone with an unknown male visitor.

Whoever he was, the boy held the door open all the way, and Liebermann went in—to a mirror-walled alcove busy with two or three himselves coming in, surprisingly seedy ("Get a haircut!" Hannah called. "Trim your mustache! Stand straight!"), and several boys in white shirts and dark trousers closing doors and hooking in chain-latches. Standing straight, Liebermann turned to the real boy. "Is Frau Döring in?"

"She's on the phone." The boy held a hand out for his hat.

Giving it to him, Liebermann smiled and asked, "Are you her grandson?"

"Her son." The boy's voice scorned the foolish question. He opened a mirror-doored closet.

Liebermann put his briefcase down and took his coat off, looking into a living room full of orange and chrome and glass, everything matching, store-like, unhuman.

He gave his coat to the boy, smiling, and the boy fitted a hanger into its sleeve, looking bored and dutiful. He was the height of Liebermann's chest. A few coats hung in the closet, one of leopard skin. A bird, a stuffed raven or some such, peered out from behind hats and boxes on the shelf. "Is that a bird back there?" Liebermann asked.

"Yes," the boy said. "It was my father's." He closed the door and stood looking at Liebermann with deep blue eyes.

Liebermann picked up his briefcase.

"Do you kill the Nazis when you catch them?" the boy asked.

"No," Liebermann said.

"Why not?"

"It's against the law. Besides, it's better to put them on trial. That way more people learn about them."

"Learn what?" The boy looked skeptical.

"Who they were, what they did."

The boy turned toward the living room.

A woman stood there, small and blond, in a black skirt and jacket and pale-blue turtleneck sweater; a pretty woman in her early forties. She cocked her head and smiled, her hands clasped tensely before her.

"Frau Döring?" Liebermann went to her. She held a hand out and he shook its small coldness. "Thank you for seeing me," he said. Her complexion was cosmetically smooth, with a few fine wrinkles at the outsides of her blue-green eyes. A pleasant perfume came from her.

"Please," she said with embarrassment, "could I ask you to show me some identification?"

"Of course," Liebermann said. "It's smart of you to ask." He shifted his briefcase to his other hand and reached into his inside jacket pocket.

"I'm sure you're . . . who you say you are," Frau Döring said, "but I . . ."

"His initials are in his hat," the boy said behind Liebermann. "Y.S.L."

Liebermann smiled at Frau Döring, handing his passport to her. "Your son's a detective," he said; and turning to the boy, "That's very good! I didn't even notice you looking."

The boy, brushing aside his dark forelock, smiled complacently.

Frau Döring returned the passport. "Yes, he's clever," she said with a smile at the boy. "Only a little bit lazy. Right now, for instance, he's supposed to be doing his practicing."

"I can't answer the door and be in my room at the same time," the boy grumbled, stalking across the living room.

Frau Döring smoothed his unruly hair as he passed her. "I know, darling; I was only teasing."

The boy stalked into a hallway.

Frau Döring smiled brightly at Liebermann, rubbing her hands as if to warm them. "Come sit down, Herr Liebermann," she said, and backed toward the windowed end of the room. A door slammed. "Would you like some coffee?"

Liebermann said, "No, thank you, I just had a cup of tea across the street."

"At the Bittner? That's where I work. I'm the hostess there from eight to three."

"That's nice and convenient for you."

"Yes, and I'm home when Erich gets here. I started Monday and so far it's perfect. I enjoy it."

Liebermann sat on an unyielding sofa, and Frau Döring sat on a chair adjacent to it. She sat erectly, her hands folded on her black skirt, her head tilted attentively.

"First of all," Liebermann said, "I'd like to express my sympathy to you. Things must be very difficult for you right now."

Looking at her folded hands, Frau Döring said, "Thank you." A clarinet darted upscale and down, readying itself to play; Liebermann looked toward the hallway, from which the woody notes flowed, and back at Frau Döring. She smiled at him. "He's very good," she said.

"I know," he said. "I heard him on the phone yesterday. I thought it was an adult. Is he your only child?"

"Yes," she said, and proudly: "He plans to make his career in music."

"I hope his father left him well provided for." Liebermann smiled. "Did he?" he asked. "Did your husband leave his money to Erich and you?"

Surprised, Frau Döring nodded. "And to a sister of his. A third each. Erich's is in trust. Why do you ask *that?*"

"I'm looking," Liebermann said, "for a reason why Nazis in South America might have wanted to kill him."

"To kill *Emil?*"

He nodded, watching Frau Döring. "And the others too."

She frowned at him. "What others?"

"The group he belonged to. In different countries."

Her frown grew more puzzled. "Emil didn't belong to any group. What are you saying, that he was a Communist? You couldn't be more wrong, Herr Liebermann."

"He didn't get mail or phone calls from outside Germany?"

"Never. Not here, anyway. Ask at his office; maybe *they* know about a group; *I* certainly don't."

"I asked there this morning; they don't know either."

"*Once,*" Frau Döring said, "three or four years ago, maybe even more, his sister called him from America, where she was visiting. That's the only foreign phone call I remember. Oh, and once, even longer ago, his first wife's brother called from somewhere in Italy, to try to get him to invest in—I don't remember, something to do with silver. Or platinum."

"Did he do it?"

"No. He was very careful with his money."

The clarinet caught Liebermann's ear, weaving the Mozart of the day before. The menuetto from the "Clarinet Quintet," being played very nicely. He thought of himself at the boy's age, putting in two and three hours a day at the old Pleyel. His mother, may she rest in peace, had also said, "He plans to make his career in music," just as proudly. Who had known what was coming? And when had he last touched a piano?

"I don't understand this," Frau Döring said. "Emil wasn't murdered."

"He might have been," Liebermann said. "A salesman got friendly with him the night before. They might have made an arrangement, to meet at the building if the salesman didn't show up at the bar by ten o'clock. That would have brought him there just at the right time."

Frau Döring shook her head. "He wouldn't have met someone at a building like that one," she said. "Not even someone he knew well. He was too suspicious of people. And why on earth would *Nazis* be interested in him?"

"Why was he carrying a gun that night?"

"He always did."

"Always?"

"*Always*, as long as I've known him. He showed it to me on our first date. Can you imagine, bringing a gun on a date? And showing it? And what's even worse, I was impressed!" She shook her head and sighed wonderingly.

"Who was he afraid of?" Liebermann asked.

"Everyone! People at the office, people who simply *looked* at him . . ." Frau Döring leaned forward confidingly. "He was a little bit—well, not crazy, but not normal either. I tried once to get him to see someone; you know, a doctor. There was a program on television about people like him, people who think they're being . . . plotted against, and after it was over I suggested in a very roundabout way —Well! *I* was plotting, right? To get him declared insane? He almost shot *me* that night!" She sat back and drew a breath, shuddered; and frowned speculatively at Liebermann. "What did he do, write to you that Nazis were after him?"

"No, no."

"Then what makes you think they were?"

"A rumor I heard."

"It was wrong. Believe me, Nazis would have *liked* Emil. He was anti-Jewish, anti-Catholic, anti-freedom, anti-everything-and-everyone except Emil Döring himself."

"*Was* he a Nazi?"

"He may have been. He said he wasn't, but I didn't meet him till 1952, so I couldn't swear. Probably he wasn't; he never joined *anything* if he could help it."

"What did he do in the war?"

"He was in the Army; a corporal, I think. He bragged about the easy jobs he managed to wangle. The main one was in a supply depot or something like that. Someplace safe."

"He was never in combat?"

"He was 'too smart.' The 'dumb ones' went."

"Where was he born?"

"In Laupendahl, on the other side of Essen."

"And lived in the area all his life?"

"Yes."

"Was he ever in Günzburg, as far as you know?"

"Where?"

"Günzburg. Near Ulm."

"I never heard him mention it."

"The name Mengele? Did he ever mention that?"

She looked at him, eyebrows up, and shook her head.

"Just a few questions more," he said. "You're being very kind. I'm afraid I'm on a wild-goose chase."

"I'm sure you are," she said, and smiled.

"Was he related to anyone of importance? In the government, say?"

She thought for a moment. "No."

"Friendly with anyone of importance?"

She shrugged. "A few Essen officials, if that's your idea of importance. He shook hands with Krupp once; that was his big moment."

"How long were you married to him?"

"Twenty-two years. Since the fourth of August, 1952."

"And in all those years you never saw or heard *anything* about an international group he belonged to, of men his own age in similar positions?"

Shaking her head, she said, "Never, not a word."

"No anti-Nazi activity of any kind?"

"None at all. He was *pro*-Nazi more than anti-. He voted National Democrat, but he didn't join them either. He wasn't a joiner."

Liebermann sat back on the hard sofa and rubbed the back of his neck.

Frau Döring said, "Would you like me to tell you who really killed him?"

He looked at her.

She leaned forward and said, "God. To set free a stupid little farm girl after twenty-two years of unhappiness. And to give Erich a father who'll help him and love him, instead of one who called him names—that's right, called him *fairy* and *imbecile*—for wanting to be a musician and not a safe fat civil servant! Do Nazis answer prayers, Herr Liebermann?" She shook her head. "No, that's God's business, and I've thanked Him every night since He pushed that wall down on Emil. He could have done it sooner, but I thank Him anyway. 'Better late than never.'" She sat back and crossed her legs —nice legs—and smiled prettily. "Well!" she said. "Doesn't he play beautifully? Remember the name: Erich Döring. Some day you'll see it on posters outside concert halls!"

When Liebermann left Frankenstrasse 12, dusk was beginning to gather. Cars and trolleys filled the street; hurrying walkers crowded the pavement. He walked among them slowly, his briefcase at his side.

Döring had been a nobody: vain, conniving, important to no one but himself. There was no conceivable reason why he should have been a target of Nazi plotters half the world away—not even in his own suspicious imaginings. The salesman in the bar? Simply a lonely salesman. The hurried exit on the night of the accident? There were a dozen reasons why a man might hurry from a bar.

Which meant that the October 16th victim had been either Chambon in France or Persson in Sweden.

Or someone else, whom Reuters had missed.

Or very possibly no one at all.

Ei, Barry, Barry! What did you have to call me for?

He walked a little faster, along the south side of crowded Frankenstrasse.

On the north side Mundt walked faster too, an unlighted cigar in his mouth, a folded newspaper under his arm.

Though the night was dry and clear, reception was poor, and what Mengele heard was, "Liebermann was *crackle-crackle-squeal* where Döring, our first man, lived. Lieber*crackle-crackle* about him, and he showed pictures of soldiers to *crackle-crackle-SQUEAL-crackle* Solingen, doing the same thing in connection with a *crackle-crackle* died in an explosion a few weeks ago. Over."

Swallowing back the sourness that was churning up into his throat, Mengele pressed the mike button and said, "Would you repeat, please, Colonel? I didn't get all that. Over."

Eventually he got it.

"I won't pretend I'm not concerned," he said, mopping his icy forehead with his handkerchief, "but if he's gone on to check on someone we had nothing to do with, then obviously he's still in the dark. Over."

"*Crackle* Döring's apartment, and it wasn't dark *there*. It was four in the afternoon and he was there for close to an hour. Over."

"Oh God," Mengele said, and pressed the button. "Then we'd better take care of him right away, just to be safe. You agree, don't you? Over."

"We're *crackle* the possibility, very carefully. I'll let you know as soon as there's a decision. I have a little good news too. Mundt *crackle-crackle*cond customer, on the exact date. Ditto Hessen. And Farnbach called in, not with questions, thank God, just with some surprising infor*crackle-squeal* seems that *his* second customer was his former commander, a captain who got himself a Swedish identity after the war. A funny twist, isn't it? Farnbach wasn't sure whether we knew or not. Over."

"He didn't let it stop him, did he? Over."

"Oh no, he *crackle-crackle* days ahead of schedule. So that's three more checks you can put on your chart. Over."

"I think it's imperative that we take care of Liebermann immediately," Mengele said. "What if he doesn't stop with this man in Solingen? If Mundt does it right, I'm sure it won't cause any trouble, at least not any more than we've got already. Over."

"If it's done while he's in Germany, I disagree. They'll *crackle-squeal-crackle* country to show they're being conscientious; they'll have to. Over."

"Then as soon as he's out of Germany. Over."

"We'll certainly take your feelings into account, Josef. Without you, nothing; we know how *crackle-crackle-squeal-crackle* off now. Over and out."

Mengele looked at the microphone, and put it down. He took the earphones off, put them down, and switched the radio off.

He went from the study into the bathroom, threw up his entire half-digested dinner, washed, and swished some Vademecum around in his mouth.

Then he went out onto the veranda, smiled and said "Sorry," and sat down and played bridge with General Fariña and Franz and Margot Schiff.

When they left, he took a flashlight and walked down to the river to think. He said a few words to the man on duty and walked a ways downriver, where he sat on the side of a rusty oil drum—to hell with his trousers—and lit a cigarette. He thought of Yakov Liebermann going into the men's homes; and of Scibert and the rest of the Organization brass facing a necessity and calling it a possibility; and of his decades-long devotion to the noblest ideals—the pursuit of knowledge and the elevation of the best of the human race—that might be robbed of its ultimate fruition by that one nosy Jew and that handful of weaseling Aryans. Who were *worse* than the Jew, because Liebermann, if one was fair about it, was doing his duty

according to his lights, while they were betraying theirs. Or thinking of betraying it.

He tossed his second cigarette into the river's glistening
blackness, and with a "Stay awake" to the guard, walked back toward the house.

On an impulse he turned aside and pushed his way into the
overgrown path to the "factory," that path down which he and the
others—young Reiter, von Sweringen, Tina Zygorny; all of them
dead now, alas—had trooped so cheerfully on those long-ago morn-
ings. Bending over the probing flashlight, he warded off broad-
leafed branches, stumbled over arching roots.

And there it was, the long low building, the trees nibbling at it.
The paint had scaled from its frame walls, every window was broken (the servants' children, damn them), and a whole section of
corrugated roof had fallen or been pulled from the dormitory end.

The front door gaped open, hanging away by its lower hinge.
Tina Zygorny laughed her masculine laugh; von Sweringen thun-
dered, "Rise and shine! You've had your beauty sleep!"

Only silence. Insects twanging, chittering.

Shining the light before him, Mengele went up the step and
through the doorway. Five years at least, since he'd last set foot . . .

Beautiful Bavaria. The poster clung to the wall, dusty and
rippled: sky, mountain, flowered foreground.

He smiled at it, and moved the light beam.

Finding gouged wallboard where shelves and cabinets had been
ripped out. Stems of plumbing standing at attention. The wall with
the brown spots that Reiter had burned into it, starting a swastika
with his microscope. Could have burned the place down, the idiot.

He walked carefully around broken glass. A rotting melon-rind,
ants feasting.

He looked into barren rooms, and remembered life and activity,
gleaming equipment. The sterilizer keened, pipettes clinked. Over
ten years ago.

Everything had been taken out, junked or perhaps given to a
clinic somewhere, so that in case the Jew-gangs got in—they were
strong in those days, "Commando Isaac" and the others—they'd have
no clues, no inkling.

He walked down the central corridor. Native attendants spoke
soothing words in primitive dialects, trying to make themselves
understood.

He came into the dormitory, fresh-smelling and cool thanks to its
open roof. The grass mats were still there, lying in disarray.

Make what you will of a few dozen grass mats, Jew-boys.

He walked among them, remembering, smiling.

Something sparked white against the wall.

He went to it, looked down at it lying there in the flashlight's beam; picked it up, blew at it, examined it on his hand. Animal claws, a circle of them; one of the women's bracelets. For good luck? The power of the animals transferred to the wearer's arm?

Odd that the children hadn't found it; surely they played in here, rolled on these mats, had disarranged them.

Yes, good luck that this bracelet had lain here all these years so that he might find it on this night of fear and uncertainty, of possible betrayal. He clustered his fingers into it, shook it down around them, pushed at it with the wrist of his flashlight-hand; the claw-circle dropped down around his gold watchband. He shook his fist; the claws danced.

He looked about at the dormitory, and up through its broken roof at treetops, and stars that came and went among them. And— maybe, maybe not—at his Führer watching him.

I won't fail you, he promised.

He looked about—at the place where so much, so gloriously much, had already been accomplished—and glaring, said aloud, "I won't."

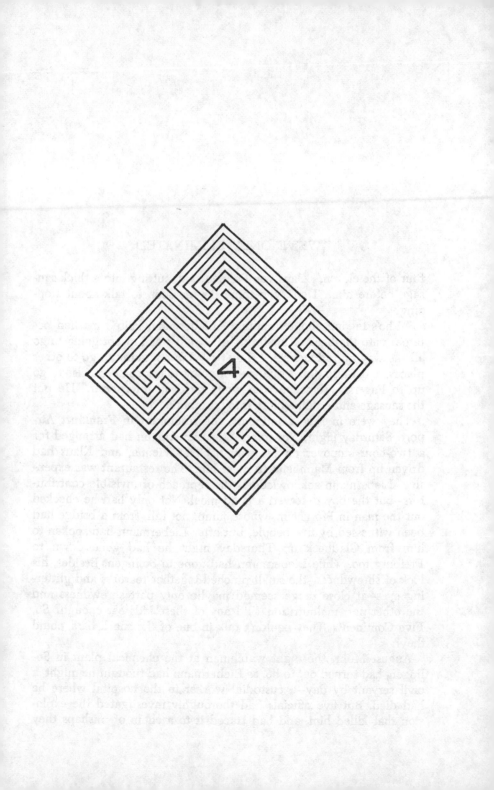

"WE'VE ONLY ELIMINATED

four of the eleven," Klaus von Palmen said, cutting into a thick sausage before him. "Don't you think it's too soon to talk about stopping?"

"Who's talking about stopping?" Liebermann knifed mashed potatoes onto the back of his fork. "All I said was I'm not going to go all the way up to Fagersta. I didn't say I'm not going to go to other places, and I also didn't say I'm not going to ask someone else to go up to Fagersta, someone who won't need an interpreter." He put the sausage-and-potatoed fork into his mouth.

They were in Five Continents, the restaurant in Frankfurt Airport. Saturday night, November 9th. Liebermann had arranged for a two-hour stopover on his way back to Vienna, and Klaus had driven up from Mannheim to meet him. The restaurant was expensive—Liebermann acknowledged the reproach of invisible contributors—but the boy deserved a good meal. Not only had he checked out the man in Pforzheim, whose jump, not fall, from a bridge had been witnessed by five people, but after Liebermann had spoken to him from Gladbeck on Thursday night he had gone down to Freiburg too, while Liebermann had gone to Solingen. Besides, his look of shrewdness—the small pinched-together features and glittering eyes—at close range seemed maybe only part shrewdness and the other part malnutrition. Did any of these kids eat enough? So, Five Continents. They couldn't talk in one of the snack bars, could they?

August Mohr, the night watchman at the chemical plant in Solingen, had turned out to be, as Liebermann had thought he might, a civil servant by day—a custodial worker in the hospital where he had died. But five officials had thoroughly investigated the explosion that killed him, and had traced it to a chain of mishaps they were certain couldn't have been prearranged. And Mohr himself was as unlikely a victim of Nazi plotting as Emil Döring had been. Semi-literate and poor, a widower for six years, he had lived with his bedridden mother in two rooms in a shabby boarding house. For most of his life, including the war years, he had worked in a Solingen steel mill. Mail or phone calls from outside the country? His landlady had laughed. "Not even from inside, sir."

Klaus, in Freiburg, had thought at first that he was on to something. The man there, a clerk in the Water Department named Josef Rausenberger, had been knifed and robbed near his home, and a neighbor had seen someone watching the house the night before.

"A man with a glass eye?"

"She wouldn't have noticed, she was too far away. A big man in a small car, smoking, was what she told the police. She couldn't even tell what make of car. Was there a man with a glass eye in Solingen?"

"In Gladbeck. Go on."

But. Rausenberger had belonged to no international organizations. He had lost both his legs below the knees in a train accident when he was a boy; as a result he hadn't done military service or even set foot—artificial foot, that is—outside Germany. ("Please," Liebermann chided.) He had been an efficient and painstaking worker, a devoted husband and father. His savings had been left to his widow. He had disapproved of the Nazis and voted against them, but nothing more. Born in Schwenningen. Never in Günzburg. One notable relation: a cousin, the managing editor of the *Berliner Morgenpost.*

Döring, Müller, Mohr, Rausenberger; none of them by any stretch of the imagination Nazi victims. Four of the eleven.

"I know a man in Stockholm," Liebermann said. "An engraver, from Warsaw originally. Very clever. He'll be glad to go up to Fagersta. The man there, Persson, and the one in Bordeaux are the two main ones to check on. October sixteenth was the one date Barry mentioned. If neither of those two was someone the Nazis could have and would have killed, then he must have been wrong."

"Unless you haven't heard about the right man. Or he was killed on the wrong day."

"'Unless,'" Liebermann said, cutting sausage. "The whole thing is 'unless' this, 'if' that, 'maybe' the other. I wish to hell he hadn't called me."

"What did he say exactly? How did it all happen?"

Liebermann went through the story.

The waiter took their plates and their dessert orders.

When he had gone, Klaus said, "Have you realized that your name might have been added to the list? Even if it wasn't Mengele, recognizing you by telepathy—which I don't for a moment believe, Herr Liebermann; I'm surprised that you do—but if *any* Nazi hung up the phone, he certainly would have made it his business to find out who Barry was talking to. The hotel operator would have known."

Liebermann smiled. "I'm only sixty-two," he said, "and I'm not a civil servant."

"Don't joke about it. If killers were being sent out, why not give them one more assignment? With top priority."

"Then the fact that I'm still alive suggests they *weren't* being sent out."

"Maybe they decided to wait awhile, Mengele and the Comrades Organization, because you knew. Or even called the whole thing off."

"You see what I mean about the 'ifs' and the 'maybes'?"

"*Did* you realize that you may be in danger?"

The waiter put cherry cake before Klaus, a Linzer torte before Liebermann. He poured Klaus's coffee, Liebermann's tea.

When he had gone, Liebermann, tearing open a packet of sugar, said, "I've been in danger for a long time, Klaus. I stopped thinking about it; otherwise I would have had to close the Center and do something else with my life. You're right; 'if' there are killers, I'm probably on the list. So finding out is still the only thing to do. I'll go to Bordeaux and have Piwowar, my friend in Stockholm, go to Fagersta. And if those men too can't have been victims, I'll check out a few more, just to be sure."

Klaus, stirring his coffee, said, "I could go to Fagersta; I speak some Swedish."

"But for you I'd have to buy a ticket, right? And for Piwowar, I won't. Unfortunately that's a factor. Also, you shouldn't skip lectures so casually."

"I could skip every lecture for a month and still graduate with honors."

"Oh my. Such a brain. Tell me about yourself; how did you become so smart?"

"I could tell you something about myself that might come as a surprise to you, Herr Liebermann."

Liebermann listened gravely and sympathetically.

Klaus's parents were former Nazis. His mother had been on close terms with Himmler; his father had been a colonel in the Luftwaffe.

Almost all the young Germans who offered to help Liebermann were children of former Nazis. It was one of the few things that made him think God might be real and at work, if only slowly.

❖

"We're awful."

"No we're not, we're smashing. Ought to be doing it on film."

"You know what I mean. Look at us; one, two, and in the kip. Tuppence says you forgot my name."

"Meg for Margaret."

"*Full name.*"

"Reynolds. Tuppence please, Nurse Reynolds."

"Too dark to find my purse. Will you settle for this?"

"Mmm, yes indeed. Mmm, that's lovely."

" 'Blushing shyly, she said, "It won't be only this one night, sir, will it?" ' "

"Is that what's on your mind?"

"No, I'm thinking about the price of pickles. Of course it's on my mind! This isn't my usual modus vivendi, you know."

"I say. 'Modus vivendi'!"

"There's a straight answer."

"I wasn't trying to be evasive, Meg. I'm afraid it *may* be only to-night, but not because I want it that way. I have no choice in the matter. I was sent up here to . . . do some business with someone, and he's laid out in your bloody hospital, on oxygen, with no visitors except the immediate fam."

"Harrington?"

"That's the chap. When I call in and report I can't get to him, I'll probably be pulled right back down to London. We're dreadfully short of staff at present."

"Will you come back when he recovers?"

"Not likely. I'll be onto another case by then; someone else'll take over. Assuming he *does* recover. It's iffy, I gather."

"Yes, he's sixty-six, you know, and it was quite a bad attack. He has a strong constitution, though. Ran round the green every morning at eight sharp; you could set your watch. They say it helps the heart, but I say it harms it at that age."

"It's a pity I can't get to him; I'd have been able to stay here a fortnight at the very least. Do you think we could get together at Christmas? We close up shop then; can you get free?"

"I might be able . . ."

"Lovely! Would you? I have a flat in Kensington, with a bed a mite softer than this one."

"Alan, what business are you *in?*"

"I told you."

"It certainly doesn't *sound* like selling. Salesmen don't have 'cases.' Except the carrying kind, and I didn't notice any of those, not that I had much time to. Selling what, eh? You're not really a salesman at all, are you."

"Clever Meg. Can you keep a secret?"

"Of course I can."

"Truly?"

"*Yes.* You can trust me, Alan."

"Well—I'm with the Inland Revenue. We've had a tip that Harrington has bilked us out of something like thirty thousand quid over the past ten or twelve years."

"I don't believe it! He's a magistrate!"

"They're the ones, more often than you'd think."

"My Lord, he's Civic Virtue on a pedestal!"

"That's as may be. I was sent to find out. Y' see, I was to put a transmitter into his home, a 'bug,' and monitor it from my room here, see what I could pick up."

"Is *that* the way you blighters operate?"

"Standard procedure in cases like this. I have the warrant in my briefcase. His hospital room would have been even better than his home. A chap's a bit nervous in hospital; tells the wife where the loot is hidden, whispers a word or two to his solicitor . . . But I can't get in to plant the bloody thing. I could show the warrant to your director, but like as not he's Harrington's pal; he'll drop a word and it's Johnny-out-the-window."

"You bastard. You ruddy old *bastard!*"

"Meg! What are—"

"You think I don't see what the game is? You want *me* to plant your whatsit for you. *That's* why we 'happened' to meet so accidentally. Fed me your line of— Oh Christ, I should have *known* you were up to something, Handsome Harry falling for a fat old cow like me."

"Meg! Don't say that, love!"

"Get your hands off. And don't call me 'love,' thank you. Oh Christ, what an *ass* I am!"

"Meg dear, please, lie back down and—"

"Keep off! I'm *glad* he did you out of something. You buggers get too much from us as it is. Ho! *There's* a joke. Remind me to laugh."

"Meg! Yes, you're right, it's true; I *was* hoping you'd lend a hand, and that *is* why we met. But it isn't why we're up here now. Do you think I'm so loyal to the bleeding Rev that I'd bed down with someone I wasn't keen on, just to get a wretched little twister like Harrington? And want to go on doing it for a fortnight or more? He's nothing compared to most we go after. I meant every word I said, Meg, about *preferring* large women, and mature ones, and wanting you to come stay with me at Christmas."

"Don't believe one bloody word."

"Oh Meg, I could . . . tear my tongue out! You're the best thing that's happened to me in fifteen years, and now I've spoiled it all with my stupidity! Will you just lie back down, love? I'm not going to mention Harrington ever again. I wouldn't let you help me now if you *begged* me."

"I shan't, so don't worry."

"Just lie back down, love—that's the girl—and let me hold you and kiss these nice big— Mmmmm! Ah, Meg, you're really heaven! Mmmmm!"

"Bastard . . ."

"You know what I'll do? I'll call in tomorrow and tell my super that Harrington's mending and I think I'll be able to plant the bug in a day or two. Perhaps I can stall him till Thursday or Friday before he pulls me back. Mmmmm! I'm queer for nurses, did y' know that? My mum was one, and so was Mary, my wife. Mmmmm!"

"Ah . . ."

"*You* mayn't like me, but your nipple does."

"Did you really mean it about Christmas, bastard?"

"I *swear* I did, love, and any other time we can manage. Maybe you could even move to London; have you ever thought of doing that? There are always posts for nurses, aren't there? That was Mary's experience."

"Oh, I couldn't. Not just pick up and move. Alan? Could you . . . really stay a fortnight?"

"I could get away with more than that, if I had the bug in; I'd have to wait till he's out of the tent and talking to people . . . But I'm not going to let you do it, Meg; I meant it."

"I already know—"

"No. I won't risk spoiling our relationship."

"Oh bosh. I already know you're a bastard, so what difference will it make? I want to help the government, not you."

"Well . . . I suppose I shouldn't stand in the way of getting my job done."

"I *thought* you'd come round. What must I do? I can't wire things."

"There's no need to. You simply bring a package into his room. The size of a sweet box. It *is* a sweet box actually, nicely done up in flowered paper. All you do is unwrap it, put it close to his bed—on a shelf or night table or such, the closer to his head the better—and you open it."

"That's all? Just open it?"

"It goes on automatically."

"I thought those things were tiny."

"The telephone ones. Not this kind."

"It won't make a spark, will it? The oxygen, you know."

"Oh no, it can't possibly. Just a microphone and a transmitter under a layer of sweets. You mustn't open it until you have it in the right place; it doesn't do to jiggle it around too much once it's broadcasting."

"Do you have it ready? I'll put it in tomorrow. Today, I should say."

"Good girl."

"Fancy old Harrington a tax cheat! What a stir it'll make if he's brought up on charges!"

"You mustn't breathe a word of this to anyone until we have evidence."

"Oh no, I'd never; I know that. We must assume he's innocent. It's quite exciting! Do you know what I'm going to do after I open the box, Alan?"

"I can't imagine."

"I'm going to *whisper something into it,* something I'd like you to do to me tomorrow night. In exchange for my helping. You will be able to hear, won't you?"

"The moment you open it. I'll be listening with bated breath. Whatever can you be thinking of, you wicked Meg? Oh yes . . . ooh, that feels very nice indeed, love."

■

Liebermann went to Bordeaux and Orléans, and his friend Gabriel Piwowar went to Fagersta and Göteborg. None of the four sixty-five-year-old civil servants who had died in those cities was any more imaginable as a Nazi victim than the four who had already been checked out.

Another batch of clippings and tear-offs came in, twenty-six this time, six of them possibles. There were now seventeen, of which eight—including the three of October 16th—had been eliminated. Liebermann was certain Barry had been wrong, but reminding himself of the gravity of the situation *if*, he decided to check out five more, the ones most easily checked. Two in Denmark he delegated to one of his contributors there, a bill collector named Goldschmidt, and one in Trittau, near Hamburg, to Klaus. Two in England he checked out himself, combining business with pleasure —a visit with his daugher Dena and her family, in Reading.

The five were the same as the other eight. Different, but the same. Klaus reported that the Widow Schreiber had propositioned him.

A few more clippings came in, with a note from Beynon: *Afraid I can't justify this to London any longer. Has anything come of it?*

Liebermann called him; he was out.

But he returned the call an hour later.

"No, Sydney," Liebermann said, "it was only wild geese. Thirteen I checked, out of seventeen that could have been. Not one was a man the Nazis would plan to kill. But it's good I checked, and I'm only sorry that I put you to so much trouble."

"Not a bit of it. The boy hasn't turned up yet?"

"No. I had a letter from his father. He's been down there twice, in Brazil, and twice to Washington; he doesn't want to give up."

"Pity. Let me know if he finds anything."

"I will. And thank you again, Sydney."

None of the final few clippings was a possible. Which was just as well. Liebermann turned his attention to a letter-writing campaign aimed at getting the West German government to renew attempts to extradite Walter Rauff—responsible for the gassing of ninety-seven thousand women and children and living then (and now) under his own name in Punta Arenas, Chile.

In January of 1975 Liebermann went to the United States for what was to have been a two-month speaking tour, a counterclockwise circuit of the eastern half of the country starting and ending in New York City. His lecture bureau had booked seventy-odd engagements for him, some at colleges and universities and the majority in temples and at luncheon meetings of Jewish groups. Before being sent on the tour he was escorted to Philadelphia and put on a television program (along with a health-food expert, an actor, and a woman who had written an erotic novel; but invaluable and hard-to-arrange publicity, Mr. Goldwasser of the bureau assured him).

On Thursday evening, January 14th, Liebermann spoke at Congregation Knesses Israel in Pittsfield, Massachusetts. A woman who had brought a paperback copy of his book for him to autograph said as he wrote in it that she was from Lenox, not Pittsfield.

"Lenox?" he asked. "That's near here?"

"Seven miles," she said, smiling. "I'd have come if it were seventy."

He smiled and thanked her.

November 16th: Curry, Jack; Lenox, Massachusetts. He hadn't brought the list with him but it was there in his head.

That night, in the guest room of the congregation's president, he lay awake, listening to snowflakes patting at the windowpanes. Curry. Something with taxes, an assessor or auditor. Killed in a hunting accident, someone's wild shot. Aimed shot?

He had checked. Thirteen out of seventeen. Including the three on October 16th. But only seven miles? The bus ride to Worcester wouldn't take more than two hours, and he didn't have to be there till dinnertime. Even after *dinnertime* in a pinch . . .

Early the next morning he borrowed his hostess's car, a big Oldsmobile, and drove to Lenox. Five inches of snow had fallen and more was coming down, but the roads were only thinly covered. Bulldozers pushed snow aside; other machines threw snow away in rushing arches. Incredible; back home everything would have been stopped dead.

In Lenox he found that no one had admitted shooting Jack Curry. And no, off the record, Police Chief DeGregorio *wasn't* sure it had been an accident. The hit had been suspiciously clean; smack through the back of the red hunting cap. That seemed more like good aim than bad luck. But Curry had been dead five or six hours when he had been found, and the area had then been walked over by at least a dozen people; so what could the police have been expected to find? Not even the shell had turned up. They had nosed around for someone with a grudge against Curry, but hadn't found anyone. He had been a fair and even-handed assessor, a respected and well-liked townsman. Had he belonged to any international group or organization? The Rotary; beyond that, Liebermann would have to ask *Mrs.* Curry. But DeGregorio didn't think she'd want to talk much; he heard she was still pretty broken up about it.

At midmorning Liebermann sat in a small untidy kitchen, sipping weak tea from a chipped mug and feeling miserable because Mrs.

Curry was going to cry any minute. Like Emil Döring's widow, she was in her early forties, but that was the only resemblance: Mrs. Curry was lank and homely, with boyishly chopped brown hair; sharp-shouldered and flat-chested in a faded floral housedress. And grieving. "*No one* would have wanted to kill him," she insisted, massaging below her flooding eyes with reddened crack-nailed fingertips. "He was . . . the finest man on God's green earth. Strong, and good, and patient, forgiving; he was a . . . *rock*, and now— Oh God! I—I'm—" And she cried; took a crumpled paper napkin and pressed it to one streaming eye and the other, laid her forehead on her hand, her sharp elbow on the tabletop; sobbed and shook.

Liebermann put his tea down and leaned forward helplessly.

She apologized in her crying.

"It's all right," he said, "it's all right." A big help. Seven miles through snow he had come, to start this woman crying. Thirteen out of seventeen wasn't enough?

He sat back, sighed, and waited; looked about dispiritedly at the small streaky-yellow kitchen with its dirty dishes and old refrigerator, carton of empty bottles by the back door. Wild Goose Number Fourteen. A fern in a red glass on the windowsill behind the sink, a can of Ajax. A drawing of an airplane, a 747, taped to a cabinet door; pretty good from where he sat. A cereal box on the counter, Cheerios.

"I'm sorry," Mrs. Curry said, wiping her nose with the napkin. Her wet hazel eyes looked at Liebermann.

"I'll only ask a few questions, Mrs. Curry," he said. "Did he belong to any international group or organization of men his own age?"

She shook her head, lowered the napkin. "American groups," she said. "The Legion, Amvets, Rotary—no, that's international. The Rotary Club. That's the only one."

"He was a World War Two veteran?"

She nodded. "The Air Force. He won the D.F.C., the Distinguished Flying Cross."

"In Europe?"

"The Far East."

"This one is personal, but I hope you won't mind. He left his money to *you?*"

Cautiously she nodded. "There's not too much . . ."

"Where was he born?"

"In Berea, Ohio." She looked beyond him, and with an effortful

smile said, "What are *you* doing out of bed?" He looked around.
The Döring boy stood in the doorway. Emil, no, Erich Döring,
gaunt and sharp-nosed, his dark hair disordered; in blue-and-white-
striped pajamas, barefoot. He scratched his chest, looking curiously
at Liebermann.

Liebermann rose, surprised; said *"Guten Morgen"* and realized
as he said it—and the boy nodded and came into the room—that
Emil Döring and Jack Curry had known each other. They *must*
have; how else could the boy be visiting? With growing excitement
he turned to Mrs. Curry and asked, "How does this boy come to *be*
here?"

"He has the flu," she said. "And there's no school anyway because of the snow. This is Jack junior. No, don't come too close,
hon. This is Mr. Liebermann from Vienna, in Europe. He's a famous man. Oh, where are your *slippers,* Jack? What do you want?"

"A glass of grapefruit juice," the boy said. In perfect English. An
accent like Kennedy's.

Mrs. Curry stood up. "Honest to Pete," she said, "you're going to
outgrow them before you ever wear them! And with the flu!" She
went to the refrigerator.

The boy looked at Liebermann with Erich Döring's deep blue
eyes. "What are you famous for?" he asked.

"He hunts for Nazis. He was on Mike Douglas last week."

"Es ist doch ganz phantastisch!" Liebermann said. "Do you
know that you have a twin? An exactly-like-you boy who lives in
Germany, in a town there called Gladbeck!"

"Exactly like me?" The boy looked skeptical.

"Exactly! I never before saw such a . . . resembling. Only twin
brothers could be so much the same!"

"Jack, you get back in bed now," Mrs. Curry said, standing by
the refrigerator with a juice carton in her hand, smiling. "I'll bring
it in."

"Wait a minute," the boy said.

"Now!" she said sharply. "You'll get *worse* instead of better,
standing around that way, no robe, no slippers; go on." She smiled
again. "Say good-by and go."

"Jesus H. *Christ,"* the boy said. "Good-*by!"* He stalked from the
room.

"You watch your tongue!" Mrs. Curry looked angrily after him,
and at Liebermann, and turned to a cabinet and yanked its door
open. "I wish that *he* paid the doctor bills," she said; *"then* he'd
think twice." She pulled out a glass.

Liebermann said, "It's amazing! I thought he was the boy in Germany visiting you! Even the voice is the same, the look in the eyes, the moving . . ."

"Everyone has a double," Mrs. Curry said, pouring a careful stream of grapefruit juice into the green glass. "Mine is in Ohio, a girl Big Jack knew before we met." She put the carton down and turned, holding the filled glass. "Well," she said, smiling, "I don't like to be inhospitable, but you can see I've got an awful lot here that needs doing. Plus having Jack at home. I'm sure nobody shot Big Jack on purpose. It was an accident. He didn't have an enemy in the world."

Liebermann blinked, and nodded, and reached for his coat on the chairback.

■

Astounding, such a sameness. Peas in a pod.

And even more astounding when, on top of the sameness of their gaunt faces and skeptical attitudes, you put the sameness of sixty-five-year-old fathers who were civil servants, dead by violence within a month of each other. *And* the sameness of their mothers' age, forty-one or -two. How could so much sameness *be*?

The wheel pulled toward the right; he straightened it, peering through the wiper's fast flickings. Concentrate on the driving!

It couldn't be only coincidence, it was too much. But what else *could* it be? Was it possible that Mrs. Curry of Lenox (who praised her dead husband's forgiveness) and Frau Döring of Gladbeck (no model of faithfulness, it seemed) had both had affairs with the same gaunt sharp-nosed man nine months before their sons were born? Even in that unlikely event (a Lufthansa pilot commuting between Essen and Boston!), the boys wouldn't be twins. And that's what they were, absolutely identical.

Twins . . .

Mengele's main interest. The subject of his Auschwitz experiments.

So?

The white-haired professor at Heidelberg: "Not one of the suggestions made so far has recognized *Dr. Mengele's* presence in the problem."

Yes, but these boys *weren't* twins; they only *looked like* twins.

He wrestled with it in the bus to Worcester.

It *had* to be a coincidence. Everyone had a double, as Mrs. Curry had said so unconcernedly; and though he doubted the statement's

truth, he had to admit he'd seen plenty of look-alikes in his life-
time: a Bormann, two Eichmanns, half a dozen others. (But look-
alikes, not look-*the-sames;* and why had she poured the grapefruit
juice so carefully? Had she been *very* concerned, and afraid a shaking hand might betray her? And then the quick kicking-him-out,
suddenly busy. Dear God, *could* the wives be involved? But how?
Why?)

The snow had stopped, the sun shone. Massachusetts swung past
—dazzlingly white hills and houses.

Mengele's obsession with twins. Every account of that subhuman
scum mentioned it: the autopsies on slaughtered twins to find genetic reasons for their slight differences, the attempts to work
changes on living twins . . .

Now listen, Liebermann, you're going a little bit overboard. More
than two months ago you saw Erich Döring. For less than five minutes. So now you see a boy who's the same type—with a strong resemblance, granted—and in your head you're doing a little mixing
and matching, and presto: identical twins, and Mengele at Auschwitz. The whole thing is that two men out of seventeen *happened*
to have sons who look alike. So what's so astounding?

But what if it's more than two? What if it's three?

You see. Overboard. Why not imagine quadruplets while you're
at it?

The widow in Trittau had given Klaus the eye, and offered him
more. In her sixties? Maybe. But probably younger. Forty-one?
Forty-two?

In Worcester he asked his hostess, a Mrs. Labowitz, if he could
make an overseas call. "I'll pay you back, of course."

"Mr. Liebermann, please! You're a guest in our home; it's *your*
telephone!"

He didn't argue. The place was a mansion practically.

It was five-fifteen. Eleven-fifteen in Europe.

The operator reported no answer at Klaus's number. Liebermann
asked her to try again in half an hour, hung up; thought for a moment, and got her back. Turning the pages of his address book, he
gave her Gabriel Piwowar's number in Stockholm and Abe
Goldschmidt's in Odense.

A call came for him just as he was sitting down to dinner with
four Labowitzes and five guests. He apologized and took it in the
library.

Goldschmidt. They spoke in German.

"What is it? More men for me to check?"

"No, it's the same two. Did they have sons about thirteen years old?"

"The one in Bramminge did. Horve. Okking in Copenhagen had two daughters in their thirties."

"How old is Horve's widow?"

"Young. I was surprised. Let me see. A little bit younger than Natalie. Forty-two, say."

"Did you see the boy?"

"He was at school. Should I have spoken to *him?*"

"No, I just wanted to know what he looks like."

"A boy, skinny. She had his picture on the piano, playing a violin. I said something, and she said it was old, when he was nine. Now he's nearly fourteen."

"Dark hair, blue eyes, sharp nose?"

"How can I remember? Dark hair, yes. The eyes I wouldn't know anyway; it wasn't colored. A skinny boy playing a violin, with dark hair. I thought you were satisfied."

"So did I. Thank you, Abe. Good-by."

He hung up; the phone rang in his hand.

Piwowar. They spoke in Yiddish.

"The two men you checked, did they have sons nearly fourteen years old?"

"Anders Runsten did. Not Persson."

"Did you see him?"

"Runsten's son? He drew my picture while I waited for his mother. I kidded him about taking him into my shop."

"What does he look like?"

"Pale, thin, dark-haired, a sharp nose."

"Blue eyes?"

"Yes."

"And the mother is in her early forties?"

"I told you?"

"No."

"So how do you know?"

"I can't talk now. People are waiting for me. Good-by, Gabriel. Be well."

The phone rang again; the operator reported that there was still no answer at Klaus's number. Liebermann told her he would place the call later.

He went into the dining room, feeling light-headed and hollow, as if his working parts were somewhere else (in Auschwitz?) and only his clothes and skin and hair there in Worcester sitting down with those whole all-there people.

He asked and answered the usual questions, told the usual stories; ate enough not to distress Dolly Labowitz.

They drove to the temple in two cars. He gave the lecture, answered the questions, signed the books.

When they got back to the house he put the call in to Klaus. "It's five A.M. there," the operator reminded him.

"I know," he said.

Klaus came on, groggy and confused. "What? Yes? Good evening! Where are you?"

"In Massachusetts in America. How old was the widow in Trittau?"

"What?"

"How old was the widow in Trittau? Frau Schreiber."

"My God! I don't know, it was hard to tell; she had a lot of make-up on. Much younger than *he* was, though. Late thirties or early forties."

"With a son almost fourteen?"

"Around that age. Unfriendly to me, but you can't blame him; she sent him off to her sister's so we could 'talk in private.' "

"Describe him."

A moment passed. "Thin, about as high as my chin, blue eyes, dark-brown hair, a sharp nose. Pale. What's going on?"

Liebermann fingered the phone's square push buttons. Round ones would look better, he thought. Square didn't make sense.

"Herr Liebermann?"

"It's not wild geese," he said. "I found the link."

"My God! What *is* it?"

He took a breath, let it blow out. "They have the same son."

"The same what?"

"Son! The *same son!* The exact same boy! I saw him here and in Gladbeck; you saw him there. And he's in Göteborg, Sweden; and Bramminge, Denmark! The exact same boy! He plays a musical instrument, or else he draws. And his mother is always forty-one, forty-two. Five different mothers, five different sons; but the son is the same, in different places."

"I . . . don't understand."

"Neither do I! The link was supposed to give us the reason, yes? And instead it's crazier than what we started out with! Five boys exactly the same!"

"Herr Liebermann—I think it may be six. Frau Rausenberger in

Freiburg is forty-one or -two. With a young son. I didn't see him or ask his age—I didn't imagine it was in any way relevant—but she said maybe *he* would go to Heidelberg too; not to study law, to study writing."

"Six," Liebermann said.

Silence stretched between them; stretched longer.

"*Ninety-four?*"

"Six is already impossible," Liebermann said, "so why not? But even if it *were* possible, and it isn't, why would they be killing the fathers? I honestly think I'll go to sleep tonight and wake up in Vienna the night this all started. Do you know what Mengele's main interest was at Auschwitz? *Twins.* He killed thousands of them, 'studying,' to learn how to breed perfect Aryans. Would you do me a favor?"

"Of course!"

"Go to Freiburg again and get a look at the boy there; see if he's the same as the one in Trittau. Then tell me whether I'm crazy or not."

"I'll go today. Where can I reach you?"

"I'll call *you*. Good night, Klaus."

"Good morning. But good night."

Liebermann put the phone down.

"Mr. Liebermann?" Dolly Labowitz smiled at him from the doorway. Would you like to watch the news with us? And have a little nosh? Some cake or fruit?"

Hannah's breasts were dry and Dena was crying, so naturally Hannah was upset. That was understandable. But was it any reason for changing Dena's name? Hannah insisted on it. "Don't argue with me," she said. "From now on we're calling her Frieda. It's the perfect name for a baby, and then I'll have milk again."

"It doesn't make *sense*, Hannah," he said patiently, trudging along beside her through the snow. "One thing has nothing to do with the other."

"Her name is Frieda," Hannah said. "We're changing it legally." The snow opened in a deep canyon before her and she slid down into it, Dena wailing in her arms. Oh God! He looked at the snow, unbroken now, and lay on his back in darkness, in a bed in a room. Worcester. Labowitz. Six boys. Dena grown up, Hannah dead.

What a dream. Where had he pulled *that* from? Frieda yet! And Hannah and Dena sliding into that canyon!

He lay still for a minute, blinking away the terrible sight, and then he got up—pale light scalloped the window shades' bottoms—and went into the bathroom.

He hadn't been up once during the night; a really good sleep. Except for that dream.

He went back into the bedroom, brought his watch over to one of the windows, squinted at it. Twenty to seven.

He got back into the warm bed, pulled the blankets up around him, and lay and thought, morning fresh.

Six identical boys—no, six very similar boys, maybe identical—lived in six different places, with six different mothers all the same age, and six different dead-by-violence fathers, all the same age, similar occupations. It wasn't impossible; it was real, a fact. So it had to be dealt with, unraveled, understood.

Lying still and at ease, he let his mind float free. Boys. Mothers. Hannah's breasts. Milk.

The perfect name for a baby . . .

Dear God, of course. It *had* to be.

He let it all come together . . .

Part of it, anyway.

It explained the grapefruit juice, and the way she'd rushed him out. The way she'd rushed the boy out too. Quick thinking, pretending his bare feet and no bathrobe were what worried her.

He lay there, hoping the rest of it would come. The main part, the Mengele part. But it didn't.

Still, one step at a time . . .

He got up and showered and shaved, trimmed his mustache, combed his hair; took his pills, brushed his teeth, put in his bridge. Dressed and packed.

At twenty after seven he went into the kitchen. The maid Frances was there, and Bert Labowitz in shirt-sleeves, eating and reading. After the good-mornings he sat down across the table from Labowitz and said, "I have to go to Boston earlier than I thought. Can I go with you?"

"Sure," Labowitz said. "I leave at five of."

"That's perfect. I have to make one phone call. Just to Lenox."

"I'll bet someone warned you about Dolly, the way she drives."

"No, something came up."

"You'll enjoy the ride more with me."

At a quarter of eight, in the library, he called Mrs. Curry. "Hello?"

"Good morning, it's Yakov Liebermann again. I hope I didn't wake you."

Silence. "I was up."

"How is your son this morning?"

"I don't know, he's still sleeping."

"That's good. That's the best thing, a lot of sleep. He doesn't know he's adopted, does he. That's why you got nervous when I told him he has a twin."

Silence.

"Don't get nervous *now*, Mrs. Curry. I won't tell him. As long as you want it a secret, I won't say a word. Just tell me one thing, please. It's very important. Did you get him from a woman named Frieda Maloney?"

Silence.

"You did, *ja?*"

"No! Just a minute." The thump of the phone being put down, footsteps going away. Silence. Footsteps coming back. Softly: "Hello?"

"Yes?"

"We got him through an agency. In New York. It was a *perfectly legal adoption.*"

"The Rush-Gaddis Agency?"

"Yes!"

"She worked there from 1960 to 1963. Frieda Maloney."

"I never heard the name before! Why are you butting in this way? What difference does it make if he *does* have a twin?"

"I'm not sure."

"Then don't bother me again! And don't come near Jack!" The phone clicked. Silence.

Bert Labowitz drove him to Logan Airport and he caught the nine-o'clock shuttle to New York.

At ten-forty he was in the office of the assistant executive director of the Rush-Gaddis Adoption Agency, a lean and handsome gray-haired woman, Mrs. Teague. "None at all," she told him.

"*None?*"

"None. She wasn't a caseworker; she wasn't qualified for that. She was a file clerk. Of course, her lawyer, when she was fighting extradition, wanted to present her in the most favorable light, so he implied that she played a more important role here than she actually did; but she was simply a file clerk. We notified the government lawyers—we were very anxious, naturally, to have our association with her put in its true perspective—and our head of personnel was subpoenaed as a witness. She was never called on to testify, though. We considered issuing some sort of statement or press release afterwards, but we decided that at that point it was better simply to let the matter fade away."

"So she *didn't* find homes for babies." Liebermann pulled at his ear.

"Not a one," Mrs. Teague said. She smiled at him. "And you have the shoe on the wrong foot: it's a question of finding babies for homes; the demand far exceeds the supply. Especially since the change in the abortion laws. We're able to help only a small fraction of the people who apply to us."

"Then too? In 1960 to '63?"

"Then and always, but it's at its worst right now."

"A lot of applications?"

"Over thirty thousand last year. From every part of the country. Of the continent, in fact."

"Let me ask you *this*," Liebermann said. "A couple comes to you, or writes to you, in that period, 1961, '62. Good people, fairly well-off. He's a civil servant, steady job. She's—now let me think a second—*she* . . . is about twenty-eight or twenty-nine, and he's fifty-two. What chance is there for them to get a baby from you?"

"None whatsoever," Mrs. Teague said. "We don't place where the husband's that old. Forty-five is our cut-off, and we'll only go *that* high if there are special factors involved. We place mostly with couples in their early thirties—old enough to be stable in their marriage and young enough to assure the child of continuing parental presence. Or the likelihood of it, I should say."

"So where would a couple like that *get* a baby?"

"Not from Rush-Gaddis. There *are* agencies a bit more flexible. And of course there's the gray market. Their lawyer or doctor might know of a pregnant teen-ager who doesn't want to abort. Or who can be paid not to."

"But if they came to *you*, you turned them down."

"Yes. We've never placed with anyone over forty-five. There are thousands of more suitable couples, waiting and praying."

"And the applications that were turned down," Liebermann said, "they were filed maybe by Frieda Maloney?"

"By her or one of the other clerks," Mrs. Teague said. "We keep all applications and correspondence for three years. It was five then, but now we've cut it down; we're short of space."

"Thank you." Liebermann stood up with his briefcase. "You helped me very much. I'm grateful to you."

At a telephone mini-booth across the street from the Guggenheim Museum, with his suitcase and briefcase on the sidewalk beside him, he called Mr. Goldwasser at the lecture bureau.

"I have some very bad news. I have to go to Germany."

"*When?*"

"Now."

"You can't! You're at Boston University tonight! Where are you?"

"In New York. And tonight I have to be on a plane."

"You *can't* be! You accepted the booking! They've sold the tickets! And tomorrow—"

"I know, I know! You think I enjoy canceling out like this? You think I don't know it's a headache for you, and for them, and you could even sue me? It's—"

"Nobody's talking about—"

"It's life or death, Mr. Goldwasser. Life or death. Maybe even more."

"God *damn* it. When will you be back?"

"I don't know. I may have to stay there awhile. And then go someplace else."

"You mean *you're canceling the whole rest of the tour?*"

"Believe me, if I didn't have to—"

"This has only happened to me once in eighteen years, and then it was a singer, not a responsible person like you! Look, Yakov, I admire you and I wish you well; I'm speaking not just as your representative now but as a fellow human, a fellow Jew. I ask you to think very carefully: if you cancel a whole tour this way, on a moment's notice—how can we possibly go on representing you? No one will represent you. No group will contract for you. You're finishing yourself as a speaker in the United States of America. I *beg* you, *please think.*"

"I thought while you was talking," he said. "I have to go. I wish I didn't."

He took a taxi out to Kennedy Airport and exchanged his return ticket to Vienna for one to Düsseldorf via Frankfurt: the earliest flight out, leaving at six o'clock.

He bought a copy of Farago's book on Bormann and spent the afternoon sitting by a window reading.

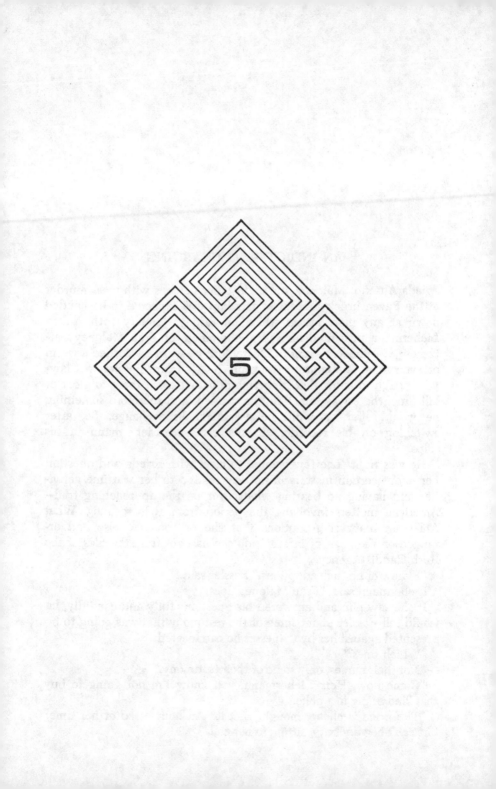

AN INDICTMENT CHARGING

Frieda Altschul Maloney and eight other persons with mass murder at the Ravensbrück concentration camp was expected to be handed down at any moment; so when, on Friday, January 17th, Yakov Liebermann presented himself at the offices of Frau Maloney's attorneys, Zweibel & Fassler of Düsseldorf, he wasn't accorded a warm or even room-temperature welcome. But Joachim Fassler was lawyer enough to know that Liebermann hadn't come there to gloat or kill time; there was something he wanted, and therefore something he would offer or could be asked for in exchange. So, after switching on his recorder, Fassler received Liebermann in his office.

He was right. The Jew wanted to meet with Frieda and question her about certain matters in no way related to her wartime activities and having no bearing whatsoever on the approaching trial—American matters involving the period from 1960 to 1963. What American matters? Adoptions that she or someone else had arranged on the basis of information she had got from the files of the Rush-Gaddis Agency.

"I know of no such adoptions," Fassler said.

Liebermann said, "Frau Maloney does."

If she saw him and answered his questions fully and candidly, he would tell Fassler about some of the testimony that was going to be presented against her by witnesses he had located.

"Which ones?"

"Not their names, only some of their testimony."

"Come now, Herr Liebermann, you know I'm not going to buy that kind of pig in a poke."

"The price is cheap enough, isn't it? An hour or so of her time? She can't be very busy, sitting in her cell."

"She may not want to talk about these alleged adoptions."

"Why not ask her? There are three witnesses whose testimony I know about. You can either hear it cold in the courtroom or have a preview tomorrow."

"I'm truly and honestly not that concerned."

"Then I guess we can't do business."

It took four days to work it all out. Frau Maloney would speak to Liebermann for half an hour about the matters that interested him, provided that A) Fassler was present; B) no fourth party was present; C) nothing was written down; and D) Liebermann permitted Fassler to search him for a recording device immediately prior to the interview. In return Liebermann would tell Fassler all he knew about the probable testimony of the three witnesses and give each one's age, sex, occupation, and present mental and physical condition, with particular regard to any scars, deformities, or disabilities resulting from experiences at Ravensbrück. The testimony and description of one witness would be supplied prior to the interview; those of the other two subsequent to it. Agreed and agreed.

On Wednesday morning, the 22nd, Liebermann and Fassler drove together in Fassler's silver-gray sports car to the federal prison in Düsseldorf where Frieda Maloney had been confined since her extradition from the United States in 1973. Fassler, a stout and well-groomed man in his mid-fifties, was almost as pink-cheeked as usual but—when they identified themselves and signed in—hadn't yet regained his customary swaggering assurance. Liebermann had told him about the most damaging witness first, hoping that the fear of worse to come would make him, and through him Frieda Maloney, anxious not to give short weight in the interview.

A guard took them up in an elevator and led them along a carpeted corridor where a few guards and matrons sat silently on benches between walnut doors marked with chrome letters. The guard opened a door marked G and showed Fassler and Liebermann into a square beige-walled room with a round conference table and several chairs. Two mesh-curtained windows gave daylight through adjacent walls, one window barred and the other not, which struck Liebermann as odd.

The guard switched on an overhead light, making scarcely a difference in the already light room. He withdrew, closing the door.

They put their hats and briefcases on the shelf of a corner coatrack, and took their coats off and hung them on hangers. Liebermann stood with his arms outstretched and Fassler searched him, looking pugnacious and determined. He felt the pockets of Lieber-

mann's hanging coat and asked him to open his briefcase. Liebermann sighed but unstrapped it and opened it; showed papers and
the Farago book, closed and restrapped it.

He satisfied himself about the windows—the unbarred one gave
on a high-walled yard far below; the barred one had black rooftop
close beneath—and then he sat down at the table with his back toward the unbarred window; but immediately got up again so he
wouldn't have to rise or not rise when Frieda Maloney came in.

Fassler opened the barred window a bit and stood looking out
through it, holding aside the beige mesh curtain.

Liebermann folded his arms and looked at a carafe and paper-
wrapped glasses on a tray on the table.

He had reported Frieda Altschul's record and whereabouts to the
German and American authorities in 1967. The record had been in
the Center's files, distilled from conversations and correspondence
with dozens of Ravensbrück survivors (the three soon-to-be
witnesses among them); the whereabouts had been given him by
two more survivors, sisters, who had spotted their former guard at a
New York racetrack and followed her to her home. He himself had
never met the woman. He didn't look forward to sitting at the same
table with her. Aside from everything else, his middle sister Ida
had died at Ravensbrück; it was entirely possible that Frieda
Altschul Maloney had had a hand in her death.

He put Ida from his mind; put everything from it except the
Rush-Gaddis Agency, and six or more boys who looked alike. A former file clerk at Rush-Gaddis is coming in, he told himself. We'll sit
at this table and talk awhile, and maybe I'll find out what the hell is
going on.

Fassler turned from the window, pushed his cuff back, frowned
at his watch.

The door opened and Frieda Maloney came in, in a light-blue
uniform dress, her hands in her pockets. A matron smiled over her
shoulder and said, "Good morning, Herr Fassler."

"Good morning," Fassler said, going forward. "How are you?"

"Fine, thanks," the matron said. She gave her smile to Liebermann, and covered it with closing door.

Fassler held Frieda Maloney's shoulder, kissed her cheek, and
backed her into the corner, speaking softly. She was gone behind
his bigness.

Liebermann cleared his throat and sat down, drew the chair in to
the table.

He had seen what photographs had shown: an ordinary-looking middle-aged woman. On the small side, graying hair combed up at the sides, curls on top. Gray-white unhealthy skin, a wide jaw, a disappointed mouth. Eyes that were tired but resolute, a lighter blue than the prison dress. She might have been an overworked chambermaid or waitress. Some day, he thought, I would like to meet a monster who *looks* like a monster.

He held the table's thick wood edge and tried to hear what Fassler was saying.

They were coming to the table.

He looked at Frieda Maloney, and she—as Fassler drew back the chair opposite—looked at him, the blue eyes measuring, the thin-lipped mouth down-drawn. She nodded, sitting.

He nodded back.

She flicked a thanking smile toward Fassler, and with her elbows on the chair arms, tapped with the flats of her fingers at the table edge, one hand's fingers and then the other's, fairly quickly; then stopped and let them rest there, looking at them.

Liebermann looked at them too.

"It's now exactly"—Fassler, seated at Liebermann's right, studied the watch on his raised wrist—"twenty-five of twelve." He looked at Liebermann.

Liebermann looked at Frieda Maloney.

She looked at him. Her thin eyebrows arched.

He found he couldn't speak. No breath was in him; only hatred. His heart pounded.

Frieda Maloney sucked at her lower lip, glanced toward Fassler, looked at Liebermann again; said, "I don't mind talking about the baby business. I made a lot of people very happy. It's nothing I'm ashamed of." She had a soft South German accent; easier to listen to than Fassler's Düsseldorf rasping. "And as far as the Comrades Organization is concerned," she said contemptuously, "they're no comrades of mine any more. If they were, I wouldn't be here, would I? I'd be down in *Sowze Amayrica*"—her eyes widened—"'living zee good life." She put a hand above her head and snapped her fingers, swaying her torso in mock-Latin rhythm.

"The best thing, I think," Fassler said to her, "would be for you to tell everything as you told it to me." He looked at Liebermann. "And then you can ask whatever questions you want. As time allows. You agree?"

Breath came back. "Yes," Liebermann said. "Provided time *does* allow for questions."

"You aren't really going to count minutes, are you?" Frieda Maloney asked Fassler.

"I certainly am," he said. "An agreement is an agreement." And to Liebermann, "There'll be enough time, don't worry." He looked at Frieda Maloney and nodded.

She folded her hands on the table, looked at Liebermann. "A man from the Organization got in touch with me," she said. "In 1960, in the spring. An uncle of mine in Argentina told them about me. He's dead now. They wanted me to get a job with an adoption agency. Alois—the man, that is—had a list of three or four of them. Any one would be all right as long as it was a job where I could look at the files. 'Alois' was the only name he ever gave me, no last name. Over seventy, white-haired; an old-soldier-type with very straight posture." Her eyes questioned Liebermann.

He gave no response, and she sat back in her chair and examined her fingernails. "I went to all the places," she said. "There were no openings. But after the summer Rush-Gaddis called me in, and they hired me. As a file clerk." She smiled musingly. "My husband thought I was crazy, taking a job in Manhattan. I was working then at a high school only eleven blocks from home. I told him that they promised me at Rush-Gaddis that in a—"

"Just the essentials, yes?" Fassler said.

Frieda Maloney frowned, nodded. "So. Rush-Gaddis." She looked at Liebermann. "What I did there was go through the mail and the files looking for applications where the husband was born between 1908 and 1912 and the wife between 1931 and 1935. The husband had to have a job in the civil service, and both of them had to be white Christians with a Nordic background. This was what Alois told me. Whenever I found one, and that was only once or twice a month, I copied it on the machine there along with all the letters between the couple and Rush-Gaddis. These were only people who hadn't been *given* babies, of course. Two sets I made, one for Alois and one for me. The ones for him I mailed to a box-number he gave me."

"Where?" Liebermann asked.

"Right there in Manhattan. The Planetarium Station, on the West Side. I kept doing that, looking for the right kind of applications and mailing them, the whole time I was there. After a year or so it got even harder to find them, because I'd been through the files by then and only had the new applications to look at. The civil-service part was changed then; as long as the job was *like* civil service it was all right. Something where the man was with a big organization and had some authority; an insurance company claim adjuster, for instance. So I had to go through the files *again*. Altogether I must have mailed off forty or forty-five applications in the three years. Copies of applications."

She leaned forward and took one of the paper-wrapped glasses from the tray, turned it in her hands. "Between . . . oh, Christmas 1960 and the end of summer 1963, which is when it ended and I left, this is what would happen. Alois or another man, Willi, would call me. Usually Willi. He'd say, 'See if . . . "the Smiths" in California want one in March.' Or whatever month, usually two months away. 'Ask "the Browns" in New Jersey too.' Maybe he'd give me three names." She looked at Liebermann, explained: "People whose applications I mailed before."

He nodded.

"So. I would call the Smiths and the Browns." She picked the wrapper-top out of the mouth of the glass. "A former neighbor of theirs told me they wanted a baby, I would say. Were they still interested? Almost always they were." She looked challengingly at Liebermann. "Not just interested. Overjoyed. The women especially." She gathered the wrapper into her hand, pushing the glass out bit by bit. "I told them I could get them one, a healthy white infant a few weeks old, in March or whenever. With New York State adoption papers. But first they had to send me as soon as possible complete medical reports—I gave them Alois's box-number— and they'd also have to agree never to tell the child it was adopted. The mother insisted on that, I said. And of course they'd have to pay me something when they came and got the baby, *if* they got it. A thousand usually, sometimes more if they could afford it. I could tell from the application. Enough so it would seem like an ordinary black-market arrangement."

She put the crushed wrapper on the tray and lifted the stopper from the carafe. "A few weeks later I'd get another call. 'Smith is no good. Brown can have it on March fifteenth.' Or maybe—" She tipped the carafe over the glass, tipped it farther; nothing came out. "Typical," she said, turning the black carafe upside down. "Typical of the way this whole damn place is run! Wrapped glasses but no water in the damn bottle! God!" She slammed the carafe down onto the tray; wrapped glasses jumped.

Fassler stood up. "I'll get some," he said, taking the carafe. "You go on." He went away toward the door.

Frieda Maloney said to Liebermann, "I could tell you things about the gross ineptness here . . . God! So. Yes. He tells me who gets the baby and when. Or maybe both couples are good, so he tells me to call the second and tell them it's too late for this one but I know another girl who's expecting in June." She rolled the glass between her palms, her lips pursed. "On the night a baby was given," she said, "everything was worked out very carefully in advance. By Alois or Willi and me, and by me and the couple. I would be in a room at the Howard Johnson Motel at the airport, Kennedy now—it was Idlewild then—using the name Elizabeth Gregory. The baby was brought to me, by a young couple or a woman alone or sometimes a stewardess. Some of them brought more than one—at different times, I mean—but usually it was someone new each time. They brought the papers too. Exactly like real ones, with the couple's names filled in. An hour or two later the couple would come and get the baby. Joyously. Grateful to me." She looked at Liebermann. "Nice people who would be good parents. They would pay me, and promise—I made them swear on the Bible there—never to tell the boy he was adopted. They were always boys. Darlings. And they would take them and go."

Liebermann said, "Don't you know where they came from? Originally, I mean?"

"The boys? From Brazil." Frieda Maloney looked away. "The people who brought them were Brazilian," she said, holding out her hand, "and the stewardesses were from the Brazilian airline, Varig." She took the carafe from Fassler, brought it to her glass, poured water. Fassler went around the table and sat down.

"From Brazil . . ." Liebermann said.

Frieda Maloney drank, putting the carafe on the tray. She drank, lowered the glass, licked her lips. "Almost always everything went like clockwork," she said. "One time the couple didn't show up. I called and they said they changed their mind. So I took the baby home with me and arranged for the next couple to come. Also new papers. I told my husband there was a mix-up at Rush-Gaddis and nobody else had room for the baby. He didn't know anything about anything. To this day he doesn't know. And that's it. Altogether there must have been about twenty babies; a few close together at the beginning, and after that, one every two or three months." She raised the glass and sipped.

"Twelve of," Fassler said, looking at his watch. He smiled at Liebermann. "You see? You have seventeen minutes left."

Liebermann looked at Frieda Maloney. "How did the babies look?" he asked her.

"Beautiful," she said. "Blue eyes, dark hair. They were all alike, even more alike than babies usually are. They looked European, not Brazilian; they had light skin, and the blue eyes."   .

"Were you *told* they were from Brazil or did you base that just on . . . ?"

"I wasn't told *anything* about them. Only what night they would be brought to the motel, and what time."

"Whose babies did you *think* they were?"

"Her opinion," Fassler said, "certainly doesn't have. any bearing on anything."

Frieda Maloney waved a hand. "What difference does it make?" she asked, and said to Liebermann, "I thought they were the children of Germans in South America. The illegitimate children, maybe, of German girls and South American boys. As to why the Organization was putting them into *North* America, and choosing the families so carefully—that I couldn't figure out at all."

"You didn't ask?"

"At the very beginning," she said, "when Alois first told me what kind of applications to look for, I asked him what it was all about. He told me not to ask questions, just to do what I was told. For the Fatherland."

"And I'm sure you were aware," Fassler reminded her, "that if you didn't cooperate, he could have exposed you to the kind of harassment that finally came years later."

"Yes, of course," Frieda Maloney said. "I was aware of that. Naturally."

Liebermann said, "The twenty couples you gave the babies to—"

"About twenty," Frieda Maloney said. "Maybe a few less. No more than twenty."

"They were all American?"

"Do you mean from the United States? No, some were Canadian. Five or six. The rest were from the States."

"No Europeans."

"No."

Liebermann sat silently, rubbing his earlobe.

Fassler glanced at his watch.

Liebermann said, "Do you remember their names?"

Frieda Maloney smiled. "It was thirteen, fourteen years ago," she said. "I remember one, Wheelock, because they gave me my dog and I called them for advice sometimes. They raised them, Dobermans. The Henry Wheelocks, in New Providence, Pennsylvania. I mentioned we were thinking of getting one, so they brought Sally, just ten weeks old then, when they came for the baby. A beautiful dog. We still have her. My husband still has her."

Liebermann said, "Guthrie?"

Frieda Maloney looked at him, and nodded. "Yes," she said. "The first one was Guthrie; that's right."

"From Tucson."

"No. In Ohio. No, Iowa. Yes, Ames, Iowa."

"They moved to Tucson," Liebermann said. "He died in an accident this past October."

"Ohh . . ." Frieda Maloney bit her lip regretfully.

"Who was next, after the Guthries?"

She shook her head. "This is when there were a few close together, only two weeks apart."

"Curry?"

She looked at Liebermann. "Yes," she said. "From Massachusetts. But not right after the Guthries. Wait a minute now. The Guthries were at the end of February; and then another couple, from someplace in the South—Macon, I think; and *then* the Currys. And then the Wheelocks."

"Two weeks after the Currys?"

"No, two or three months. After the first three they were spread out."

Liebermann asked Fassler, "Would it kill you if I wrote this down? It's not going to hurt her, in America so long ago."

Fassler scowled and sighed. "All right," he said.

"Why is it important?" Frieda Maloney asked.

Liebermann got out his pen and found a piece of paper in his pocket. "How is 'Wheelock' spelled?" he asked.

She spelled it for him.

"New Providence, Pennsylvania?"

"Yes."

"Try to remember: exactly how long after the Currys did they get their baby?"

"I can't remember exactly. Two or three months; it wasn't a regular schedule."

"Was it closer to two months or to three?"

"She can't remember," Fassler said.

"All right," Liebermann said. "Who came after the Wheelocks?"

Frieda Maloney sighed. "I can't remember who came when," she said. "There were twenty, over two and a half years. There was a Truman, not related to Truman the President. I think they were one of the Canadian couples. And there was . . . 'Corwin' or 'Corbin,' something like that. Cor*bett*."

She remembered three more names, and six cities. Liebermann wrote them down.

"Time," Fassler said. "Would you mind waiting for me outside?"

Liebermann put his pen and paper away. He looked at Frieda Maloney, nodded.

She nodded back.

He got up and went to the coatrack; put his coat over his arm and took his hat and briefcase from the shelf. He went to the door, and stopped and stood motionless; turned. "I'd like to ask one more question," he said.

They looked at him. Fassler nodded.

He looked at Frieda Maloney and said, "When is your dog's birthday?"

She looked blankly at him.

"Do you know?" he asked her.

"Yes," she said. "April twenty-sixth."

"Thank you," he said; and to Fassler: "Please don't be too long; I want to get this over with." He turned and opened the door and went out into the corridor.

He sat on a bench doing some figuring with his pen and a pocket calendar. The matron, sitting on the other side of his folded coat, said, "Do you think you'll get her off?"

"I'm not a lawyer," he said.

Fassler, nudging his car restlessly against stalled traffic, said, "I'm totally mystified. Would you tell me, please, what the Organization was doing in the baby business?"

"I'm sorry," Liebermann said, "but that's not in our agreement."

As if he knew.

He went back to Vienna. Where, in the face of a court order, the desks and file cabinets were being moved to an office Max had found, two small rooms in a run-down building in the Fifteenth District. And where *he*, therefore, had to move at once—Lili was already looking—to a smaller and cheaper apartment (good-by, Glanzer, you bastard). And where, what with one thing and another—two months' advance on the office, legal fees, moving costs, the phone bill—there was hardly enough left in the kitty to buy a ticket to Salzburg, let alone Washington.

Which was where he had to go the week after next, February 4th or 5th.

He explained to Max and Esther while they made the new office look more like the War Crimes Information Center and less like H. Haupt & Son, Advertising Specialties. "The Guthries and the Currys," he said, scraping the second *H* from the doorpane with a paper-pinched razor blade, "got their babies about four weeks apart, at the end of February and the end of March, 1961. And Guthrie and Curry were *killed* four weeks apart, one day over, in the same order. The Wheelocks got their baby around July fifth—this I know because they gave Frieda Maloney a ten-week-old puppy that was born on April twenty-sixth—"

"What?" Esther turned and looked at him. She held a map to the wall while Max pushed thumbtacks in.

"—and from the end of March to July fifth," Liebermann said, scraping, "is roughly fourteen weeks. So it's a good bet that Wheelock is supposed to be killed around February twenty-second, fourteen weeks after Curry. And I want to be in Washington two or three weeks before."

Esther said, "I *think* I follow you," and Max said, "What's not to follow? They're being killed in the same order they got the babies, and the same time apart. The question is—why?"

The question, Liebermann felt, would have to wait. Stopping the killings, whatever their reason, was what mattered, and his best chance of doing that was through the U.S. Federal Bureau of Investigation. They could confirm easily enough that two men who had died in "accidents" were the fathers of illicitly adopted look-alike sons, and that Henry Wheelock was a third (or fourth, if they turned up the one in Macon-maybe). On February 22nd, give or take a few days, they could capture Wheelock's intended killer, and learn from him the identities, and maybe even the schedules, of the other five. (Liebermann believed now that the six killers were working singly, not in pairs, because of the closeness in time of the murders of Döring, Guthrie, Horve, and Runsten—all in different countries.)

He might also, more easily, go to the Federal Criminal Investigation Department in Bonn, since he was certain that a German adoption agency (and an English and three Scandinavian ones) had had a Frieda Maloney searching its files and distributing babies. Klaus had found the boy in Freiburg identical to the one in Trittau, and Liebermann himself, while in Düsseldorf, had called the Frauen Döring, Rausenberger, and Schreiber, getting, in response to "Tell me, please, is your son adopted?," two surprised and wary yesses, one furious no, and three orders to mind his own business.

But in Bonn he would have no next victim to offer, and the explanation of how he had got Frieda Maloney to talk wouldn't be well received. He himself wouldn't be well received either, as he hoped he might be in Washington. Besides, in his Jewish heart of hearts, he didn't trust German authorities as much as American where Nazi matters were concerned.

So, Washington and the F.B.I.

He sat at the phone in the new office calling old contributors. "I don't like to buttonhole you this way, but believe me, it's important. Something that's going on *now*, with six SS men and Mengele." Inflation, they told him. Recession. Business was awful. He began bringing in dead parents, the Six Million—which he hated doing, using guilt as a fund-raiser. He got a few promises. "Please, right away," he said. "It's important."

"But it's not *possible*," Lili said, spooning a second deadly portion of potato kugel onto his plate. "How can there be *so many boys* who look alike?"

"Darling," Max said to her across their table, "don't say it's not possible. Yakov *saw*. His *friend from Heidelberg* saw."

"Frieda Maloney saw," Liebermann said. "The babies were all alike, more than babies usually are."

Lili made a spit-sound at the floor beside her. "She should die."

"The name she used," Liebermann said, "was Elizabeth Gregory. I meant to ask her if it was given to her or if she picked it herself, but I forgot."

"What's the difference?" Max asked, chewing.

Lili said, "*Gregory*. The name Mengele used in Argentina."

"Oh, of course."

"It *must* have come from him," Liebermann said. "*Everything* must have come from him, the whole operation. He was signing it, even if he didn't mean to."

Some money came in—from Sweden and the States—and he booked a ticket to Washington via Frankfurt and New York, for Tuesday, February 4th.

■

On Friday evening, January 31st, Mengele was using the name Mengele. He had flown with his bodyguards to Florianópolis on the island of Santa Catarina, roughly midway between São Paulo and

Pôrto Alegre, where in the ballroom of the Hotel Novo Hamburgo, decorated for the occasion with swastikas and red and black streamers, the Sons of National Socialism were holding a hundred-cruzeiros-a-head dinner dance. What excitement when Mengele made his appearance! Big Nazis, the ones who had played stellar roles in the Third Reich and were known throughout the world, tended to be snobbish toward the Sons, declining their invitations on grounds of ill health and making testy comments about their leader, Hans Stroop (who even the Sons would admit sometimes overdid his Hitler act). But here was Herr Doktor Mengele himself, in the flesh and white dinner jacket, shaking hands, kissing cheeks, beaming, laughing, repeating new names. How kind of him to come! And how healthy and happy he looked!

And was. And why not? It was the 31st, wasn't it? Tomorrow he would paint four more checks on the chart and be more than half-way down the first column—eighteen. He was going to every dance and party available these days; a reaction, of course, to the anguish and depression he had gone through back in November and early December, when it had looked for a while as if Jew-bastard Liebermann was going to spoil everything. Sipping champagne in this festive ballroom full of admiring Aryans, some of the men in Nazi uniforms (squint a little: Berlin in the thirties), he was amazed to remember the state he'd been in scarcely two months back. Absolutely Dostoevskian! Plotting, planning, making arrangements to leap into the breach if the Organization betrayed him (which they had been on the verge of doing, there was no doubt of *that*). But then Liebermann had led Mundt off on a tour of France, and Schwimmer through the wrong cities in England; and finally, thank God, had given up and stayed home, assuming, no doubt, that his young American stooge had been mistaken. (Thank God, too, that they had got to *him* before he had actually played the tape for Liebermann.) So we sip champagne and eat these delicious little whatever-they-ares ("A pleasure to *be* here! Thank you!") while poor Liebermann, according to *The New York Times,* is off in the wilds of America on what, reading between the lines of Jew-controlled puffery, is surely a very small-potatoes lecture tour. And it's winter there! Snow, please, God; plenty of snow!

He sat on the dais with Stroop at his left; was toasted by him most eloquently—the man wasn't as much of an idiot as he'd expected—and turned his attention to the ravishing blonde on his right. Last year's Miss Nazi she turned out to be, and small wonder. Though wedding-ringed now and—no fooling *his* eye—pregnant, four months. Husband in Rio on business; thrilled to be sitting next to such a distinguished . . . Maybe? He could always stay over; fly back bright and early.

While he was dancing with pregnant Miss Nazi, working his hand down gradually onto her really marvelous ass, Farnbach danced close and said, "Good evening! How are you? We heard you were here and came gate-crashing. May I present my wife Ilse? Sweetheart, Herr Doktor Mengele."

He kept dancing in place and smiling, thinking he had had too much to drink, but Farnbach didn't disappear or turn into someone else; he stayed Farnbach—became *more* Farnbach, in fact; shaven-headed, thick-lipped, introducing himself hungry-eyed to Miss Nazi while the ugly little woman in his arms yammered about "honor" and "pleasure" and "though you took Bruno away from me!"

He stopped dancing, freed his arms.

Farnbach explained cheerfully to him: "We're at the Excelsior. A little second honeymoon."

He stared at him, and said, *"You're supposed to be in Kristianstad. Getting ready to kill Oscarsson."*

Gasp from the ugly woman. Farnbach went white, stared back at him.

"Traitor!" he screamed. *"Pig of a—"* Words couldn't do it; he flung himself at Farnbach and grabbed his thick neck; pushed him backward through dancers, strangling him, while Farnbach's hands pulled at his arms. Red-faced the no-word-for-him now, blue eyes bulging. Scream of a woman; people turning: "Oh my God!" A table stopped Farnbach, lifted its far side; people retreated. He pushed Farnbach down, strangling him; the table shot up, pouring dishes-glasses-cutlery as they fell before it, spilling soup and wine on Farnbach's shaven head, washing his purpling face.

Hands pulled at Mengele; women screamed; the music splintered and died. Rudi tore at Mengele's wrists, looking pleadingly at him.

He let go, allowed himself to be pulled up and away, set on his feet. "This man is a traitor!" he shouted at them all. "He betrayed *me*, he betrayed *you!* He betrayed the *race! He betrayed the Aryan race!"*

A scream from the ugly woman kneeling at Farnbach's side as, red-faced and wet, he rubbed his throat, gasping. "There's glass in his head!" she cried. "Oh my God! Get a doctor! Oh Bruno, Bruno!"

"This man should be killed," Mengele explained breathily to the men around him. "He betrayed the Aryan race. He was given a job to do, a soldier's duty. He chose not to do it."

The men looked confused and concerned. Rudi rubbed Mengele's blotched wrists.

Farnbach coughed, trying to say something. He pushed his wife's napkin-hand from his face and raised himself on one arm, looking up toward Mengele. He coughed and rubbed at his throat. His wife clutched his wet-darkened shoulders. "Don't move!" she told him. "Oh God! Where's a doctor?"

"They!" Farnbach barked. "Called! Me back!" A drop of blood slid down in front of his right ear and became a small ruby earring, hanging, growing.

Mengele pushed men away, looked down.

"Monday!" Farnbach told him. "I was *in* Kristianstad! Setting things up for"—he looked at the others, looked at Mengele—"for what I had to do!" His blood-earring dropped; another began growing in its place. "They called me in Stockholm and told"—he glanced toward his wife, looked at Mengele—"someone I knew there that I should come back. To my company's office. At once."

"You're lying," Mengele said.

"No!" Farnbach cried; his blood-earring dropped. "*Everyone's* back! One was at—the office when I got there! Two had already been! The other two were coming!"

Mengele stared at him, swallowed. "Why?" he asked.

"*I don't know,*" Farnbach told him scornfully. "*I don't ask questions any more. I do as I'm told.*"

"Where's a *doctor?*" his wife screamed; "He's on his way!" someone called from the door.

Mengele said, "I . . . am a doctor."

"Don't you come near him!"

He looked at Farnbach's wife. "Shut up," he said. He looked around. "Does anyone have a pair of tweezers?"

In the banquet manager's office he picked slivers of glass out of the back of Farnbach's head with tweezers and a magnifying glass, while Rudi held a lamp close beside. "Just a few more," he said, dropping the largest sliver into an ashtray.

Farnbach, sitting bent over, said nothing.

Mengele dabbed the cuts with disinfectant and taped a gauze square over them. "I'm very sorry," he said.

Farnbach stood up, straightened his damp jacket. "And when," he asked, "do we find out *why* we were sent?"

Mengele looked at him for a moment and said, "I thought you stopped asking questions."

Farnbach turned on his heel and went out.

Mengele gave the tweezers to Rudi and sent him out too. "Find Tin-tin," he said. "We'll be leaving soon. Send him ahead to warn Erico. And close the door."

He put things back in the first-aid kit, sat down at the slovenly desk, took his glasses off, palmed his forehead dry. He got out his cigarette case; lit a cigarette and drew on it, dropped the match on the slivers of glass. He put his glasses back on and got out his address book.

He called Seibert's private number. A Brazilian maid with the giggles told him that the senhor and senhora were out, she didn't know where.

He tried headquarters, expecting no answer; got none.

Ostreicher's son Siegfried gave him another number, where Ostreicher himself answered the phone.

"This is Mengele. I'm in Florianópolis. I just saw Farnbach."

Silence, and then: "*Damn* it. The colonel was going to tell you in the morning; he's been putting it off. He's very unhappy about it. He fought like hell."

"I can imagine," Mengele said. "What happened?"

"It's that son of a bitch Liebermann. He saw Frieda Maloney sometime last week."

"He's in America!" Mengele cried.

"Not unless they moved it to Düsseldorf. She must have told him the whole story of her end of things. Her lawyer asked some of our friends there how come we were black-marketing babies in the 1960's. He convinced them it was true, and *they* asked *us*. Rudel flew in last Sunday, there was a three-hour meeting—Seibert very much wanted you to be there; Rudel and some of the others didn't —and that was it. The men came in on Tuesday and Wednesday."

Mengele pushed his glasses up and groaned, holding his eyes. "*Why couldn't they simply have killed Liebermann?*" he asked. "Are they lunatics, or Jews themselves, or what? Mundt would have *leaped* at the chance. He wanted to do it on his own, at the very beginning. He, alone, is smarter than all your colonels put together."

"Would you like to hear their reasoning?"

"Go ahead. If I vomit while you're speaking, please excuse me."

"Seventeen of the men are dead. This means, according to *your figures*, that we can be sure of one or even two successes. And maybe one or two more among the others, since some of the men will die *naturally* at sixty-five. Liebermann still doesn't know everything, because Maloney doesn't. But she may have remembered *names*, and if she did, his next logical step is to try to trap Hessen."

"Then just bring *him* in! Why all six?"

"That's what Seibert said."

"And?"

"This is where you'll vomit. The whole thing has become too risky. That's Rudel. It's going to end up putting the Organization in the limelight, and so would Liebermann's murder. Better to settle for the one or two successes or even more—which are enough, aren't they?—and close everything down. Let Liebermann spend the rest of his life Hessen-hunting."

"But he *won't.* He'll catch on eventually and concentrate on the boys."

"Maybe and maybe not."

"The truth is," Mengele said, taking his glasses off, "they're a bunch of tired old men who've lost their balls. They want only to die of old age in their villas by the sea. If their grandchildren become the last Aryans in a world of human shit, they couldn't care less. I would line them up in front of a firing squad."

"Come on now, they helped bring us this far."

"What if my figures were wrong? What if the chance isn't one out of ten but one out of twenty? Or thirty? Or *ninety-four?* Where are we then?"

"Look, if it were up to me I would kill Liebermann regardless of the consequences and go on with the others. I'm on your side. Seibert is too. I know you don't believe it, but he put up one hell of a battle. It would have been settled in five minutes if not for him."

"That's very comforting," Mengele said. "I have to go now. Good night." He hung up.

He sat with his elbows on the desk, his chin on the thumbs of his finger-locked hands, his lips kissing his inmost knuckle. So it always is, he thought, when one depends on others. Was there ever a man of vision, of genius (yes, *genius,* damn it!), who was well served by the Rudels and Seiberts of this world?

Outside the closed door of the office, Rudi waited, and Hans Stroop and his lieutenants; and the banquet manager and general manager of the hotel; and, at a discreet distance, Miss Nazi, not listening to the young man in uniform talking to her.

When Mengele came out, Stroop went to him with open arms and an ingratiating smile. "That poor fellow's gone off into the night," he said. "Come, we're holding the main course for you."

"You shouldn't have," Mengele said. "I have to go." He took Rudi by the arm and hurried toward the exit.

■

Klaus called and said he knew everything: how ninety-four boys could be as alike as twins and why Mengele would want their adoptive fathers killed on specific dates.

Liebermann, who had been up the night before with rheumatic aches and diarrhea, was spending the day in bed, and the first thing that struck him was the nice *symmetry* of it: a question put to him by one young man, by telephone while he was in bed, would be answered for him by another young man, by telephone while he was in bed. He was certain Klaus would be right. "Go ahead," he said, gathering the pillows up behind him.

"Herr Liebermann"—Klaus sounded uncomfortable—"it's not the sort of thing I can rattle off over the phone; it's complicated, and I really don't understand it thoroughly myself. I've only had it at second hand, from Lena, this girl I live with. It was her idea, and she spoke about it to a professor of hers. He's the one who really knows. Could you come up here and I'll arrange a meeting? I promise you it *has* to be the explanation."

"I'm leaving for Washington on Tuesday morning."

"Then fly up tomorrow. Or better yet, come Monday, stay over, and go on from here Tuesday. You must be going through Frankfurt anyway, yes? I'll pick you up at the airport there and bring you back again. We can meet with the professor Monday night. You'll stay here with Lena and me; you get the bed, we get the sleeping bags."

Liebermann said, "Give me at least the gist of it now."

"No. Really, it has to be explained by someone who knows what he's talking about. Is this why you're going to Washington?"

"Yes."

"Then you certainly want as much information as possible, don't you? I promise you, you won't be wasting your time."

"All right, I trust you. I'll let you know what time I'll be getting in. You'd better check with this professor and make sure he's free."

"I will, but I'm sure he will be. Lena says he's anxious to meet you and help. So is she. She's Swedish, so she has a vested interest. Because of the one in Göteborg."

"What does he teach, her professor—political science?"

"Biology."

"Biology?"

"That's right. I have to go out now, but we'll be in all day tomorrow."

"I'll call. Thank you, Klaus. Good-by."

He hung up.

So much for nice symmetry.

A professor of *biology?*

■

Seibert was relieved not to have had to be the one to break the news to Mengele, but he also felt he had got off the hook perhaps too easily; his long association with Mengele, and his admiration of his truly remarkable talent, suggested that he offer some sort of expression of commiseration and good cheer, and in fairness to himself he also wanted to present a fuller description than Ostreicher claimed to have given of the heated battle he had fought against Rudel, Schwartzkopf, et al. He tried to raise Mengele on the radio during the weekend, and unable to do so, flew out to the compound early Monday afternoon, taking his six-year-old grandson Ferdi along for the flight and bringing with him new recordings of *Die Walküre* and *Götterdämmerung*.

The landing strip was empty. Seibert doubted that Mengele had stayed on in Florianópolis, but it was possible that he was in Asunción or Curitiba for the day. Or he might only have sent his pilot into Asunción for supplies.

They walked along the pathway toward the house, Seibert and prancing Ferdi, with the co-pilot, who wanted to use the bathroom, walking behind them.

No one was about—no guards, no servants. The barracks, whose door the co-pilot tried, was locked, and the servants' house was closed and shuttered. Seibert grew uneasy.

The main house's back door was locked, and its front door too. Seibert pounded and waited. A small toy tank lay on the floorboards; Ferdi bent to it, but Seibert said sharply, "Don't touch!"—as if infection might lurk.

The co-pilot kicked in one of the windows, elbowed away the remaining peaks of glass, and carefully put himself through. A moment later he unlocked and opened the door.

The house was deserted but in good order, with no signs of a hasty departure.

In the study, the glass-topped desk was as Seibert had seen it last, the painting things lined up on a towel at a corner. He turned to the chart.

It was raped with red. Slashes like blood tore down through the boxes in the third and second columns. The first column's boxes held neat red checks halfway down, then larger and wilder checks, stabbing beyond the boxes.

Ferdi, looking worried, said, "He went outside the lines."

Seibert gazed at the ravaged chart. "Yes," he said. "Outside the lines. Yes." He nodded.

"What is it?" Ferdi asked.

"A list of names." Seibert turned and put the package of records on the desk. A bracelet of animal claws lay at its center. "Hecht!" he called; and louder, "*Hecht!*"

The co-pilot's answering "sir?" came faintly.

"Finish what you're doing and go back to the plane!" Seibert picked up the bracelet. "Bring me a can of gas!"

"Yes, sir!"

"Bring Schumann back with you!"

"Yes, sir!"

Seibert examined the bracelet and tossed it back onto the desk. He sighed.

"What are you going to do?" Ferdi asked him.

He nodded toward the chart. "Burn that."

"Why?"

"So no one ever sees it."

"Will the house catch on fire?"

"Yes, but the man who owns it isn't coming back."

"How do you know? He'll be angry if he does."

"Go play with that little toy outside."

"I want to watch."

"Do as I say!"

"Yes, sir." Ferdi hurried from the room.

"Stay on the porch!" Seibert called after him.

He pushed the long table with its stacks of magazines close against the wall. Then he went to the file drawers under the laboratory window, crouched and opened one, and took out a thick handful of folders and another thick handful. He brought them to the table and fitted them between magazine stacks. He looked ruefully at the red-slashed chart, shook his head.

He brought several loads of folders to the table, and when there was room for no more, opened the remaining drawers. He unlocked and opened the windows behind the desk.

He stood looking at the Hitler memorabilia above the sofa, took three or four items from the wall, looked speculatively at the large central portrait.

The co-pilot came in with a red fuel can; the pilot stood in the doorway.

Seibert put the things he had taken on the package of records. "Take out the portrait," he told the co-pilot. He sent the pilot off to make sure no one was in the house and to open all the windows.

"May I stand on the sofa?" the co-pilot asked.

Seibert said, "My God, why on earth not?"

He poured gasoline over the folders and magazines, standing well back, and tossed a few splashes up onto the chart itself. Names gleamed wetly: *Hesketh, Eisenbud, Arlen, Looft.*

The co-pilot carried the portrait out.

Seibert put the can outside the door and went to the open file drawers. He took from one a few sheets of paper and twisted them into a white branch as he moved to the desk. He picked up the lighter there, a cylindrical black one, and pressed flame from it a few times.

The pilot reported no one in the house and the windows open. Seibert had him take out the records and mementos and the fuel can. "Make sure my grandson's there," he told him.

He waited a moment, lighter in one hand, white paper branch in the other. *"Is he with you, Schumann?"* he called.

"Yes, sir!"

He lit the tip of the branch and put the lighter back behind him; dipped the branch to strengthen the flame, and stepping forward, threw it onto the flame-bursting folders and magazines. Flame sheared up the wall.

Seibert stepped back and watched the red-slashed center column of the chart blister and go brown. Names, dates, and lines, sheeted with flame, died away as blackness grew around them.

He hurried out.

Behind the house they stopped and watched awhile, well back from the wavering heat and the crackling: Seibert holding Ferdi's hand, the co-pilot resting a forearm on the frame of Hitler's portrait, the pilot with his arms full and the red can by his feet.

Esther had her hat and coat on and one foot out the door—literally—when the phone rang. This was *not* her day. Would she *ever* get home? Sighing, she drew the foot back, closed the door, and went and answered the ringing phone in the faint light from the doorpane.

An operator, with a call for Yakov from São Paulo; Esther told her Herr Liebermann was out of town. The caller, in good German, said he would speak to *her*. "Yes?" she said.

"My name is Kurt Koehler. My son Barry was—"

"Oh yes, I *know*, Herr Koehler! I'm Herr Liebermann's secretary, Esther Zimmer. Is there any news?"

"Yes, there is, and it's bad news. Barry's body was found last week."

Esther groaned.

"Well, we've been expecting it—no word in all this time. I'm starting home now. With . . . it."

"Ei! I'm so sorry, Herr Koehler!"

"Thank you. He was stabbed, and then dumped in the jungle. From a plane, apparently."

"Oh my God . . ."

"I thought Herr Liebermann would want to know—"

"Of course, of course! I'll tell him."

"—and I also have some information for him. They took Barry's wallet and passport, of course—those filthy Nazi pigs—but there was a piece of paper in his jeans that they overlooked. It looks to me as if he wrote down some notes while he was listening to that tape recording, and there's a great deal here that I'm sure Herr Liebermann can make use of. Could you tell me where I can get in touch with him?"

"Yes, he's at Heidelberg tonight." Esther switched on the lamp and turned her phone index. "In Mannheim, actually. I've got the number right here."

"Tomorrow he'll be back in Vienna?"

"No, he's going to Washington from there."

"Oh? Well, perhaps I ought to call him in Washington. I'm a little . . . shaken up right now, as you can imagine, but I'll be home tomorrow and able to talk more easily. Where will he be staying?"

"At the Benjamin Franklin Hotel." She turned the index. "I have that number too." She found it and read it off slowly and clearly.

"Thank you. What time is he due there?"

"His plane lands at six-thirty, God willing; he should be at the hotel by seven or seven-thirty. Tomorrow night."

"Is he going there about this business Barry was investigating?"

"Yes," Esther said. "Barry was *right*, Herr Koehler. A lot of men have been murdered, but Yakov's going to put a stop to it. You can rest assured that your son didn't die in vain."

"It's good to hear that, Fräulein Zimmer. Thank you."

"Don't mention it. Good-by."

She hung up, sighed, and shook her head sadly.

Mengele hung up too, picked up his brown canvas suitcase, and got on the shorter of the two lines at the Pan Am ticket counter. He had brown hair combed to the side and a full brown mustache, and was wearing a high padded neck-brace. So far it seemed to be doing its job of making people avoid his eyes.

According to his Paraguayan passport he was Ramón Aschheim y Negrín, a *comerciante en antigüedades,* a dealer in antiquities; which was why he had a gun in his suitcase, a nine-millimeter Browning Hi-Power Automatic. He had a permit for it, as well as a driver's license, a full complement of social and business credentials, and in his passport, page after page of visas. Señor Aschheim y Negrín was setting off on a multinational buying trip: the States, Canada, England, Holland, Norway, Sweden, Denmark, Germany, and Austria. He was well supplied with money (and diamonds). His visas, like his passport, had been issued in December, but they were still valid.

He bought a ticket for New York on the next flight out, leaving at 7:45, which in conjunction with an American Airlines flight would get him into Washington at 10:35 the next morning.

Plenty of time to get settled in at the Benjamin Franklin.

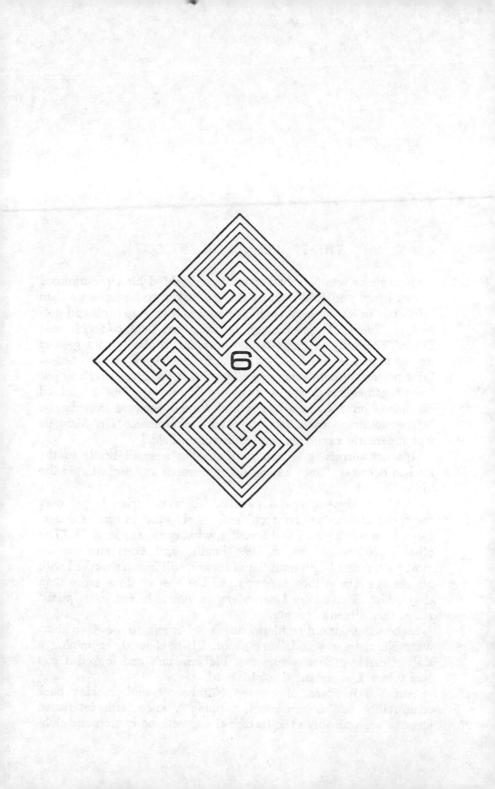

THE PROFESSOR OF BIOLOGY

—whose name was Nürnberger and who, behind his close-trimmed brown beard and gold-rimmed glasses, looked to be no more than thirty-two or -three—bent back his pinky as if to snap it off and present it. "Identical appearance," he said, and bent back his next finger. "Similarity of interests and attitudes, probably to a greater degree than you're presently aware." He bent back his next finger. *"The placement with similar families:* this is the giveaway. You put these together and there's only one possible explanation." He folded his hands on his crossed legs and leaned forward confidingly. "Mononuclear reproduction," he told Liebermann. "Dr. Mengele was apparently a good ten years ahead of the field."

"It's not surprising," Lena said, shaking a small bottle in the kitchen doorway, "since he was doing research at Auschwitz, in the forties."

"Yes," Nürnberger agreed (while Liebermann tried to get over the shock of hearing "research" and "Auschwitz" in one sentence; forgive her, she's young and Swedish, what could she know?). "The others," Nürnberger was saying, "English and Americans for the most part, didn't begin until the fifties and still haven't worked with human ova. Or so they say; you can bet they've done more than they admit. That's why I say Mengele was only ten years ahead rather than fifteen or twenty."

Liebermann looked at Klaus, sitting at his left, to see if *he* knew what Nürnberger was talking about. Klaus chewed, examining a stub of carrot-stick. His eyes met Liebermann's and looked a *you see?* at him. Liebermann shook his head.

"And the Russians, of course," Nürnberger said, rocking back comfortably on his campstool, cupping a knee with interlaced fingers, "are probably even farther along, with no church and public opinion to contend with. They probably have a whole *school* of perfect little Vanyas somewhere in Siberia; even older, perhaps, than these boys of Mengele's."

"Excuse me," Liebermann said, "but I don't understand what you're talking about."

Nürnberger looked surprised. Patiently he said, "Mononuclear reproduction. The breeding of genetically identical copies of an individual organism. Have you studied any biology at all?"

"A little," Liebermann said. "About forty-five years ago."

Nürnberger smiled a young man's smile. "That's just when the possibility of it was first recognized," he said. "By Haldane, the English biologist. He called it *cloning*, from a Greek word meaning 'a cutting,' as from a plant. 'Mononuclear reproduction' is a far more explicit term. Why coin a new word when the old ones convey more?"

"*Cloning* is shorter," Klaus said.

"Yes," Nürnberger conceded, "but isn't it better to use a few more syllables and say exactly what you mean?"

Liebermann said, "Tell me about 'mononuclear reproduction.' But bear in mind please that I studied biology only because I had to; my real interest was music."

"Try singing it," Klaus suggested to Nürnberger.

"It wouldn't make much of a song if I could," Nürnberger said. "Not a pretty love song like ordinary reproduction. There we have an ovum, or egg cell, and a sperm cell, each with a nucleus containing twenty-three chromosomes, the filaments on which the genes, hundreds of thousands of them, are strung like beads. The two nuclei merge, and we have a fertilized egg cell, forty-six chromosomes. I'm speaking now of human cells; the number is different in different species. The chromosomes duplicate themselves, duplicating *each of their genes*—it really is miraculous, isn't it?—and the cell divides, one set of identical chromosomes going into each resulting cell. This duplication and division occurs again and again—"

"Mitosis," Liebermann said.

"Yes."

"The things that stay in the mind!"

"And in nine months," Nürnberger said, "we have the billions of cells of the complete organism. They've evolved to perform different functions—to become bone or flesh or blood or hair; to respond to light or heat or sweetness, and so on—but *each* of those cells, each of the billions of cells that constitute the body, contains in its nucleus exact duplicates of an original set of forty-six chromosomes, half from the mother, half from the father: a mix that, except in the case of identical twins, is absolutely unique—the blueprint, as it were, of an absolutely unique individual. The only exceptions to the forty-six-chromosomes rule are the sex cells, sperm and ova, which have twenty-three, so that they can merge, fulfill each other, and begin a new organism."

Liebermann said, "So far it's clear."

Nürnberger leaned forward. "That," he said, "is ordinary reproduction as it occurs in nature. Now we go into the laboratory. In mononuclear reproduction, the nucleus of an egg cell is destroyed, leaving the body of the cell unharmed. This is done by radiation and is, of course, microsurgery of the most sophisticated order. Into the enucleated egg cell is put *the nucleus of a body cell of the organism to be reproduced*—the nucleus of a *body* cell, not a sex cell. We now have exactly what we had at this point in natural reproduction: an egg cell with forty-six chromosomes in its nucleus; a fertilized egg cell which, in a nutrient solution, proceeds to duplicate and divide. When it reaches the sixteen- or thirty-two-cell stage—this takes four or five days—it can be implanted in the uterus of its 'mother'; who isn't its mother at all, biologically speaking. She supplied an egg cell, and now she's supplying a proper environment for the embryo's growth, but she's given it nothing of her own genetic endowment. The child, when it's born, has neither father *nor* mother, only a donor—the giver of the nucleus—of whom it's an exact genetic duplicate. Its chromosomes and genes are identical to the donor's. Instead of a new and unique individual, we have an existing one repeated."

Liebermann said, "This . . . can be done?"

Nürnberger nodded.

"It's *been* done," Klaus said.

"With frogs," Nürnberger said. "A far simpler procedure. That's the only *acknowledged* instance, and it caused such a flap—at Oxford in the sixties—that all later work has been done on the quiet. I've heard reports, every biologist has, of rabbits, dogs, and monkeys; in England, America, here in Germany, everywhere. And as I said before, I'm sure they've already done it with humans in Russia. Or at least tried. What planned society could resist the idea? Multiply your superior citizens and prohibit the inferior ones from reproducing. Think of the savings in medical care and education! And the improved quality of the population in two or three generations."

Liebermann said, "Could Mengele have done it with humans in the early sixties?"

Nürnberger shrugged. "The theory was already known," he said. "All he needed was the right equipment, some healthy and willing young women, and a high degree of microsurgical skill. Others have had it: Gurdon, Shettles, Steptoe, Chang . . . And of course, a place where he could work without interference or publicity."

"He was in the jungle by then," Liebermann said. "He went in in '59. I drove him in . . ."

Klaus said, "Maybe you didn't. Maybe he *chose* to go."

Liebermann looked uneasily at him.

"But it's pointless," Nürnberger said, "to talk about whether or not he *could* have done it. If what Lena told me is true, he obviously *did* do it. The fact that the boys were placed with similar families proves it." He smiled. "You see, genes aren't the only factor in our ultimate development; I'm sure you know that. The child conceived by mononuclear reproduction will grow up looking like his donor and sharing certain characteristics and propensities with him, but if he's raised in a different environment, subjected to different domestic and cultural influences—as he's bound to be, if only by being born years later—well, he can turn out to be quite different *psychologically* from his donor, despite their genetic sameness. Mengele was obviously interested not in breeding a particular biological strain, as I think the Russians might be, but in reproducing *himself*, a particular individual. The similar families are an attempt to maximize the chances of the boys' growing up in the right environment."

Lena came to the kitchen doorway.

"The boys," Liebermann said, "are . . . duplicates of Mengele?"

"Exact duplicates, genetically," Nürnberger said. "Whether or not they'll grow up to be duplicates *in toto* is, as I said, another question."

"Excuse me," Lena said. "We can eat now." She smiled apologetically; her plain face became pretty for an instant. "In fact, we have to," she said, "otherwise things will be ruined. If they aren't already."

They got up and went from the small room of scavenged furniture, animal posters, paperback books, into an almost-the-same-size kitchen, with more animal posters, a steel-gated window, and a red-covered table—bread, salad, red wine in mismatched tumblers.

Liebermann, uncomfortable on a small wire-backed chair, looked across the table at Nürnberger buttering bread. "What did you mean," he asked, "about the boys' growing up in 'the right environment'?"

"One as much like Mengele's as possible," Nürnberger said, looking at him. He smiled in his brown beard. "Look," he said, "if I wanted to make another Eduard Nürnberger, it wouldn't be enough simply to scrape a bit of skin from my toe, pluck a nucleus from a cell, and go through that whole procedure I described—assuming I had the ability and equipment—"

"And the woman," Klaus said, putting a plate before him.

"Thank you," Nürnberger said, smiling. "I could get the woman."

"For *that* kind of reproduction?"

"Well, assuming. It only means two tiny incisions, one to extract the ovum and one to implant the embryo." Nürnberger looked at Liebermann. "But that would be only *part* of the job," he said. "I would then have to find a suitable *home* for Baby Eduard. He would require a mother who's very religious—almost a maniac, in fact—and a father who drinks too much, so that there's constant fighting between them. And there would also have to be in the house a wonderful uncle, a math teacher, who takes the boy out of there as often as he can: to museums, to the country . . . These people would have to treat the boy like their own, not like someone conceived in a laboratory, and furthermore, the 'uncle' would have to die when the boy was nine and the 'parents' would have to separate two years later. The boy would have to spend his adolescence shuttling between the two with his younger sister."

Klaus was sitting down with a plate at Liebermann's right. A plate lay before Liebermann—dry-looking meat loaf, carrots steaming a minty smell.

"And even *then*," Nürnberger said, "he might turn out very different from *this* Eduard Nürnberger. His biology teacher might not take a shine to him, as mine did. A girl might let him go to bed with her sooner than one let me. He'd read different books, watch television where I listened to radio, be subject to thousands of chance encounters that might make him more or less aggressive than I am, more or less loving, witty, et cetera, et cetera."

Lena sat down with a plate at Liebermann's left, looked across the table at Klaus.

Nürnberger, breaking meat loaf with his fork, said, "Mengele was aware of the chanciness of the whole thing, so he produced and found homes for *many* boys. He'll be happy, I suppose, if a few, or even only one, turns out exactly right."

"Do you see now," Klaus asked Liebermann, "why the men are being killed?"

Liebermann nodded. "To—I don't know what word to use—to *shape* the boys."

"Exactly," Nürnberger said. "To shape them, to try to make them *psychological* Mengeles as well as genetic ones."

Klaus said, "He lost his father when he was a certain age, so the boys must do the same. Or lose the men they *think* are their fathers."

"The event," Nürnberger said, "surely was of paramount importance in shaping his psyche."

"It's like unlocking a safe," Lena said. "If you can turn the knob to all the right numbers, in the right order, the door opens."

"Unless," Klaus said, "the knob was turned to a wrong number in between. These carrots are great."

"Thank you."

"Yes," Nürnberger said. "Everything's delicious."

"Mengele has brown eyes."

Nürnberger looked at Liebermann. "Are you sure?"

Liebermann said, "I've held his Argentine identity card in my hand. 'Eyes, brown.' And his father was a manufacturer, not a civil servant. Farm machines."

"He's related to *those* Mengeles?" Klaus asked.

Liebermann nodded.

Nürnberger, taking salad onto his plate, said, "No wonder he could afford the equipment. Well, he can't have been the donor himself, if the eyes don't match."

Lena said to Liebermann, "Do you know who's the head of the Comrades Organization?"

"A colonel named Rudel, Hans Ulrich Rudel."

"Blue eyes?" Klaus asked.

"I don't know. I'll have to check. And his family background." Liebermann looked at the fork in his hand, put its tines into a slice of carrot, raised the carrot, put it into his mouth.

"At any rate," Nürnberger said, "you know now why those men are being killed. What are you planning to do next?"

Liebermann sat silently for a moment. He put his fork down and took the napkin from his lap and put it on the table. "Excuse me," he said, and got up and went out of the kitchen.

Lena looked after him, looked at his plate, looked at Klaus.

"It's not that," he said.

"I hope not," she said, and pressed the side of her fork into her meat loaf.

Klaus looked beyond her; watched Liebermann go to the bookshelves in the other room.

"Not that this isn't excellent meat," Nürnberger said, "but we'll all be eating much better meat some day, and much cheaper, thanks to mononuclear reproduction. It'll revolutionize cattle-breeding. And it'll also preserve our endangered species, like that beautiful leopard there."

"You're defending it?" Klaus asked.

"It doesn't need defending," Nürnberger said. "It's a technique, and like any other technique you can mention, it can be put to either good or bad uses."

"I can think of two good ones," Klaus said, "and you just mentioned them. Give me a pencil and paper and five minutes and I'll give you fifty bad ones."

"Why must you always take the opposite side?" Lena asked. "If the professor had said it's a terrible thing, you'd be talking now about cattle-breeding."

"That's not true at all," Klaus said.

"It is so. He'll argue against his own statements."

Klaus looked beyond Lena; saw Liebermann standing in profile, head bent to an open book, rocking slightly: Jew at prayer. Not a Bible, though; they didn't have one. Liebermann's own book? He was standing just about where it was. Checking on the colonel's eyes? "Klaus?" Lena offered the salad bowl.

He took it.

Lena turned and looked, turned back to the table.

Nürnberger said, "I'm going to have a hard time keeping my mouth shut about this."

"You must, though," Klaus said.

"I know, I know, but it won't be easy. Two of the men in the department have tried it themselves, with rabbit ova."

Liebermann stood in the doorway, ashen and beaten-looking, his glasses hanging from the hand at his side.

"What is it?" Klaus put the bowl down.

Nürnberger looked; Lena turned in her chair.

Liebermann said to Nürnberger, "Let me ask you a foolish question."

Nürnberger nodded.

"The one who gives the nucleus," Liebermann said. "The donor. He has to be alive, yes?"

"No, not necessarily," Nürnberger said. "Individual cells are neither alive nor dead, only intact or not intact. With a lock of Mozart's hair—not even a lock; with a single hair from Mozart's head—someone with the skill and equipment"—he smiled at Klaus—"*and* the women"—he looked back at Liebermann—"could breed a *few hundred* infant Mozarts. Find the right homes for them and we'd wind up with five or ten adult Mozarts, and a lot more beautiful music in this world."

Liebermann blinked, took an unsteady step forward, shook his head. "Not music," he said. "Not Mozart." He brought his hand from behind his back and showed them *Hitler;* the paperback book bore three black brush-strokes: mustache, sharp nose, forelock.

Liebermann said, "His father was a civil servant, a customs officer. He was fifty-two when . . . the boy was born. The mother was twenty-nine." He looked around for someplace to put the book, found no place, put it on one of the stove's burners. He looked at them again, wiped his hand against his side. "The father died at sixty-five," he said. "When the boy was thirteen, almost fourteen."

They left everything on the table and went in and sat in the other room, Liebermann and Klaus on the daybed again, Nürnberger on the campstool, Lena on the floor.

They looked at the empty glasses on the trunk before them, the bowls of carrot-sticks and almonds. They looked at one another.

Klaus picked up a few almonds, tossed them on his palm.

Liebermann said, "Ninety-four Hitlers," and shook his head. "No," he said. "No. It's not possible."

"Of course it isn't," Nürnberger said. "There are ninety-four boys with the *same genetic inheritance as Hitler*. They could turn out very differently. Most of them probably will."

"Most," Liebermann said. He nodded at Klaus and at Lena. "*Most*." He looked at Nürnberger. "That leaves *some*," he said.

"How many?" Klaus asked.

"I don't know," Nürnberger said.

"You said five or ten Mozarts out of a few hundred. How many Hitlers out of ninety-four? One? Two? Three?"

"I don't *know*," Nürnberger said. "I was talking. No one really knows." He smiled wryly. "The frogs weren't given personality tests."

"Make a guess," Liebermann said.

"If the parents were matched only by age, race, and the father's occupation, I'd say the prospects were pretty poor. From Mengele's viewpoint, I mean; pretty good from ours."

"But not perfect," Liebermann said.

"No, of course not."

"Even if there were only one," Lena said, "there would still be a chance of his . . . being influenced the right way. The *wrong* way."

Klaus said to Liebermann, "Do you remember what you said at the lecture? Someone asked you if the neo-Nazi groups were dangerous, and you said not now, only if social conditions got worse—which God knows they're doing every day—and another leader like Hitler appeared."

Liebermann nodded. "Speaking to the whole world at once," he said, "by television satellite. God in heaven." He closed his eyes, put his hands to his face, and wiped his fingers across his eyelids, pressing hard.

"How many of the fathers have actually been killed?" Nürnberger asked.

"That's *right!*" Klaus said. "Only six! It's not as bad as it seems!"

"Eight," Liebermann said, lowering his hands, blinking his reddened eyes. "You're forgetting Guthrie in Tucson, and the one between him and Curry. Others, too, that we don't know about in the other countries. More at the beginning than later on; that's how it was in the States."

Nürnberger said, "The initial batch must have had a higher success-ratio than he expected."

"I can't help feeling," Klaus said, "that you're a little bit pleased by the achievement."

"Well, you have to admit that strictly from a scientific viewpoint, it's a step forward."

"Jesus Christ! Do you mean you can sit there and—"

"Klaus," Lena said.

"Oh—shit." Klaus slapped the almonds down.

Liebermann said to Nürnberger, "I'm going to Washington tomorrow to speak to their Federal Bureau of Investigation. I know who the next father there is; they could trap the killer, they *have to* trap him. Will you come with me and help convince them?"

"Tomorrow?" Nürnberger said. "I can't *possibly.*"

"To prevent a new Hitler?"

"God!" Nürnberger rubbed his brow. "Yes, of course," he said, "if you absolutely need me. But look, there are men there, at Harvard, Cornell, Cal Tech, whose credentials are much more impressive than mine and who would in any case carry more weight with American authorities simply by virtue of being American. I can give you names and schools if you'd like—"

"I would, yes."

"—and if for any reason you do want me, I *will* come over."

"Good," Liebermann said. "Thank you."

Nürnberger took a pen and a black leather memo pad from inside his jacket. "Shettles himself would probably help you," he said.

"Put his name down," Liebermann said. "And where I can reach him. Put down everyone you can think of." To Klaus he said, "He's right, an American is better. Two foreigners, they'll kick us out on our asses."

"Don't you have any contacts there?" Klaus asked.

"Dead contacts," Liebermann said. "Not-with-the-Justice-Department-any-more contacts. I'll manage, though. I'll break down doors. God in heaven! Think of it! Ninety-four young Hitlers!"

"Ninety-four *boys*," Nürnberger said, writing, "with the same *genetic inheritance* as Hitler."

The Benjamin Franklin, as a hotel, a place to stop at, rated about one tenth of a star in Mengele's judgment, and that only because the sink in the bathroom had a certain antique charm. As a place to rid oneself of an enemy bent on destroying one's life work and the last hope (correction, certainty) of Aryan supremacy, however, it rated three and a half stars, possibly a full four.

For one thing, the clientele in the lobby was partly black, which meant, of course, that crime on the premises wasn't unheard of. As proof of this, if proof were needed, the door of his room, 404, bore the gouge-marks of forcible entry, and *For your own protection please keep door bolted at all times*, a red-lettered sticker on the inside urged. He complied.

For another thing, the place was ill-attended; at 11:40 in the morning, breakfast trays still lay outside the doors of some of the rooms. As soon as he had taken off the damn neck-brace (only for border-crossing and *maybe* in Germany) he nipped outside and got himself a tray and a breadbasket and a *Do Not Disturb* sign. He hid the tray between the mattress and the box spring, the breadbasket in a paper laundry bag on the closet shelf; put the *Do Not Disturb* sign in the writing drawer with the one already there. He checked the floor plan on the door; there were three stairways, one right around a corner from arrow-marked 404. He went out again and found it; opened the door, went onto the landing, looked up and down the gray-painted flights.

Room service was abominable. By the time his lunch appeared he had excreted and cleaned the tube of diamonds, washed up, powdered his chafed neck, unpacked as much as he meant to unpack, tried the television, and made a list of everything he had to buy and do. But the waiter who brought the lunch—a full star right here—was a white man almost as old as he, sixty or so, wearing a plain white linen mess jacket such as might be bought, surely, in any working-class clothing store. He added it to the list; easier than filching one.

The food, sole *à la bonne femme*—forget it.

He left the hotel at a little after one, by a side door. Dark glasses, no mustache, hat, wig, overcoat with turned-up collar. Gun in shoulder holster. He would leave nothing of value in that vulnerable room, and besides, it was wise to go armed in the States; not only for himself, for anyone.

Washington was cleaner than he had expected and quite attractive, but the wide streets were wet with day-old snow. The first thing he did was stop in a shoestore and buy a pair of rubbers. He had flown from summer into winter and had always been susceptible to colds; vitamins were on his list too.

He walked until he came to a bookstore, and went in and browsed, exchanging the dark glasses for his regular ones. He found a paperback copy of Liebermann's book; studied the stamp-size photo on the back of it. There would be no mistaking that Jewish beak. He flipped through the section of photos at the book's center and found his own; Liebermann, on the other hand, would be hard put to recognize *him*. It was the Buenos Aires photo of '59, obviously the best Liebermann had been able to come up with; neither with the brown wig and mustache nor his own cropped gray hair and newly shaven upper lip did he look much at all, alas, like this handsome sixteen-years-younger himself. And Liebermann, of course, wouldn't even be watching for him.

He put the book back in its place in the rack and found a section of travel books. He selected road atlases of the States and Canada; paid for them with a twenty-dollar bill and accepted his change, bills and coins, with a casual glance and a nod.

In dark glasses again, he walked into less spacious streets with brighter, more gaudy shop windows. He couldn't find what he wanted, and finally asked a young black man—who would know better? He walked on, following the surprisingly well-spoken directions.

"What kind of knife?" a black man behind a counter asked him.

"For hunting," he said.

He chose the best. German-made, good in the hand, really beautiful. And so sharp it whisked ribbons from loosely held paper. Two more twenties and a ten.

A drugstore was next door. He bought his vitamins.

And in the next block, *Uniforms & Work Clothes.*

"I'd say you're about a thirty-six?"

"Yes."

"Would you like to try it on?"

"No." Because of the gun.

He bought a pair of white cotton gloves too.

A food store was impossible to find. Nobody knew; they didn't eat, apparently.

He found one finally, a glary supermarket full of blacks. He bought three apples, two oranges, two bananas, and for his own consumption, a lovely-looking bunch of green seedless grapes.

He took a taxi back to the Benjamin Franklin—the side entrance, please—and at 3:22 was back in that dismal one-tenth-of-a-star room.

He rested awhile, eating grapes and looking at the atlases in the easy (ha!) chair, consulting now and again the typed sheets of names and addresses, dates. He could get Wheelock—assuming he was still in New Providence, Pennsylvania—almost on schedule; but from then on, it would have to be catch-as-catch-can. He would try to keep within six months of the optimum dates. Davis in Kankakee, then up into Canada for Stroheim and Morgan. Then Sweden. Would he have to renew the visa?

After he had rested, he rehearsed. Took off the wig and put on the white jacket and gloves; practiced carrying the basket of fruit on the tray; said, "Compliments of the management, sir"—again and again till he got the *th*-sound right.

He stood with his back to his bolted door, hung the *Do Not Disturb* sign on air and let it fall, knocked at air. "Compliments of the management, sir." He carried the tray across the room, set it on the dresser, drew the knife from the sheath in his belt; turned, keeping the knife behind him; walked, stopped, put out his left hand. "Sank you, sir." Grabbed with his left hand, stabbed with his right.

"Thank you, sir. *Thank* you. *Th, th, th.*" Grab with the left hand, stab with the right.

Do Jews tip?
He worked out some alternative movements.

The sunlit plateau of clouds ended abruptly; blue-black ocean
lay below, wrinkled and white-flecked, immobile. Liebermann
gazed down at it, his chin in his hand.

Ei.

He had lain awake all night, sat awake all day, thinking of a full-
grown Hitler hurling his demonic speeches at mobs too discon-
tented to care about history. Two or *three* Hitlers even, maneu-
vering to power in different places, recognized by their followers
and themselves as the first human beings bred by what in 1990 or
so would be a widely known, maybe widely practiced, procedure.
More alike than brothers, the same man multiplied, wouldn't they
join forces and wage again (with 1990 weapons!) their first one's
racial war? Certainly that was Mengele's hope; Barry had said so:
"It's supposed to lead to the triumph of the Aryan race, for God's
sake!" Words to that effect.

A lovely package to bring to an F.B.I. that's had an almost
hundred-percent turnover since Hoover died in '72. He could hear
the puzzled question: "Yakov *who?*"

It had been easy enough last night to tell Klaus he would manage,
would break down doors; and in truth he wasn't wholly without
contacts. There were senators he had met who were still in office;
one of them, surely, would unlock the right doors for him. But now,
having weighed the horror, he was afraid that even with unlocked
doors too much time might be lost. Guthrie's and Curry's deaths
would have to be investigated, their widows questioned, the
Wheelocks questioned . . . Now it was the utmost necessity to capture Wheelock's would-be killer and find through him the five
others. The rest of the ninety-four men had to stay alive; the knobs
of the safes, to follow Lena's comparison (a good one to remember
and use in the days ahead), must not be allowed to be turned to
what was maybe the last and most crucial number in the combina-
tion.

And making matters even worse, the 22nd was only an approxi-
mation of Wheelock's death date. What if the real date was earlier?
What if—laughable, the small thing future history might hinge on—
Frieda Maloney had been wrong about the puppy being ten weeks
old? What if it had been nine weeks old, or eight weeks old, when

the Wheelocks got their baby? The killer might kill and be gone a few days from now.

He looked at his watch: 10:28. Which was wrong; he hadn't set it back yet. He did it now—spun the hands and gave himself six extra hours, at least as far as watches were concerned: 4:28. New York in half an hour, customs, and the short hop to Washington. He'd get some sleep tonight, he hoped—he was a little punchy already—and in the morning he would call the senators' offices; call Shettles too, some others on Nürnberger's list.

If only he could arrange *now* to have Wheelock's killer watched for, without any waiting, explaining, checking, questioning. He should have come sooner; would have, of course, if he had known the full enormity . . .

Ei.

What he needed, really, was a Jewish F.B.I. Or a U.S. branch of Israel's Mossad. Someplace where he could go in tomorrow and say, "A Nazi is coming to kill a man named Wheelock in New Providence, Pennsylvania. Guard him; capture the Nazi. Don't ask me questions, I'll explain later. I'm Yakov Liebermann—would I steer you wrong?" And they would go ahead and do it.

Dream! If only such an organization existed!

People in the plane fastened their seat belts and made comments to one another; the sign had lit up.

Liebermann sat frowning at the window.

■

After a refreshing hour's nap, Mengele washed and shaved, put on the wig and mustache, and got into his dark suit. He laid everything out on the bed—white jacket, gloves, knife in sheath, tray with basket of fruit and *Do Not Disturb* sign—so that as soon as he saw Liebermann check in and learned his room number, he could zip up and assume his waiter role with no delay.

When he left the room he tried the knob and hung the other *Do Not Disturb* sign on it.

At 6:45 he was seated in the lobby, leafing through a copy of *Time* and keeping an eye on the revolving door. The occasional suitcase-bearing new arrivals who went to the registration desk across the lobby were almost all unaccompanied men, a veritable textbook of inferior racial types; not only Blacks and Semites, but a pair of Orientals as well. One fine-looking young Aryan checked in, but a few minutes later, as if to compensate for an error, a black dwarf appeared, striding along beside a suitcase in a wheeled metal frame.

At twenty past seven Liebermann came in—tall, round-shouldered, dark-mustached, in a tan cap and belted tan overcoat. Or *was* this Liebermann? A Jew, yes, but too young-looking and with not quite the Liebermann beak.

He got up and strolled across the lobby, took a *This Week in Washington* from a stack of them on the cracked marble counter.

"You're staying through Friday night?" the clerk asked the possible Liebermann at his back.

"Yes."

A bell pinged. "Would you take Mr. Morris to seven-seventeen?"

"Yes, sir."

He strolled back cross the lobby. A Lebanese or some such had taken his seat—fat and greasy-looking, rings on every finger.

He found another seat.

The beak of all beaks came in, but it was attached to the face of a young man holding the elbow of a gray-haired woman.

At eight o'clock he stepped into a phone booth and called the hotel. He asked—taking care not to let his lips touch the mouthpiece, laden with God knew what germs—if Mr. Yakov Liebermann was expected.

"Just a moment." A click, and ringing. The clerk across the lobby picked up a phone and said in Mengele's ear, "Front desk."

"Have you a room reserved for Mr. Yakov Liebermann?"

"For this evening?"

"Yes."

The clerk looked down as if reading. "Yes, we do. Is this Mr. Liebermann speaking?"

"No."

"Would you like to leave a message for him?"

"No, thank you. I shall call later."

He could keep watch just as well from inside the booth, so he put another ten-cent coin into the phone and asked the operator how he could get the number of someone in New Providence, Pennsylvania. She gave him a long number to call; he wrote it down on *Time*'s red border, took the coin from the receptacle at the bottom of the phone, put it in at the top again, dialed.

There was a Henry Wheelock in New Providence. He wrote the number down below the other one. The woman gave him the address too, Old Buck Road, no house number.

A Latin with a suitcase and a leashed poodle went to the registration desk.

He thought for a moment, then called the operator and got instructions. He examined his array of coins on the booth's small shelf, picked out the right ones.

It was only when the phone at the other end gave its first ring that he realized that if this was the Henry Wheelock he wanted, the boy himself might answer. In another instant he could actually be speaking with his Führer reborn! A dizzying joy swept his breath away, tipped him against the side of the booth as the phone rang again. Oh please, dear Boy, come and answer your telephone!

"Hello." A woman.

He drew in breath, sighed it out.

"Hello?"

"Hello." He straightened up. "Is Mr. Henry Wheelock there?"

"He's here, but he's out in back."

"Is this Mrs. Wheelock?"

"It is, yes."

"My name is Franklin, madam. I believe you have a son approaching the age of fourteen?"

"We do . . ."

Praise God. "I conduct tours for boys of that age. Would you be interested in sending him to Europe this summer?"

A laugh. "Oh no, I don't think so."

"May I send you a brochure?"

"You may, but it's not going to do you much good."

"Old Buck Road is the address?"

"Really, he's staying right here this summer."

"Good night, then. I'm sorry to have troubled you."

He took a pamphlet from the unattended car-rental booth and sat studying it, glancing up whenever the revolving door whisked.

Tomorrow he would rent a car and drive to New Providence. When Wheelock was taken care of he would drive on up to New York, turn in the car, sell a diamond, and fly to Chicago. If Robert K. Davis was still in Kankakee.

But where the hell was *Liebermann*?

At nine o'clock he went into the coffee shop and took a counter seat from which he could see the revolving door through the glass shop-door. He ate scrambled eggs and toast, drank the world's worst coffee.

He got a dollar's worth of change when he left, went into the phone booth again, and called the hotel. Maybe Liebermann had come in through the side entrance.

He hadn't. They were still expecting him.

He called both airports, hoping—it was possible, wasn't it?—that there had been a crash.

No such luck. And all incoming flights were on schedule.

The son of a bitch must have stayed on in Mannheim. But for how long? It was too late to call Vienna and find out from that Fräulein Zimmer. Too early, rather; not quite four in the morning there.

He began to worry about someone remembering him sitting in the lobby all evening watching the door.

Where are you, you goddamned Jew-bastard? Come let me kill you!

On Wednesday afternoon, at a few minutes after two o'clock, Liebermann got out of a traffic-locked taxi in the middle of Manhattan's garment center and took to the sidewalk despite the freezing rain. His umbrella, borrowed from the people he had stayed the night with, Marvin and Rita Farb, was another bold color in each of its panels (it's an umbrella, he told himself; be glad you've got it).

He splatted briskly down the west side of Broadway, weaving past other umbrellas (black) and men pushing plastic-covered racks of dresses. He looked at the numbers of the office buildings he passed; walked faster.

He walked seven or eight blocks, crossed a street and looked at the building there—an Off-Track Betting office, a lamp showroom, twenty or so stories of grimy stonework and narrow windows—and went to its arched entrance and backed open a heavy glass swingdoor, pulling the multicolored umbrella closed.

He crossed the black-matted lobby—small, a magazine-and-candy-stand taking up most of it—and joined the half-dozen people waiting for the elevators; stamped his sodden shoes, tapped the umbrella's tip against the wet rubber matting, making rain on it.

On the twelfth floor—dingy, paint peeling—he followed the numbers on pebbled doorpanes: *1202, Aaron Goldman, Artificial Flowers; 1203, C. & M. Roth, Imported Glassware; 1204, Youthcraft Dolls, B. Rosenzweig.* Room 1205 had *YJD* on the pane, stick-on metallic letters, the *D* a little higher than the *Y* and the *J.* He knuckled the glass.

A flesh-and-white blur came to the pane. "Yes?" A young woman's voice.

"It's Yakov Liebermann."

The mail slot below the pane clinked and gave light. "Would you put your I.D. through?"

He got out his passport and put it into the slot; it was taken from his fingers.

He waited. The door had two locks, one that looked like the original, and beneath it, a bright-brassed new-looking one.

A bolt clicked and the door opened.

He went in. A fat girl of sixteen or so with pulled-back red hair smiled at him and said, "Shalom," offering him his passport.

He took it and said, "Shalom."

"We have to be careful," the girl apologized. She closed the door and turned its bolt. She wore a white sweatshirt and blue swollen-tight jeans; her hair hung down her back, a glistening orange-red horsetail.

They were in a tiny cluttered anteroom: a desk, a mimeograph machine on a table with stacks of white and pink paper; raw wood shelves piled with handbills and newspaper reprints; in the wall opposite, an almost-closed door with a *Young Jewish Defenders* poster taped to it, a hand brandishing a dagger in front of a blue Jewish star.

The girl reached for the umbrella; Liebermann gave it to hér and she put it in a metal wastebasket with two others, black, wet.

Liebermann, taking his hat and coat off, said, "Are you the young lady who was on the phone?"

She nodded.

"You handled things very efficiently. Is the Rabbi here?"

"He just came in." She took the hat and coat from Liebermann.

"Thank you. How's his son?"

"They don't know yet. His condition is stable."

"Mm." Liebermann shook his head sympathetically.

The girl found places for the hat and coat on a full coat-tree. Liebermann, straightening his jacket, smoothing his hair, glanced at piles of handbills on a shelf beside him: *Tho Now Jew; KISSInger OF DEATH: No Compromise—Ever!*

The girl excused herself past Liebermann and knocked at the postered door; opened it farther and looked in. "Reb? Mr. Liebermann's here."

She pushed the door all the way open, and smiling at Liebermann, stepped aside.

A stocky blond-bearded man glared grimly at Liebermann as he came into an overheated office of men and desks and clutter; and coming out from behind the corner desk, Rabbi Moshe Gorin, handsome, dark-haired, compact, smiling, blue-jawed; in a tweed jacket and an open-necked yellow shirt. He took Liebermann's hand, gripped it in both his own, and looked at him with magnetic brown eyes weighted with shadows. "I've wanted to meet you ever since I was a kid," he said in a soft but intense voice. "You're one of the few men in this world I really admire, not only because of what you've done, but because you did it without any help from the establishment. The *Jewish* establishment, I'm talking about."

Liebermann, embarrassed but pleased, said, "Thank you. I wanted to meet you too, Rabbi. I appreciate your coming in this way."

Gorin introduced the other men. The blond-bearded one, hawk-nosed, with a crushing handshake, was his second-in-command, Phil Greenspan. A tall balding one with glasses was Elliot Bachrach. Another, big, a black beard: Paul Stern. The youngest—twenty-five or so—a thick black mustache, green eyes, another crushing handshake: Jay Rabinowitz. All were in shirtsleeves, and like Gorin, skullcapped.

They brought chairs from the other desks and put them around the end of Gorin's desk; seated themselves. The tall one with glasses, Bachrach, sat against a windowsill behind Gorin, his arms folded, the buff shade all the way down behind him. Liebermann, across from Gorin, looked at the sober strong-looking men and the shabby cluttered office with its wall maps of the city and the world, a blackboard easel, stacks of books and papers, cartons. "Don't look at this place." Gorin waved it away.

"It's not so different from *my* office," Liebermann said, smiling. "A little bigger, maybe."

"I'm sorry for you."

"How is your son doing?"

"I think he'll be all right," Gorin said. "His condition is stable."

"I appreciate your coming in."

Gorin shrugged. "His mother is with him. I did my praying." He smiled.

Liebermann tried to get comfortable in the armless chair. "Whenever I speak," he said, "in public, I mean—they ask me what I think of you. I always say 'I never met him personally, so I have no opinion.'" He smiled at Gorin. "Now I'll have to make a new answer."

"A favorable one, I hope," Gorin said. The phone on the desk rang. "Nobody's here, Sandy!" Gorin shouted toward the door. "Unless it's my wife!" To Liebermann he said, "You're not expecting any calls, are you?"

Liebermann shook his head. "Nobody knows I'm here. I'm supposed to be in Washington." He cleared his throat, sat with his hands on his knees. "I was on my way there yesterday afternoon," he said. "To go to the F.B.I. about some killings I'm investigating. Here and in Europe. By former SS men."

"Recent killings?" Gorin looked concerned.

"Still going on," Liebermann said. "Arranged for by the *Kameradenwerk* in South America and Dr. Mengele."

Gorin said, "*That* son of a bitch . . ." The other men stirred. The blond-bearded one, Greenspan, said to Liebermann, "We have a new chapter in Rio de Janeiro. As soon as it's big enough we're going to set up a commando team and get him."

"I wish you luck," Liebermann said. "He's still alive all right, running this whole business. He killed a young fellow there, a Jewish boy from Evanston, Illinoise, in September. The boy was on the phone to me, telling me about this, when it happened. My problem now is, it's going to take time for me to convince the F.B.I. I know what I'm talking about."

"Why did you wait so long?" Gorin asked. "If you knew in September . . ."

"I *didn't* know," Liebermann said. "It was all . . . ifs and maybes, uncertainty. I only now have the whole thing put together." He shook his head and sighed. "So it dawned on me on the plane," he said to Gorin, "that maybe you, the Y.J.D."—he looked at all of them—"could help out in this thing while I go on to Washington."

"Whatever we can do," Gorin said, "just ask, you've got it." The others agreed.

"Thank you," Liebermann said, "that's what I was hoping. It's a job of guarding someone, a man in Pennsylvania. In a town there, New Providence, a dot on the map near the city Lancaster."

"Pennsylvania—Dutch country," the man with the black beard said. "I know it."

"This man is the next one to be killed in this country," Liebermann said. "On the twenty-second of this month, but maybe sooner. Maybe only a few days from now. So he has to be guarded. But the man who comes to kill him mustn't be scared away or killed himself; he has to be captured, so he can be questioned." He looked at Gorin. "Do you have people who could do a job like that? Guard someone, capture someone?"

Gorin nodded. Greenspan said, "You're looking at them," and to Gorin, "Let Jay take over the demonstration. I'll manage this."

Gorin smiled, tilted his head toward Greenspan and said to Liebermann, "This one's main regret is he missed World War Two. He runs our combat classes."

"It will only be for a week or so, I hope," Liebermann said. "Just till the F.B.I. comes in."

"What do you want *them* for?" the young one with the mustache asked, and Greenspan said to Liebermann, "*We'll* get him for you, and get more information out of him, quicker, than they will. I guarantee it." The phone rang.

Liebermann shook his head. "I have to use them," he said, "because from them it has to go to Interpol. Other countries are involved. There are five other men besides this one."

Gorin was looking toward the door; he looked at Liebermann. "How many killings have there been?" he asked.

"Eight that I know of."

Gorin looked pained. Someone whistled.

"*Seven* that I know of," Liebermann corrected himself. "One very probable. Maybe others."

"Jews?" Gorin asked.

Liebermann shook his head. "Goyim."

"Why?" Bachrach at the window asked. "What's it for?"

"Yes," Gorin said. "Who are they? Why does Mengele *want* them killed?"

Liebermann drew a breath, blew it out. He leaned forward. "If I tell you it's very, very important," he said, "more important in the long run than Russian anti-Semitism and the pressure on Israel— would that be enough for now? I promise you I'm not exaggerating."

In silence, Gorin frowned at the desk before him. He looked up at Liebermann, shook his head, and smiled apologetically. "No," he said. "You're asking Moshe Gorin to lend you three or four of his best men, maybe more. Men, not boys. At a time when we're spread thin already and when the government's breathing down my neck because I'm lousing up their precious détente. No, Yakov"—he shook his head—"I'll give you all the help I can, but what kind of a leader would I be if I committed my men blindly, even to Yakov Liebermann?"

Liebermann nodded. "I figured you'd at least want to know," he said. "But don't ask me for proof, Rabbi. Just listen and trust me. Or else I wasted my time." He looked at all of them, looked at Gorin, cleared his throat. "By any chance," he said, "did you ever study a little biology?"

"God!" the one with the mustache said.

Bachrach said, "The English word for it is 'cloning.' There was an article about it in the *Times* a few years ago."

Gorin smiled faintly, winding a loose thread around a cuff-button. "This morning," he said, "by my son's bedside, I said 'What next, oh Lord?'" He smiled at Liebermann, gestured ruefully at him. "Ninety-four Hitlers."

"Ninety-four boys with Hitler's genes," Liebermann said.

"To me," Gorin said, "that's ninety-four Hitlers."

Greenspan said to Liebermann, "Are you sure this man Wheelock hasn't been killed *already?*"

"I am."

"And that he hasn't moved away?"—the black-bearded one.

"I got his phone number," Liebermann said. "I didn't want to talk to him myself yet, until I knew you would do what I wanted you to"—he looked at Gorin—"but I had the woman from the couple I'm staying with call him this morning. She said she wanted to buy a dog and heard he raised them. It's him. She got directions how to get there."

Gorin said to Greenspan, "We're going to have to work this out of Philadelphia." And to Liebermann: "The one thing we *won't* do is take guns across a state border. The F.B.I. would love to get *us* along *with* the Nazi."

Liebermann said, "Should I call Wheelock now?"

Gorin nodded. Greenspan said, "I'm going to want to put someone right in his house with him." The young man with the mustache moved the phone over near Liebermann.

Liebermann put his glasses on and got an envelope out of his jacket pocket. Bachrach at the window said, "Hi, Mr. Wheelock, your son is Hitler."

Liebermann said, "I'm not going to mention the boy at all. It might make him hang up on me, because of the way the adoption was. I just dial, yes?"

"If you have the area code."

Liebermann dialed the phone, reading the number from the envelope.

"School's probably out by now," Gorin said. "The boy is liable to answer."

"We're friends," Liebermann said drily. "I met him twice already." The phone at the other end rang.

Rang again. Liebermann looked at Gorin looking at him.

"Hay-lo," a man said in a deep-throated voice.

"Mr. Henry Wheelock?"

"Speaking."

"Mr. Wheelock, my name is Yakov Liebermann. I'm calling from New York. I run the War Crimes Information Center in Vienna—maybe you heard of us? We collect information on Nazi war criminals, help find them and help with the prosecution?"

"I've heard. That Eichmann."

"That's right, and others. Mr. Wheelock, I'm after someone now, someone who's in this country. I'm on my way to Washington to see the F.B.I. about it. This man killed two or three men here not so long ago, and he's planning to kill more."

"Are you looking for a guard dog?"

"No," Liebermann said. "The next one this man is planning to kill, Mr. Wheelock"—he looked at Gorin—"it's you."

"All right, who is this? Ted? That's a real good Choiman agzent, you shithead."

Liebermann said, "This isn't someone joking. I know you think a Nazi would have no reason to kill you—"

"Says who? I killed plenty of *them*; I bet they'd be damn happy to get even. If any were still around."

"One *is* around—"

"Come on now, who is this?"

"It's *Yakov Liebermann*, Mr. Wheelock." "Christmas!" Gorin said; the others spoke, groaned. Liebermann stuck a finger in his ear. "I *swear* to you," he said, "that a man is coming to New Providence to kill you, a former SS man, maybe in only a few days. I'm trying to save your life."

Silence.

Liebermann said, "I'm here in the office of Rabbi Moshe Gorin of the Young Jewish Defenders. Until I can get the F.B.I. to protect you, which could take a week or so, the Rabbi wants to send some of his men down. They could be there—" He looked questioningly at Gorin, who said, "Tomorrow morning." "Tomorrow morning," Liebermann said. "Will you cooperate with them until F.B.I. men get there?"

Silence.

"Mr. Wheelock?"

"Look, Mr. Liebermann, if this *is* Mr. Liebermann. All right, maybe it is. Let me tell you something. You happen to be speaking to one of the safest men in the U.S.A. Firstly, I'm a former correction officer at a state penitentiary, so I know a little about taking care of myself. And secondly, I've got a houseful of trained Dobermans; I say the word and they tear the throat out of anyone who looks cross-eyed at me."

"I'm glad to hear that," Liebermann said, "but can they stop a wall from falling on you? Or someone shooting at you from far away? That's what happened to two of the other men."

"What the *hell* is this *about?* No Nazi is after me. You've got the wrong Henry Wheelock."

"Is there another in New Providence who raises Dobermans? Sixty-five years old, a wife much younger, a son almost fourteen?"

Silence.

"You need protection," Liebermann said. "And the Nazi has to be captured, not killed by dogs."

"I'll believe it when the F.B.I. tells me. I'm not going to have any Jew kids with baseball bats around."

Liebermann was silent for a moment. "Mr. Wheelock," he said, "could I come see you on my way to Washington? I'll explain a little more." Gorin looked questioningly at him; he looked away.

"Come ahead if you want to; I'm always here."

"When is your wife *not* there?"

"She's away most of the day. She teaches."

"And the boy is in school too?"

"When he's not playing hooky to make movies. He's going to be the next Alfred Hitchcock, he thinks."

"I'll be there around noon tomorrow."

"Suit yourself. But just *you.* I see any 'Jewish Defenders' around, I let the dogs loose. You got a pencil? I'll give you directions."

"I have them," Liebermann said. "I'll see you tomorrow. And I hope tonight you stay home."

"I was planning to."

Liebermann hung up.

"I have to tell him it involves the adoption," he told Gorin, "and it's better if he can't hang up on me." He smiled. "I also have to convince him the Y.J.D. isn't 'Jew kids with baseball bats.'" To Greenspan he said, "You'll have to wait someplace there and then I'll call you."

"I have to go to Philadelphia first," Greenspan said. "To pick my men and get my equipment." To Gorin he said, "I want to take Paul along."

They worked things out. Greenspan and Paul Stern would go to Philadelphia in Stern's car as soon as they could get packed, and Liebermann would drive Greenspan's car to New Providence in the morning. When he had persuaded Wheelock to accept Y.J.D. protection, he would call Philadelphia and the team would drive out and meet him at Wheelock's home. Once things were settled there, he would drive on to Washington, keeping Greenspan's car till the F.B.I. relieved the team. "I should call my office," he said, stirring tea. "They think I'm there already."

Gorin gestured at the phone.

Liebermann shook his head. "No, not now, it's too late there. Early in the morning I'll call." He smiled. "I won't stick the Y.J.D."

Gorin shrugged. "I'm on the phone to Europe all the time," he said. "Our chapters there."

Liebermann nodded thoughtfully. "The contributors went from me to you."

"I suppose some did," Gorin said. "But the fact that we're sitting here together, working together, proves that they're still helping the same cause, doesn't it?"

"I guess so," Liebermann said. "Yes. Sure."

Later he said, "Wheelock's boy doesn't paint pictures. It's 1975; he makes movies." He smiled. "But he picked himself the right initials. He wants to be another Alfred Hitchcock. And the father, the civil servant, doesn't think it's such a good idea. Hitler and his father had big arguments about his wanting to be an artist."

■

Mengele had gone across the street early Wednesday morning and taken a room at another hotel, the Kenilworth, registering as Mr. Kurt Koehler of 18 Sheridan Road, Evanston, Illinois. He had been asked, fairly enough, to pay in advance, since all he carried was a slim leather portfolio (papers, knife, clips for the Browning, diamonds) and a small paper bag (grapes).

He couldn't call Liebermann's office from the room of Sr. Ramón Aschheim y Negrín, for after Liebermann's death the calls from Koehler might well be checked into, nor did he especially care to gather seven dollars' worth of coins and spend an hour blackening his thumb as he fed them into a booth phone. And as Kurt Koehler he could receive a return call, should one be necessary.

In his second room (*no* tenths of a star) he had reached Fräulein Zimmer and explained to her that he had flown from New York to Washington, sending Barry's body on its way unescorted, because of the overriding importance of getting the poor boy's notes—even more significant than he had originally realized—into Herr Liebermann's hands as quickly as possible. But where, pray tell, *was* Herr Liebermann?

Not at the Benjamin Franklin? Fräulein Zimmer had been surprised but not alarmed. She would call Mannheim and see what she could find out. Perhaps Herr Koehler might try some other hotels, though why Herr Liebermann should have gone elsewhere she couldn't imagine. No doubt he would call in soon; he usually did when he changed his plans. (*Usually!*) Yes, she would call Herr Koehler as soon as she had information. At the Kenilworth, kind Fräulein; the Benjamin Franklin had been full when he arrived. But holding a room for Herr Liebermann, of course.

By the time she had called back he had called more than thirty hotels, and the Benjamin Franklin six times.

Liebermann had left Frankfurt on his intended flight Tuesday morning; so he was either in Washington or had stopped off in New York.

"Where does he stay there?"

"Sometimes the Hotel Edison but usually with friends, contributors. He has a lot of them there. It's a big Jewish city, you know."

"I know."

"Don't worry, Herr Koehler; I'm sure I'll hear soon and I'll tell him you're waiting. I'm staying here late, just in case."

He called the Edison in New York, more hotels in Washington, the Benjamin Franklin every half-hour; dashed back there through freezing rain to make sure his clothes and suitcase were still in his *Do Not Disturb*-signed room.

He slept Wednesday night at the Kenilworth. *Tried* to sleep. Grew depressed. Thought of the gun on the bedside table . . . Did he *really* expect to get Liebermann and the other men still to be killed (seventy-seven of them!) before being killed himself? Or even worse, captured and made to endure the kind of hideous mock-trial that had befallen poor Stangl and Eichmann? Why not end all the struggling, planning, worrying?

He found, at one in the morning on American television—and surely this was God's doing, a sign sent to raise him from despair— a glorious film of the Führer and General von Blomberg watching a

Luftwaffe flyover; silenced the loathsome English narration and watched the grainy old soundless images, so heart-wrenchingly bittersweet, so reinspiring . . .

Slept.

At a few minutes after eight on Thursday morning, just as he was about to place another call to Vienna, the phone rang. "Hello?"

"Kurt Koehler?" A woman, American, not Fräulein Zimmer.

"Yes . . ."

"Hello, this is Rita Farb! I'm a friend of Yakov Liebermann's. He's been staying with us. I'm in New York. He asked me to call you. He called his office in Vienna a little while ago and found out you were there in Washington waiting for him. He'll be there tonight, around six. He'd like you to have dinner with him. He'll call you as soon as he gets in."

Relieved, joyful, Mengele said, "That's fine!"

"And could you do him a favor, please? Would you call the Hotel Benjamin Franklin and tell them he'll definitely be coming?"

"Yes, I'll be glad to! Do you know what flight he's arriving on?"

"He's driving, not flying. He just left. That's why *I'm* calling. He was a little rushed."

Mengele frowned. "Won't he be here earlier than six?" he asked. "If he left already?"

"No, he has to make a detour into Pennsylvania. He might even be a little later than six, but he'll definitely be there and he'll call you first thing."

Mengele was silent; then said, "Is he going to speak to Henry Wheelock? In New Providence?"

"Yes, I'm the one who got the directions for him. It certainly is interesting having Yakov in your house! I gather something really big is going on."

"Yes," Mengele said. "Thank you for calling. Oh, do you know what time Yakov and Henry are getting together?"

"Noon."

"Thank you. Good-by." He pushed the phone's button down, held it, looked at his watch, closed his eyes and pressed the side of his fist against his forehead; opened his eyes, released the button, tapped at it. Got the cashier and told her to get his food-and-phone bill ready.

Put the mustache on, the wig. The gun. Jacket, coat, hat; grabbed the portfolio.

He ran across the street and into the Benjamin Franklin; paused at the cashier's window to give instructions and hurried to the car-rental booth. A pretty young woman in a yellow-and-black uniform smiled radiantly at him.

And only a little less radiantly when she learned he was Paraguayan and had no credit card. The estimated cost of the rental would have to be paid in cash in advance; around sixty dollars, she thought; she would work it out more accurately. He threw bills down, left his license, told her to have the car ready within ten minutes, no later; hurried to the elevators.

By nine o'clock he was on the highway to Baltimore, in a white Ford Pinto under a bright blue sky. Gun under his arm, knife in his coat pocket, God at his side.

Driving at the fifty-five-mile-per-hour speed limit, he would reach New Providence almost an hour before Liebermann.

Other cars slowly passed him. Americans! The limit is fifty-five, they go sixty. He shook his head and allowed himself to drive faster. When in Rome . . .

He reached New Providence—a clutch of drab houses, a shop, a one-story brick post office—at ten of eleven, but then he had to find Old Buck Road without asking directions of someone who might later describe him and/or his car to the police. The road map he had picked up at a gas station in Maryland, more detailed than the atlas map, showed a town named Buck to the southwest of New Providence; he explored in that direction, following a bumpy two-lane road that curved through winter-bare farmland; slowed at each cross road and peered at all-but-illegible signs and markers. Occasional cars and trucks passed him.

He found Old Buck Road branching right and left; chose the right-hand branch and headed back toward New Providence, watching for mailboxes. Passed *Gruber,* and *C. Johnson.* Leafless trees locked branches over the narrow road. A horse-drawn black buggy came toward him. He had seen similar ones on billboards on the main road; Amish people were apparently a local tourist attraction. A bearded black-hatted man and a black-bonneted woman sat within the black-canopied buggy, looking straight ahead.

The mailboxes, near drives leading into trees, were few and far apart. Which was good; he could use the gun.

H. Wheelock. The red flag-signal was down at the side of the box. *GUARD DOGS,* a board below warned (or advertised?) in crude black-painted letters.

Which was bad. Though not wholly bad, since it gave him a

more acceptable reason for being there than the summer-tour-for-the-boy business which he had intended to repeat.

He turned right, guiding the car's wheels into the deep ruts of a humpbacked dirt drive that led gradually uphill through trees. The car's bottom scraped against the hump: Herr Hertz's problem. But his own, too, should the car be disabled. He drove slowly. Looked at his watch: 11:18.

Yes, he vaguely remembered one of the American couples listing dog-breeding among their interests. No doubt it had been the Wheelocks; and the prison guard, retired by now certainly, had perhaps made a full-time occupation of his former pastime. "Good morning!" Mengele said aloud. "The sign down below says 'guard dogs,' and a guard dog is exactly what I'm looking for." He pressed the full mustache down tight, patted the wig at side and back, tilted the mirror and glanced at himself; put the mirror right and followed the rutted drive slowly; reached under coat and jacket, unsnapped the holster's side so the gun could be whipped free.

Dogs' barking, a tumult of it, challenged him from a sunlit clearing where a two-story house—white shutters, brown shingles—stood at an angle to him; and at its back a dozen dogs flinging themselves at high mesh fence, barking, yipping. A white-haired man stood behind them, looking toward him.

He drove on to the foot of the house's stone-paved walk and stopped the car there; shifted to P and turned the key. One dog yipped now, a puppy by the sound of it. At the far side of the house a red pickup truck stood in a two-car garage, the other half empty.

He unlocked the car door, opened it, got out; stretched and rubbed his back while the car whined at him to take the key. The gun stirred under his arm. He slammed the door and stood looking at the white-trimmed porch at the head of the walk. This is where one of them lives! Perhaps a photo of the boy would be around somewhere. How wonderful to see that nearly-fourteen-year-old face! God in heaven, what if he's not in school today? Upsetting but thrilling thought!

The white-haired man came loping around the side of the house, a dog at his side, a gleaming black hound. The man wore a bulky brown jacket, black gloves, brown trousers; he was tall and broad, his ruddy face sullen, unfriendly.

Mengele smiled. "Good morning!" he called. "The—"

"You Liebermann?" the man asked in a deep-throated voice, loping nearer.

Mengele smiled more widely. "*Ja,* yes!" he said. "Yes! Mr. Wheelock?"

The man stopped near Mengele and nodded his head of wavy white hair. The dog, a handsome blue-black Doberman, snarled at Mengele, showing sharp white teeth. Its chain collar was hooked by a black leather finger. Rips and tears shredded the sleeves of the coarse brown jacket, fibers of white quilting sticking out.

"I'm a little early," Mengele apologized.

Wheelock looked beyond him, toward the car, and looked directly at him with squinting blue eyes under bushy white brows. Wrinkles seamed his white-stubbled cheeks. "Come on in," he said, tilting his white-haired head toward the house. "I don't mind admitting you've got me goddamn curious." He turned and led the way up the walk, finger-holding the blue-black Doberman's chain.

"That's a beautiful dog," Mengele said, following.

Wheelock went up onto the porch. The white door had a dog's-head knocker.

"Is your son at home?" Mengele asked.

"Nobody is," Wheelock said, opening the door. "Excepting them." Dobermans—two, three of them—came licking his glove, growling at Mengele. "Easy, boys," Wheelock said. "It's a friend." He gestured the dogs back—they retreated obediently—and he went in with the other dog, beckoning to Mengele. "Close the door."

Mengele came in and closed the door; stood looking at Wheelock crouching among crowding black Dobermans, stroking their heads and clapping their firm flanks while they tongued and nuzzled him. Mengele said, "How beautiful."

"These young fellows," Wheelock said happily, "are Harpo and Zeppo—my son named them; only litter I ever let him—and this old boy is Samson—easy, Sam—and this one is Major. This is Mr. Liebermann, fellows. A friend." He stood up and smiled at Mengele, pulling at glove fingertips. "You can see now why I don't wet my pants when you say someone's out to get me."

Mengele nodded. "Yes," he said. He looked down at two Dobermans sniffing his thighs. "Wonderful protection," he said, "dogs like these."

"Tear the throat out of anyone who looks cross-eyed at me." Wheelock unzipped his jacket; red shirt was inside it. "Take your coat off," he said. "Hang it there."

A high coat-stand with large black hooks stood at Mengele's right; its oval mirror showed a chair and the end of a dining table in the room opposite. Mengele put his hat on a hook, unbuttoned his coat; smiled down at the Dobermans, smiled at Wheelock taking his jacket off. Beyond Wheelock a narrow stairway rose steeply.

"So you're the one that caught that Eichmann." Wheelock hung up his shredded-sleeved jacket.

"The Israelis caught him," Mengele said, taking his coat off. "But I helped them, of course. I found where he was hiding down there in Argentina."

"Get a reward?"

"No." Mengele hung his coat up. "I do these things for the satisfaction," he said. "I hate all Nazis. They should be hunted down and destroyed like vermin."

Wheelock said, "It's the boogies not the Nazis we have to worry about now. Come on in here."

Mengele, adjusting his jacket, followed Wheelock into a room on the right. Two of the Dobermans escorted him, nosing at his legs; the other two went with Wheelock. The room was a pleasant sitting room, with white-curtained windows, a stone fireplace, and to the left, a wall of all-colored prize ribbons, gilded trophies, black-framed photos. "Oh, this is very impressive," Mengele said, and went and looked. The photos were all of Dobermans, none of the boy.

"Now why is a Nazi coming for me?"

Mengele turned. Wheelock was sitting on a Victorian settee between the two front windows, pinching tobacco out of a cut-glass jar on a low table before him, packing it into a chunky black pipe. A Doberman stood with his front paws on the table, watching.

Another Doberman, the largest one, lay on a round hooked rug between Wheelock and Mengele, looking up at Mengele placidly but with interest.

The other two Dobermans nosed Mengele's legs, his fingertips.

Wheelock looked over at Mengele and said, "Well?"

Smiling, Mengele said, "You know, it's very hard for me to talk with . . ." He gestured at the Dobermans beside him.

"Don't worry," Wheelock said, working at his pipe. "They won't bother *you* unless you bother *me*. Just sit down and talk. They'll get used to you."

Mengele sat down on a wheezing leather sofa. One of the Dobermans jumped up beside him and turned around and around, getting ready to lie down. The Doberman on the rug got up and came and pushed his sleek black head between Mengele's knees, sniffing toward his crotch.

"Samson," Wheelock warned, sucking match-flame into his pipe bowl.

The Doberman withdrew his head and sat on the floor looking at Mengele. Another Doberman, sitting by Mengele's feet, scratched with a hind leg at his chain collar. The Doberman beside Mengele on the sofa lay watching the Doberman sitting before Mengele.

Mengele cleared his throat and said, "The Nazi who's coming is Dr. Mengele himself. He'll probably be here—"

"A doctor?" Wheelock, holding his pipe, shook out the match.

"Yes," Mengele said. "Dr. Mengele. Mr. Wheelock, I'm sure these dogs are perfectly trained—I can tell as much from all these marvelous prizes"—he pointed a finger at the wall behind him—"but the fact is, when I was eight years old I was attacked by a dog; not a Doberman, a German shepherd." He touched his left thigh. "This entire thigh," he said, "is still today a mass of scars. And there are mental scars too. I'm very uncomfortable when a dog is in the room with me, and to have *four* of them present—well, this is a nightmare for me!"

Wheelock put his pipe down. "You should've said so right off the bat," he said, and stood up and snapped his fingers. Dobermans jumped, sprang, jostled to his side. "Come on, boys," he said, leading the pack across the room toward a doorway by the sofa. "We've got another Wally Montague on our hands. In you go." He pointed the Dobermans through the doorway, toed something away from the bottom of the door and closed it, tried the knob.

"They can't come in another way?" Mengele asked.

"Nope." Wheelock walked back across the room.

Mengele breathed a sigh and said, "Thank you. I feel much better now." He sat forward on the sofa and unbuttoned his jacket.

"Tell your story quickly," Wheelock said, sitting on the settee, picking up his pipe. "I don't like to keep them cooped up in there too long."

"I'll come directly to the point," Mengele said, "but first"—he raised a finger—"I should like to lend you a gun, so you can defend yourself at moments like this when the dogs are not with you."

"Got a gun," Wheelock said, sitting back with the pipe between his teeth, his arms along the settee's frame, his legs crossed. "A Luger." He took the pipe from his mouth, blew smoke. "And two shotguns and a rifle."

"This is a Browning," Mengele said, taking the gun from the holster. "Similar to the Luger except that the clip holds thirteen cartridges." He thumbed the safety catch down, and holding the gun in firing position, turned it toward Wheelock. "Raise the hands," he said. "Put the pipe down first, slowly."

Wheelock frowned at him, white eyebrows bristling.

"Now," Mengele said. "I don't want to hurt you. Why should I? You're a complete stranger to me. Liebermann is the one I'm interested in. 'The one in whom I'm interested,' I should say."

Wheelock uncrossed his legs and leaned forward slowly, glaring at Mengele, his face flushed. He put his pipe down and raised his open hands above his head.

"On the head," Mengele suggested. "You have beautiful hair; I envy you. This is a wig, unfortunately." He got up from the sofa, wagged the gun's barrel upward.

Wheelock got up, his hands folded across the top of his head. "I don't care doodily-shit about Jews and Nazis," he said.

"Good," Mengele said, keeping the gun aimed at Wheelock's red-shirted chest. "But nevertheless I should like to put you someplace where you can't give Liebermann a signal. Is there a cellar?"

"Sure," Wheelock said.

"Go to it. At a not-alarming pace. Are there any other dogs in the house besides those four?"

"No." Wheelock walked slowly toward the hallway, his hands on his head. "Lucky for you."

Mengele followed after him with the gun. "Where is your wife?" he asked.

"At school. Teaching. In Lancaster." Wheelock walked into the hallway.

"Have you pictures of your son?"

Wheelock paused for a moment, walked toward the right. "What do you want them for?"

"To look at," Mengele said, following after him with the gun. "I'm not thinking of hurting him. I'm the doctor who delivered him."

"What the *hell* is this *about?*" Wheelock stopped beside a door in the side of the stairway.

"Have you pictures?" Mengele asked.

"There's an album in there. Where we were. On the bottom of the table where the phone is."

"That is the door?"

"Yes."

"Lower one hand and open it, only a little."

Wheelock turned to the door, lowered a hand, opened the door slightly; put the hand back on his head.

"The rest with your foot."

Wheelock toed the door all the way open.

Mengele moved to the wall opposite and stood against it, the gun close to Wheelock's back. "Go in."

"I have to put the light on."

"Do so."

Wheelock reached, pulled a string; harsh light came on inside the doorway. Putting his hand back on his head, Wheelock ducked and stepped down onto a landing of household implements clipped to plank wall.

"Go down," Mengele said. "Slowly."

Wheelock turned to the left and started slowly down stairs.

Mengele moved to the doorway, stepped down onto the landing; turned toward Wheelock, drew the door closed.

Wheelock walked slowly down cellar stairs, his hands on his head.

Mengele aimed the gun at the red-shirted back. He fired and fired again; deafeningly loud shots. Shells flew and bounded.

The hands left the white-haired head, groped down, found wooden rails. Wheelock swayed.

Mengele fired another deafening shot into the red-shirted back.

The hands slipped from the rails and Wheelock toppled forward. The front of his head banged floor below; his shoe-soled feet spread apart and his legs and trunk slid farther down the stairs.

Mengele looked, reaming at an ear with a forefinger.

He opened the door and went out into the hallway. The dogs were barking wildly. "Quiet!" Mengele shouted, finger-reaming his other ear. The dogs kept barking.

Mengele pushed the safety catch up and put the gun into the holster; got out his handkerchief, wiped the door's inside knob, pulled the light string, elbowed the door closed. "Quiet!" he shouted, putting the handkerchief in his pocket. The dogs kept barking. They scratched and thumped at a door at the end of the hallway.

Mengele hurried to the front door, looked out through a narrow pane beside it; opened the door and ran out.

Got into his car, started it, and drove it past the house and around into the empty half of the garage.

Ran back into the house, closed the door. The dogs were barking and whining, scratching, thumping.

Mengele looked at himself in the coat-stand's mirror; detached the wig and took it off, peeled the mustache from his upper lip; put mustache and wig into a pocket of his hanging coat, pulled the flap out and over.

Looked at himself again as he palmed his cropped gray hair with both hands. Frowned.

Took his jacket off, hung it on a hook; took the coat and hung it over the jacket.

Unknotted his black-and-gold-striped tie, whipped it off, rolled it up and stuffed it into another coat pocket.

Unbuttoned the collar of his light-blue shirt, the next button too; spread the collar, pressed down its wings.

The dogs barked and whined behind the door.

Mengele worked at the holster's back-strap. Looked at himself in the mirror and asked, "You Liebermann?"

Asked it again, more American, less German: "You Liebermann?" Tried to make his voice more Wheelock-like, more down-in-the-throat: "Come on in. I have to admit I'm goddamn curious. Ignore sem, sey always bark like sat. *Them. They. Th, th, th. That, that.* Ignore them, they always bark like that. You Liebermann? Come on in."

The dogs barked.

"Quiet!" Mengele shouted.

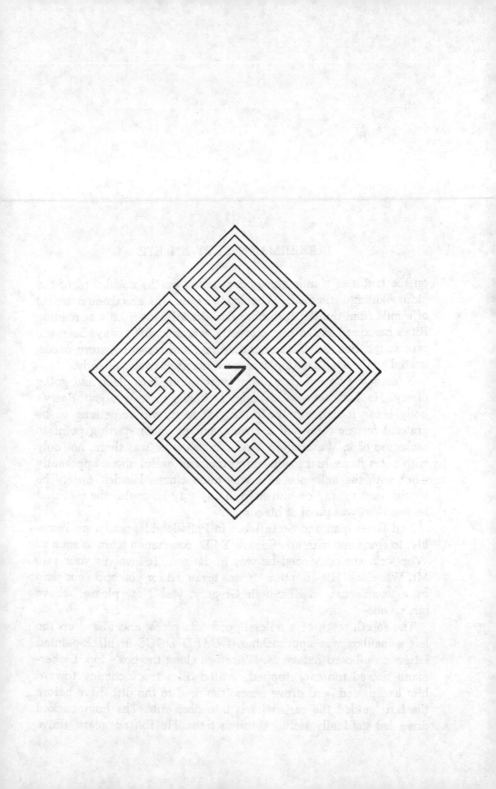

on the tenths of a mile slowly registering on the dashboard of the kidney-killing little Saab. Wheelock's house was exactly four tenths of a mile from the left turn onto Old Buck Road—*if* he was reading Rita's baroque handwriting correctly, which hadn't always been the case so far. Between Rita's handwriting, and rest-room stops necessitated by the Saab's jolting, it was twenty after twelve already.

Nonetheless he felt that things were falling into place and going nicely. He had been saddened, of course, to hear about Barry's body being found, but the timing, at least, was something to be grateful for; now he had a strong and provable starting point to make use of in Washington. And Kurt Koehler was there, not only with notes Barry had made—important and useful notes, apparently —but with the influence of a well-to-do citizen besides. Surely he would want to stay on and help in any way he could; the fact that he was there was proof of his concern.

And Greenspan and Stern were in Philadelphia, ready, presumably, to come out with an effective Y.J.D. commando team as soon as Wheelock was convinced he was in danger. "It involves your son, Mr. Wheelock. His adoption. It was arranged for you and your wife by a woman named Elizabeth Gregory, yes? Now please believe me, no one—"

The fourth tenth of a mile slipped into place, and ahead on the left a mailbox was approaching. *GUARD DOGS* in black-painted letters on a board below; *H. Wheelock* along the box's top. Liebermann slowed the car, stopped, waited till a truck coming toward him had passed, and drove across the road to the dirt drive before the box; guided the car's wheels into deep ruts. The humpbacked drive led gradually uphill through trees. He shifted gears, drove slowly. The car's bottom scraped against the hump. He glanced at his watch: almost twenty-five after.

Half an hour, say, to convince Wheelock (without going into genes: "I don't know *why* they're killing the boys' fathers; they *are*, that's all"), and then an hour or so for the Y.J.D. to get there. That would be two o'clock, a little after. He could probably leave by three, and be in Washington by five, five-thirty. Call Koehler. He looked forward to meeting him, and seeing those notes of Barry's. Surprising that Mengele had missed them. But maybe Koehler was overestimating their importance . . .

Dogs' barking, a tumult of it, challenged him from a sunlit clearing where a two-story house—white shutters, brown shingles—stood at an angle to him; and at its back a dozen dogs flinging themselves at high mesh fence, barking, yipping.

He drove to the foot of the house's stone-paved walk and stopped the car there; shifted into neutral, turned the key, pulled up the hand brake. The dogs out in back still barked. At the far side of the house a red pickup truck and a white sedan stood in a garage.

He got out of the car—a real relief—and with his briefcase in his hand, stood looking at the white-trimmed brown house. It would be easy enough to protect Wheelock here; the dogs—still barking— were a built-in alarm system. And deterrent. The killer would probably make his move somewhere else—in town or on the road. Wheelock would have to follow a normal routine and allow the killer an opportunity to show himself. Problem: scare him enough so that he accepts Y.J.D. protection, but not so much that he stays at home and locks himself in a closet.

He drew a breath and marched up the walk and onto the porch. The door had a knocker, a dog's head of iron, and a black bell button at the side. He chose the knocker; worked it twice. It was old and tight; the knocks weren't very loud. He waited a moment—dogs were barking *in* the house now—and put a finger toward the button; but the door opened and a man smaller than he expected, with cropped gray hair and vivid and cheery brown eyes, looked at him and said in a deep-throated voice, "You Liebermann?"

"Yes," he said. "Mr. Wheelock?"

A nod of the cropped gray head, and the door opened wider. "Come on in."

He went in, to a dog-smelling hallway with stairs going up. He took his hat off. Dogs—five or six of them, it sounded like—were barking, whining, scratching behind a door at the hallway's end. He turned toward Wheelock, who had closed the door and stood smil-

ing at him. "Nice to meet you," Wheelock said, spruce-looking in a
light-blue shirt with the collar open and the cuffs turned up, well-
fitting dark-gray trousers, good-looking black shoes. No recession in
the guard-dog business. "I was beginning to think you wouldn't
come."

"I read the directions wrong," Liebermann said. "The lady who
called you from New York?" He shook his head, smiling apologetically. "She was calling for me."

"Oh," Wheelock said, and smiled. "Take your coat off." He
pointed at a coat-stand; a black hat and coat hung on it, and a
brown quilted jacket, its sleeves shredded with rips and tears.

Liebermann hung his hat up, put his briefcase on the floor, unbuttoned his coat. Wheelock was friendlier than he had been on the
phone—seemed genuinely pleased to see him in fact—but something
in the way he spoke ran counter to the friendliness; Liebermann
felt it, but he couldn't pinpoint what it was. Glancing at the door
where the dogs barked and whined, he said, "You meant it when
you said 'a houseful of dogs.'"

"Yes," Wheelock said, going past him, smiling. "Ignore them.
They always bark like that. I put them in there so they wouldn't
annoy you. Some people get nervous. Come in here." He gestured
toward a room at the right.

Liebermann hung his coat up, picked up his briefcase, and with a
pondering look at Wheelock's back, followed him into a pleasant
sitting room. The dogs began bumping and barking behind a door
on the left, next to a black leather sofa above which all-colored
prize ribbons hung on wood-paneled wall amid trophies and black-
framed photos. A stone fireplace stood at the end of the room, more
trophies on its mantel, a clock. White-curtained windows in the
right-hand wall, an old-fashioned settee between them; in the
corner by the doorway, a chair and table, telephone, ledgers, pipes
in a rack.

"Sit down," Wheelock said, gesturing toward the sofa as he went
to the settee. "And tell me why a Nazi is coming to get me." He sat
down. "I have to admit I'm goddamn curious."

Curhious—the *r* slightly roughened. *That* was what was bothering
him; friendly Henry Wheelock was *mimicking* him, shading his
American speech with a hint of a "Choiman agzent"; nothing
broad, just the hardly-at-all roughening of the *r*'s, the lightest dart
of a *v* inside the *w*'s. Liebermann sat on the sofa—the cushion
wheezed—and looked across at Wheelock leaning forward on the
settee, elbows on spread knees, fingertips gliding back and forth

along the edge of a green album or scrapbook on a low table before him; smiling at him, waiting.

Could the mimicry be unintended? He himself had sometimes echoed the rhythm and inflections of a foreigner's awkward German; had caught himself doing it and been embarrassed.

But no, this was intentional, he was sure of it. Hostility was coming at him from smiling Wheelock. And what would you expect from an anti-Semitic former penitentiary guard who trains dogs to tear people's throats out? Loving kindness? Good manners?

Well, he hadn't come here to make a new friend. He put his briefcase by his feet, rested his hands on his knees.

"To explain this, Mr. Wheelock," he said, "I have to go into personal matters. Personal regarding *you*. About your son, and his adoption."

Wheelock's eyebrows lifted questioningly.

"I know," Liebermann said, "that you and Mrs. Wheelock got him in New York City from 'Elizabeth Gregory.' Now please believe me"—he leaned forward—"no one is going to make trouble about it. No one is going to try to take your son away from you or charge you with any law-breaking. It's long ago and not important any more, not *directly* important. I give you my word on this."

"I believe you," Wheelock said gravely.

A very cool customer, this momzer, taking it so calmly; sitting there running the tips of his forefingers apart and together, apart and together, along the edge of the green album cover. The spine of the album lay toward Liebermann; the cover sloped upward, resting, apparently, on something inside. "'Elizabeth Gregory,'" Liebermann said, "wasn't her real name. Her real name was Frieda Maloney, Frieda Altschul Maloney. You have heard it?"

Wheelock frowned thoughtfully. "Do you mean that Nazi?" he asked. "The one they sent back to Germany?"

"Yes." Liebermann picked up his briefcase. "I have here some pictures of her. You'll see that—"

"Don't bother," Wheelock said.

Liebermann looked at him.

"I saw her picture in the newspaper," Wheelock explained. "She looked familiar to me. Now I know why." He smiled. The "why" had almost been "vy."

Liebermann nodded. (*Was* it intentional? Except for the mimicry Wheelock was behaving pleasantly enough . . .) He put back the loosened briefcase strap; looked at Wheelock. "You and your wife," he said, trying to un-*v* his own *w*'s, "weren't the only couple that got babies from her. A couple named Guthrie did, and Mr. Guthrie was murdered last October. A couple named Curry did; Mr. Curry was murdered in November."

Wheelock looked concerned now. His fingertips were motionless on the edge of the album cover.

"There is a Nazi going about in this country," Liebermann said, holding the briefcase on his lap, "a former SS man, killing the fathers of the boys adopted through Frieda Maloney. Killing them in the same order as the adoptions, and the same time apart. You're the next one, Mr. Wheelock." He nodded. "Soon. And there are many more after. This is why I go to the F.B.I., and this is why, *while* I go, you should be protected. And by more than your dogs." He gestured at the door beyond the sofa end; the dogs were whining behind it now, one or two barking half-heartedly.

Wheelock shook his head in amazement. "Hmm!" he said. "But this is so strange!" He looked wonderingly at Liebermann. "The *fathers* of the boys are being killed?"

"Yes."

"But *why?*" Perfect pronunciation this time; he too was trying.

Dear God, of course! Not mimicry at all, intended or unintended, but a real accent, like his own, being suppressed!

He said, "I don't know . . ."

And the shoes and the trousers, of a city man not a country man; the hostility coming from him; the dogs closed away so as not to "annoy" . . .

"You don't know?" the-Nazi-not-Wheelock asked him. "All these killings are taking place and you *don't know the rheason?*"

But the killers were in their fifties, and this man was sixty-five, maybe a little less. *Mengele?* Impossible. He was in Brazil or Paraguay and wouldn't *dare* come north, couldn't *possibly* be sitting here in New Providence, Pennsylvania.

He shook his head at no-not-Mengele.

But Kurt Koehler had been in Brazil, and had come to Washington. The name would have been in Barry's passport or wallet as next-of-kin . . .

A gun came out from behind the album cover, aiming its muzzle at him. "Then I must tell it to you," the man holding the gun said. Liebermann looked at him; darkened and lengthened his hair, gave him a thin mustache, filled him out and made him younger . . . Yes, Mengele. Mengele! The hated, the so-long-hunted; Angel of Death, child-killer! Sitting here. Smiling. Aiming a gun at him. "Heaven forbid," *Mengele* said in German, "that you should die in ignorance. I want you to know exactly what's coming in twenty years or so. Is that ossified stare only for the gun, or have you recognized me?"

Liebermann blinked, took a breath. "I recognize you," he said.

Mengele smiled. "Rudel and Seibert and the others," he said, "are a bunch of tired old ladies. They called the men home because Frieda Maloney talked to you about babies. So I have to finish the job myself." He shrugged. "I really don't mind; the work will keep me young. Listen, put the briefcase down very slowly and sit back with your hands on your head and relax; you have a good minute or so before I kill you."

Liebermann put the briefcase down slowly, to the left of his feet, thinking that if he got a chance to go quickly to the right and open the door there—assuming it wasn't locked—maybe the dogs whimpering on the other side would see Mengele with the gun and go for him before he could get off too many shots. Of course, maybe the dogs would go for *him too;* and maybe they wouldn't go for either of them without Wheelock (dead in there) giving a command. But he couldn't think of anything else to try.

"I wish it could be longer," Mengele said. "Truly I do. This is one of the most satisfying moments in my life, as I'm sure you can appreciate, and if it were at all practical to do so, I would gladly sit and talk with you like this for an hour or two. Refute some of the grotesque exaggerations in that book of yours, for instance! But alas . . ." He shrugged regretfully.

Liebermann folded his hands on top of his head, sitting erect on the front of the sofa. He began working his feet farther apart, very slowly. The sofa was low, and getting up from it quickly wasn't going to be easy. "Is Wheelock dead?" he asked.

"No," Mengele said. "He's in the kitchen making lunch for us. Listen closely now, dear Liebermann; I'm going to tell you something that's going to sound totally incredible to you, but I swear to you on my mother's grave that it's the absolute truth. Would I bother to lie to a Jew? And a dead one?"

Liebermann flicked his eyes to the window at the right of the settee and looked back at Mengele attentively.

Mengele sighed and shook his head. "If I want to look out the window," he said, "I'll kill you and then look. But I don't *want* to look out the window. If someone were coming, the dogs out in back would be barking, yes? Yes?"

"Yes," Liebermann said, sitting with his hands on his head.

Mengele smiled. "You see? Everything goes my way. God is with me. Do you know what I saw on television at one o'clock this morning? Films of Hitler." He nodded. "At a moment when I was severely depressed, virtually suicidal. If that wasn't a sign from heaven, there's never been one. So don't waste your time looking at windows; look at me, and listen. He's alive. This album"—he pointed with his free hand, not taking his eyes or his gun off Liebermann—"is full of pictures of him, ages one through thirteen. The boys are exact genetic duplicates of him. I'm not going to take the time to explain to you how I achieved this—I doubt whether you'd have the capacity to understand it if I did—but take my word for it, I did achieve it. *Exact genetic duplicates.* They were conceived in my laboratory, and carried to term by women of the Auiti tribe; healthy, docile creatures with a businesslike chieftain. The boys bear no taint of them; they're pure Hitler, bred entirely from his cells. He allowed me to take half a liter of his blood and a cutting of skin from his ribs—we were in a Biblical frame of mind—on the sixth of January, 1943, at Wolf's Lair. He had denied himself children"—the phone rang; Mengele kept his eyes and his gun on Liebermann—"because he knew that no son could flourish in the shadow of so"—the phone rang—"godlike a father; so when he heard what was theoretically possible, that I could"—the phone rang—"create some day not his son but another himself, not even a carbon copy but"—the phone rang—"another original, he was as thrilled by the idea as I was. It was then that he gave me the position and facilities I required to begin my pursuit of the goal. Did you really think my work at Auschwitz was aimless insanity? How simple-minded you people are! He commemorated the occasion, the giving of the blood and skin, with a beautifully inscribed cigarette case. 'To my friend of many years Josef Mengele, who has served me better than most men and may serve me some day better than all. Adolf Hitler.' My most cherished possession, naturally; too risky to take through customs, so it sits in my lawyer's safe in Asunción, waiting for me to come home from my travels. You see? I'm giving you more than a minute"—he looked at the clock—

Liebermann got up and—a gunshot roared—stepped around the sofa end, reaching. A gunshot roared, a gunshot roared; pain flung him against hard wall, pain in his chest, pain farther down. Dogs barked loud in his wall-pressing ear. The brown wood door thumped and quivered; he reached across it for its glass-diamond knob. A gunshot roared; the knob burst apart as he caught it, a small hole in the back of his hand filling with blood. He clutched a sharp part of knob—a gunshot roared; the dogs barked wildly—and wincing in pain, eyes shut tight, he twisted the part-knob, pulled. The door threw itself open against his arm and shoulder, dog-howling; gunshots roared, a thundering salvo. Barks, a cry, clicks of an empty gun; a thud and clatter, snarls, a cry. He let go the cutting part-knob, turned himself back gasping against the wall; let himself slide downward, opened his eyes . . .

Black dogs drove Mengele into a spread-legged side-sprawl on the settee; big Dobermans, teeth bared, eyes wild, sharp ears back. Mengele's cheek slammed against the settee arm. His eye stared at a Doberman before him, shifting amid the legs of the overturned table, jaw-grappling his wrist; the gun fell from his fingers. His eye rolled to stare at Dobermans snarling close against his cheek and underjaw. The Doberman at his cheek stood between his back and the settee's back, its forepaws treading for purchase at his shoulder. The Doberman at his underjaw stood hind-legged on the floor be-tween his spread legs, leaning in over his updrawn thigh, body down low against his chest. Mengele raised his cheek higher against the settee arm, eye staring down, lips trembling.

A fourth Doberman lay big on the floor between the settee and Liebermann, on its side, black ribs heaving, its nose on hooked rug. A light-reflecting flatness spread out from beneath it; a puddle of urine.

Liebermann slid all the way down the wall, and wincing, sat on the floor. He straightened his legs out slowly before him, watching the Dobermans threatening Mengele.

Threatening, not killing. Mengele's wrist had been let go; the Doberman that had held it stood snarling at him almost nose to nose.

"Kill!" Liebermann commanded, but only a whisper came out. Pain lancing his chest enlarged and sharpened.

"Kill!" he shouted against the pain. A hoarse command came out.

The Dobermans snarled, not moving.

Mengele's eye clenched tight; his teeth bit his lower lip.

"KILL!" Liebermann bellowed—and the pain ripped his chest, tore it apart.

The Dobermans snarled, not moving.

A high-pitched squealing came from Mengele's bitten-closed mouth.

Liebermann threw his head back against the wall and closed his eyes, gasping. He tugged his tie knot down, unbuttoned his shirt collar. Undid another button under the tie and put his fingers to the pain; found wetness on his chest at the edge of his undershirt.

Brought the fingers out, opened his eyes; looked at blood on his fingertips. The bullet had gone right through him. Hitting what? The left lung? Whatever it had hit, every breath swelled the pain. He reached down for the handkerchief in his trouser pocket, rolled leftward to get at it; worse pain exploded below, in his hip. He winced as it gored him. Ei!

He got the handkerchief out, brought it up, pressed it against the chest wound and held it there.

Raised his left hand. Blood leaked from both sides of it, more from the ragged break in the palm than from the smaller puncture in the back. The bullet had gone through below the first and second fingers. They were numb and he couldn't move them. Two scratches bled across the palm.

He wanted to keep the hand up to slow the bleeding but couldn't; let it fall down. No strength was in him. Only pain. And tiredness . . . The door beside him drifted slowly toward closing.

He looked at Mengele.

Mengele's eye watched him.

He closed his eyes, breathing shallowly against the pain burning in his chest.

■

"Away . . ."

He opened his eyes and looked across the room at Mengele lying side-sprawled on the settee among the close-snarling Dobermans.

"Away," Mengele said, softly and warily. His eye moved from the Doberman before him to the Doberman at his underjaw, the Doberman at his cheek. "Off. No more gun. No gun. Away. Off. Good dogs."

The blue-black Dobermans snarled, not moving.

"Nice dogs," Mengele said. "Samson? Good Samson. Off. Go away." He turned his head slowly against the settee arm; the Dobermans withdrew their heads a little, snarling. Mengele made a shaky smile at them. "Major?" he asked. "Are you Major? Good Major, good Samson. Good dogs. Friend. No more gun." His hand, red-wristed, caught the front of the settee arm; his other hand held the frame of the settee's back. He began turning himself up slowly from his side. "Good dogs. Off. Away."

The Doberman in the middle of the room lay motionless, its black ribs still. The urine puddle around it had fragmented into a scatter of small puddles glinting on wide floorboards.

"Good dogs, nice dogs . . ."

Lying on his back, Mengele began pulling himself up slowly into the corner of the settee. The Dobermans snarled but stayed where they were, finding new paw-holds as he moved himself higher, away from their teeth. "Away," he said. "I'm your *friend*. Do I hurt you now? No, no, I *like* you."

Liebermann closed his eyes, breathed shallowly. He was sitting in blood that leaked down behind him.

"Good Samson, good Major. Beppo? Zarko? Good dogs. Away. Away."

Dena and Gary were having some kind of trouble between them. He had kept his mouth shut when he was there in November, but maybe he shouldn't have; maybe he—

"Are you alive, Jew-bastard?"

He opened his eyes.

Mengele sat looking at him, erect in the corner of the settee, one leg up, one foot on the floor. Holding the settee's arm and back; scornful, in command. Except for the three Dobermans leaning at him, softly snarling.

"Too bad," Mengele said. "But you won't be for long. I can see it from here. You're gray as ashes. These dogs will lose interest in me if I sit calmly and talk nicely to them. They'll want to go pee or get a drink of water." To the Dobermans he šaid in English, "Water? Drink? Don't you want water? Good dogs. Go get a drink of water."

The Dobermans snarled, not moving.

"Sons of bitches," Mengele said pleasantly in German. And to Liebermann: "So you've accomplished nothing, Jew-bastard, except to die slowly instead of quickly, and to scratch my wrist a little. In fifteen minutes I'll walk out of here. Every man on the list will die at his time. The Fourth Reich is coming: not just a German Reich but a pan-Aryan one. I'll live to see it, and to stand beside its leaders. Can you imagine the awe they'll inspire? The mystical authority they'll wield? The trembling of the Russians and Chinese? Not to mention the Jews." The phone rang.

Liebermann tried to move from the wall—to crawl if he could to the wire hanging down from the table by the doorway—but the pain in his hip spiked him and held him, impossible to move against. He settled back into the stickiness of his blood. Closed his eyes, gasping.

"Good. Die a minute sooner. And think while you die of your grandchildren going into ovens."

The phone kept ringing.

Greenspan and Stern, maybe. Calling to see what was happening, why *he* hadn't called. Getting no answer, wouldn't they worry and come, get directions in the town? If only the Dobermans would hold Mengele . . .

He opened his eyes.

Mengele sat smiling at the Dobermans—a relaxed, steady, friendly smile. They weren't snarling now.

He let his eyes close.

Tried not to think of ovens and armies, of heiling masses. Wondered if Max and Lili and Esther would manage to keep the Center going. Contributions might come in. Memorials.

Barking, snarling. He opened his eyes.

"No, no!" Mengele said, sitting back down on the settee, clutching the arm and back of it while the Dobermans pushed and snarled at him. "No, no! Good dogs! Good dogs! No, no, I'm not going! No, no. See how still I sit? Good dogs. Good dogs."

Liebermann smiled, closed his eyes.

Good dogs.

Greenspan? Stern? Come on . . .

"Jew-bastard?"

The handkerchief would stick to the wound by itself, so he kept his eyes closed, not breathing—let him *think*—and then he got his right hand up and gave the middle finger.

Faraway barking. The dogs out in back.

He opened his eyes.

Mengele glared at him. The same hatred that had come at him over the telephone that night so long ago.

"Whatever happens," Mengele said, "I win. Wheelock was the eighteenth one to die. *Eighteen of them* have lost their fathers when he lost his, and at least *one* of the eighteen will grow to manhood as *he* grew, become who he became. You won't leave this room alive to stop him. *I* may not leave it either, but *you* won't; I swear it."

Footsteps on the porch.

The Dobermans snarled, leaning at Mengele.

Liebermann and Mengele stared across the room at each other.

The front door opened.

Closed.

They looked at the doorway.

A weight dropped in the hallway. Metal clinked.

Footsteps.

The boy came and stood in the doorway—gaunt and sharp-nosed, dark-haired, a wide red stripe across the chest of his blue zipper jacket.

He looked at Liebermann.

Looked at Mengele and the Dobermans.

Looked at the dead Doberman.

Looked back and forth, deep blue eyes wide.

Pushed his dark forelock aside with a blue plastic mitten.

"Sh*eeesh*!" he said.

◼

"*Mein*—dear boy," Mengele said, looking adoringly at him, "my dear, dear, dear, dear boy, you can not *possibly* imagine how happy I am, how *joyous* I am, to see you standing there so fine and strong and handsome! Will you call off these dogs? These most loyal and admirable dogs? They've kept me motionless here for *hours*, under the mistaken impression that *I*, not that vicious Jew over there, am the one who came here to do you harm. Will you call them off, please? I'll explain everything." He smiled lovingly, sitting among the snarling Dobermans.

The boy stared at him, and turned his head slowly toward Liebermann.

Liebermann shook his head.

"Don't be deceived by him," Mengele warned. "He's a criminal, a killer, a terrible man who came here to hurt you and your family. Call off these dogs, Bobby. You see, I know your name. I know all about you—that you visited Cape Cod last summer, that you have a movie camera, that you have two pretty girl cousins named . . . I'm an old friend of your parents. In fact I'm the doctor who delivered you, just back from abroad! Dr. Breitenbach. Have they mentioned me? I left long ago."

The boy looked uncertainly at him. "Where's my father?" he asked.

"I don't know," Mengele said. "I suspect, since that person had a gun that I succeeded in taking away from him—and the dogs saw us fighting and reached their wrong conclusion—I suspect that he may have"—he nodded gravely—"done away with your father. I came to call, having just come back from abroad, as I said, and he let me in, pretending to be a friend. When he drew his gun I was able to overpower him and get it, but then he opened that door and let the dogs out. Call them off and we'll look for your father. Perhaps he's only tied up. Poor Henry! Let's hope for the best. It's a good thing your mother wasn't here. Does she still teach school in Lancaster?"

The boy looked at the dead Doberman.

Liebermann wagged his finger, trying to catch the boy's eye.

The boy looked at Mengele. "Ketchup," he said; the Dobermans turned and came jumping and hurrying to him. They ranked themselves two at one side of him, one at the other. His mittens touched their blue-black heads.

"Ketchup!" Mengele exclaimed happily, lowering his leg from the settee, sitting forward and rubbing his upper arms. "Never in a *thousand years* would I have thought to say ketchup!" He marched his feet against the floor, rubbing his thighs, smiling. "I said *off*, I said *away*, I said *go*, I said *friend;* not *once* did it enter my mind to say ketchup!"

The boy, frowning, pulled his mittens off. "We . . . better call the police," he said. The dark forelock fell aslant his forehead.

Mengele sat gazing at him. "How marvelous you are!" he said. "I'm so—" He blinked, swallowed, smiled. "Yes," he said, "we certainly must call the police. Do a favor for me, *mein*—Bobby dear. Take the dogs and go in the kitchen and get me a glass of water. You might also find me something to eat." He stood up. "I shall call the police, and then I'll look for your father."

The boy stuffed his mittens into his jacket pockets. "Is that your car in front?" he asked.

"Yes," Mengele said. "And his is the one in the garage. Or so I assume. Is it yours? The family's?"

The boy looked skeptically at him. "The one in front," he said, "has a bumper sticker about Jews not giving up any of Israel. You called *him* a Jew."

"And so he is," Mengele said. "At least he looks like one." He smiled. "This is hardly the time to talk about what words I used. Go get the water, please, and I'll call the police."

The boy cleared his throat. "Would you sit down again?" he said. "I'll call them."

"Bobby dear—"

"Pickles," the boy said; the Dobermans rushed snarling at Mengele. He backed down onto the settee, forearms crossed before his face. "Ketchup!" he cried. "Ketchup! *Ketchup!*" The Dobermans leaned at him, snarling.

The boy came into the room, unzipping his jacket. "They're not going to listen to *you*," he said. He turned toward Liebermann, pushed his dark forelock aside.

Liebermann looked at him.

"He switched it around, didn't he?" the boy said. "*He* had the gun, and let *you* in."

"No!" Mengele said.

Liebermann nodded.

"Can't you talk?"

He shook his head, pointed at the phone.

The boy nodded and turned.

"That man is your enemy!" Mengele cried. "I swear to God he is!"

"You think I'm retarded?" The boy moved to the table, picked up the phone.

"Don't!" Mengele leaned toward him. The Dobermans snapped and snarled at him but he stayed leaning. "Please! I beg you! For *your* sake, not mine! I'm your *friend!* I came here to help you! Listen to me, Bobby! Only for one minute!"

The boy faced him, the phone in his hand.

"Please! I'll explain! The truth! I *did* lie, yes! *I* had the gun. To help *you!* Please! Only listen to me for one minute! You'll thank me, I swear you will! One minute!"

The boy stood looking at him, and lowered the phone, hung it up.

Liebermann shook his head despairingly. "Call!" he said. A whisper, not even getting out of his mouth.

"Thank you," Mengele said to the boy. "Thank you." He sat back, smiling ruefully. "I should have known you would be too clever to lie to. Please"—he glanced at the Dobermans, looked at the boy—"call them off. I'll stay here, sitting."

The boy stood by the table looking at him. "Ketchup," he said; the Dobermans turned and hurried to him. They ranked themselves beside him, all three at the side toward Liebermann, facing Mengele.

Mengele shook his head, ran a hand back over his cropped gray hair. "This is . . . so difficult." He lowered his hand, looked anxiously at the boy.

"Well?" the boy said.

Mengele said, "You *are* clever, are you not?"

The boy stood looking at him, fingers moving at the head of the nearest Doberman.

"You don't do well in school," Mengele said. "You did when you were little, but not now. This is because you're *too* clever, too"—he raised a hand, tapped at his temple—"thinking your own thoughts. But the fact is, you're smarter than the teachers, yes?"

The boy looked toward the dead Doberman, frowning, his lips pursed. He looked at Liebermann.

Liebermann poked his finger at the phone.

Mengele leaned toward the boy. "If *I* am to be truthful with *you*," he said, "*you* must be truthful with *me!* Are you not smarter than the teachers?"

The boy looked at him, shrugged. "Except one," he said.

"And you have high ambitions, yes?"

The boy nodded.

"To be a great painter, or an architect."

The boy shook his head. "To make movies."

"Oh yes, of course." Mengele smiled. "To be a great movie-maker." He looked at the boy; his smile faded. "You and your father have fought about this," he said. "A stubborn old man with a limited viewpoint. You resent him, with good reason."

The boy looked at him.

"You see," Mengele said, "I *do* know you. Better than anyone else on earth."

The boy, bewildered-looking, said, "Who are you?"

"The doctor who delivered you. That much was true. But I'm not an old friend of your parents. In fact, I've never met them. We are strangers."

The boy tipped his head as if to hear better.

"Do you see what that means?" Mengele asked him. "The man you think of as your father"—he shook his head—"is not your father. And your mother—though you love her and she loves you, I'm sure —she is not your mother. They adopted you. It was I who arranged for the adoption. Through intermediaries. Helpers."

The boy stared at him.

Liebermann watched the boy uneasily.

"That's distressing news to receive so suddenly," Mengele said, "but perhaps . . . not wholly unpleasing news? Have you never felt that you were superior to those around you? Like a prince among commoners?"

The boy stood taller, shrugged. "I feel . . . different from every-one sometimes."

"You *are* different," Mengele said. "Infinitely different, and infinitely superior. You have—"

"Who are my real parents?" the boy asked.

Mengele looked thoughtfully at his hands, clasped them, looked at the boy. "It would be better for you," he said, "not to know yet. When you're older, more mature, you'll find out. But this I can tell you now, Bobby: you were born of the finest blood in all the world. Your inheritance—I'm speaking not of money but of character and ability—is incomparable. You have it within you to fulfill ambitions a *thousand times greater* than those of which you presently dream. And you *shall* fulfill them! But only—and you must bear in mind how well I know you, and trust me when I say this—*only* if you will go out of here now with the dogs, and let me . . . do what I must and go."

The boy stood looking at him.

"For *your* sake," Mengele said. "*Your well-being* is all that I con-sider. You *must* believe that. I have consecrated my life to you and your welfare."

The boy stood looking at him. "Who are my real parents?" he asked.

Mengele shook his head.

"I want to know," the boy said.

"In this you must bow to my judgment; at the—"

"Pickles!" The Dobermans rushed snarling at Mengele. He cow-ered back behind crossed forearms. The Dobermans leaned at him, snarling.

"Tell me," the boy said. "Right now. Or else I'll . . . say some-thing else to them. I mean it! I can make them kill you if I want."

Mengele stared at him over crossed wrists.

"Who are my parents?" the boy asked. "I'll give you three. One . . ."

"You have none!" Mengele said.

"Two . . ."

"It's true! You were born from a cell of the greatest man who ever lived! *Reborn!* You are *he,* reliving his life! And that Jew over there is his sworn enemy! And yours!"

The boy turned toward Liebermann, blue eyes confounded.

Liebermann got his hand up, circled a finger at his temple, pointed at Mengele.

"No!" Mengele cried as the boy turned to him. The Dobermans

snarled. "I am not mad! Smart though you are, there are things you don't know, about science and microbiology! You're the living duplicate of the greatest man in all history! And he"—his eyes jumped toward Liebermann—"came here to kill you! I to protect you!"

"Who?" the boy challenged. "Who am I? What great man?"

Mengele stared at him over the heads of the snarling Dobermans.

The boy said, "One . . ."

"Adolf Hitler; you've been told he was evil," Mengele said, "but as you grow and see the world engulfed by Blacks and Semites, Slavs, Orientals, Latins—and your own Aryan folk threatened with extinction—from which you shall save them!—you'll come to see that he was the best and finest and wisest of all mankind! You'll rejoice in your heritage, and bless me for creating you! As he himself blessed me for trying!"

"You know what?" the boy said. "You're the biggest nut I ever met. You're the weirdest, craziest—"

"I am telling you the truth!" Mengele said. "Look in your heart! The strength is there to command armies, Bobby! To bend whole nations to your will, to destroy without mercy all who oppose you!"

The boy stood looking at him.

"It's true," Mengele said. "All his power is in you, or will be when the time comes. Now do as I tell you. Let me protect you. You have a destiny to fulfill. The highest destiny of all."

The boy looked down, rubbing at his forehead. He looked up at Mengele. "Mustard," he said.

The Dobermans leaped; Mengele flailed, cried out.

Liebermann looked. Winced. Looked.

Looked at the boy.

The boy thrust his hands into the pockets of his red-striped blue jacket. He moved from the table, walked slowly to the side of the settee; stood looking down. He wrinkled his nose. Said, "Sheesh."

Liebermann looked at the boy, and at the burrowing Dobermans pushing Mengele down onto the floor.

He looked at his slowly bleeding left hand, both sides of it.

Growls sounded. Wet partings. Scrapings.

After a while the boy came away from the settee, his hands still in his pockets. He looked down at the dead Doberman, prodded its rump with a sneaker-toe. He glanced at Liebermann, and turned and looked back. "Off," he said. Two of the Dobermans raised their heads and came walking toward him, tongues lapping bloody mouths.

"Off!" the boy said. The third Doberman raised its head.

One of the Dobermans sniffed at the dead Doberman.

The other Doberman came past Liebermann, nosed open the door beside him, and went out.

The boy came and stood between Liebermann's feet, looking down at him, the forelock aslant his forehead.

Liebermann looked up at him. Pointed at the phone.

The boy took his hands from his pockets and crouched down, elbows on brown-corduroy thighs, hands hanging loose. Dirty fingernails.

Liebermann looked at the gaunt young face: the sharp nose, the forelock, the deep blue eyes looking at him.

"I think you're going to die soon," the boy said, "if someone doesn't come help you, get you to the hospital." His breath smelled of chewing gum.

Liebermann nodded.

"I could go out again," the boy said. "With my books. And come back later. Say I was . . . just walking somewhere. I do that sometimes. And my mother doesn't get home till twenty to five. I bet you'd be dead by then."

Liebermann looked at him. Another Doberman went out.

"If I stay, and call the police," the boy said, "are you going to tell them what I did?"

Liebermann considered. Shook his head.

"Ever?"

He shook his head.

"Promise?"

He nodded.

The boy put out his hand.

Liebermann looked at it.

He looked at the boy; the boy looked at him. "If you can point, you can shake," the boy said.

Liebermann looked at the hand.

No, he told himself. Either way you're going to die. What kind of doctors can they have in a hole like this?

"Well?"

And maybe there's an afterlife. Maybe Hannah's waiting. Mama, Papa, the girls . . .

Don't kid yourself.

He brought his hand up.

Shook the boy's hand. As little as possible.

"He was a real nut," the boy said, and stood up.

Liebermann looked at his hand.

"*Scram!*" the boy shouted at a Doberman busy on Mengele.

The Doberman ran out into the hallway, then back crazily, bloody-mouthed, and past Liebermann and out.

The boy went to the phone.

Liebermann closed his eyes.

Remembered. Opened them.

When the boy was done talking, he beckoned to him.

The boy came over. "Water?" he asked.

He shook his head, beckoned.

The boy crouched down beside him.

"There's a list," he said.

"What?" The boy leaned his ear close.

"There's a list," he said as loud as he could.

"A list?"

"See if you can find it. In his coat maybe. A list of names."

He watched the boy go into the hallway.

My helper Hitler.

He kept his eyes open.

Looked at Mengele in front of the settee. White and red where his face was. Bone and blood.

Good.

After a while the boy came back looking at papers.

He reached.

"My father's on it," the boy said.

He reached.

The boy looked uneasily at him, put the papers down into his hand. "I forgot. I better go look for him."

Five or six typed sheets. Names, addresses, dates. Hard to read without his glasses. Döring, crossed out. Horve, crossed out. Other pages, no crossings.

He folded the papers against the floor, got them into his jacket pocket.

Closed his eyes.

Stay alive. Not finished yet.

Faraway barking.

"I found him."

■

Blond-bearded Greenspan glared at him. Whispered, "He's *dead!* We can't question him!"

"It's all right. I have the list."

"What?"

Crinkly blond hair, pinned-in embroidered skullcap. As loud as he could: "It's all right. I have the list. All the fathers."

He was lifted—ei!—and put down.

On a stretcher. Being carried. Dog's-head knocker, daylight, blue sky.

A shiny lens looking at him, keeping up, humming. Sharp nose next to it.

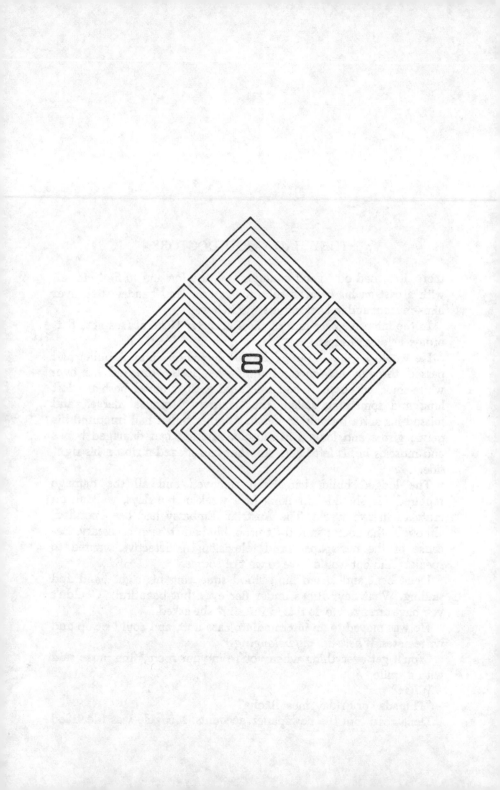

THEY HAD GOOD DOCTORS

there, it turned out; good enough, anyway, for him to find himself with a cast on his hand, a tube in his arm, and bandages all over him—in front and in back, above and below.

In the intensive care unit of the Lancaster General Hospital. Saturday. Friday was lost.

He would be fine, a pudgy Indian doctor told him. A bullet had passed through his "mediastinum"—the doctor touched his own white-smocked chest. It had fractured a rib, injured both the left lung and something called "the recurrent laryngeal nerve," and missed his aorta by only *so much*. Another bullet had fractured his pelvic girdle and lodged in muscle. Another had damaged bones and muscles in his left hand. Another had grazed a rib on his right side.

The lodged bullet had been removed and all the damage repaired. He should be talking in a week or ten days, walking on crutches in two weeks. The Austrian Embassy had been notified, although—the doctor smiled—it probably hadn't been necessary. Because of the newspapers and television. A detective wanted to speak to him but would have to wait of course.

Dena bent and kissed him; stood squeezing his right hand and smiling. What day? Rings under her eyes, but beautiful. "Couldn't you have arranged to do this in Britain?" she asked.

He was moved to an intermediate care unit, and could sit up and write notes. *Where are my belongings?*

"You'll get everything when you're in your room," the nurse said with a smile.

When?

"Thursday or Friday, most likely."

Dena read him the newspaper accounts. Mengele was identified as Ramón Aschheim y Negrín, a Paraguayan. He had killed Wheelock, wounded Liebermann, and been killed by Wheelock's dogs. Wheelock's son, Robert, thirteen, had summoned the police on his return from school. Five men who had arrived immediately after the police had identified themselves as members of the Young Jewish Defenders and friends of Liebermann; they had intended to meet him there, they said, and accompany him on a trip to Washington. They expressed the opinion that Aschheim y Negrín was a Nazi, but could offer no explanation of his or Leibermann's presence at Wheelock's home, or of Wheelock's murder. The police hoped that Liebermann, if and when he recovered, would be able to shed light on the matter.

"Can you?" Dena asked.

He tilted his head, made a "maybe" mouth.

"When did you become friendly with the Y.J.D.?"

Last week.

A nurse told Dena someone wanted to see her.

Dr. Chavan came by, studied Liebermann's chart, held his chin and looked closely at him, and told him that the worst thing wrong with him was that he needed a shave.

Dena came back, leaning against the weight of Liebermann's suitcase. "Speak of the devil," she said, setting it down by the partition. Greenspan had dropped it off. He had come down to get his car, which the police hadn't let him take on Thursday. He had given Dena a message for Liebermann: "One, get well; and two, Rabbi Gorin will call you as soon as he can. He has problems of his own. Watch the newspapers."

He hurt all over. Slept a lot.

He was moved into a nice room with striped curtains and a television set up on the wall, his briefcase on a chair. As soon as he was settled in the bed, he opened the night-table drawer. The list was there, along with his other things. He put his glasses on and looked at it. Numbers one through seventeen crossed out. Cross out Wheelock too. Wheelock's date had been February 19th.

A barber came and shaved him.

He could talk, hoarsely, but wasn't supposed to. It was just as well; it gave him time to think.

Dena wrote letters. He read the *Philadelphia Inquirer* and *The New York Times*, watched the news on the push-button television. Nothing on Gorin. Kissinger in Jerusalem, meeting with Rabin. Crime, unemployment.

"What's wrong, Pa?"

"Nothing."

"Don't talk."

"You asked."

"Don't talk! Write! That's what you've got the pad for!"

NOTHING'S WRONG!

She could be a pest sometimes.

Cards and flowers came: from friends, contributors, the lecture bureau, the Sisterhood of the local temple. A letter from Klaus, who had got the hospital address from Max: *Please write as soon as you're able. Needless to say, Lena and I, and Nürnberger too, are most anxious to learn more than was in the newspapers.*

The day after he was allowed to talk, a detective named Barnhart came to see him, a big redheaded young man, polite and soft-spoken. Liebermann didn't have much light to shed; he had never met Ramón Aschheim y Negrín before the day the man shot him. He hadn't even heard the name. Yes, Mrs. Wheelock was right; he had called Wheelock the day before and told him a Nazi *might* be coming to kill him. That was in response to a tip he had got from a not-too-reliable source in South America. He had come to see Wheelock to try to find out if there could really be anything in it; Aschheim had let him in, fired at him. He had let the dogs in. The dogs killed Aschheim.

"The Paraguay government says his passport's a fake. They don't know who he is either."

"They have no record of his prints?"

"No, sir, they don't. But whoever he was, it looks like you're the one he was after, not Wheelock. You see, he died only a little while before we got there. You must have come around two-thirty, right?"

Liebermann considered, nodded. "Yes," he said.

"But Wheelock died between eleven and noon. So 'Ashheim' waited over two hours for you. That tip of yours looks mighty like a trap, sir. Wheelock had nothing at all to do with the kind of people you go after, we're sure of that. You'd better be leery of future tips, if you don't mind my saying so."

"I don't mind at all. It's good advice. Thank you. To be 'leery.' Yes."

Gorin was in the news that evening. He had been on probation since 1973, when he had been given a three-year suspended sentence on a bombing-conspiracy charge to which he had pleaded guilty; now the federal government was trying to have his probation revoked on the grounds that he had conspired again, this time to kidnap a Russian diplomat. A judge had scheduled a hearing for

February 26th. Revocation would mean Gorin would have to go to prison for the balance of his sentence, a year. Yes, he had problems, all right.

Liebermann did too. He studied the list when he was alone. Five thin pages, neatly typed. Ninety-four names. He sat looking at the wall; shook his head and sighed; folded the list up small and slid it into his passport case.

He wrote letters to Max and Klaus, not saying much. Began taking and making phone calls, though he was still hoarse and couldn't talk at normal volume.

Dena had to go home. She had arranged about the hospital bill. Marvin Farb and some others were going to take care of it, and when Liebermann got back to Austria and collected on his insurance, he would pay them back. "Don't forget the copy of the bill," she warned him. "And don't try to walk too soon. And don't leave until they *say* you should leave."

"I won't, I won't, I won't."

After she left he realized that he hadn't brought up the business about her and Gary; felt bad about it. Some father.

He crutched himself up and down the corridor, hard work with the cast still on his hand. Got to know some of the other patients, griped about the food.

Gorin called. "Yakov? How are you?"

"All right, thanks. I'll be out in a week. How are you?"

"Not so hot. You see what they're doing to me?"

"Yes. I'm sorry."

"We're trying to get a postponement but it doesn't look good. They're really out to get me. And *I'm* supposed to be the conspirator! Oh man. Listen, what's doing? Can you talk? I'm in a booth, so it's all right here."

In Yiddish he said, "We'd better speak in Yiddish. There aren't going to be any more killings. The men were called home."

"They were?"

"And the one who shot me, the one the dogs got, it was . . . the Angel. You understand who I mean?"

Silence. "You're *sure?*"

"Positive. We talked."

"Oh my God! *Thank* God! *Thank* God! Dogs were too good for him! And you're sitting on it? I would call the biggest press conference in history!"

"And what do I say when they ask me what he was doing there? A blank from Paraguay is no problem, but him? And if I *don't* explain, the F.B.I. comes in to find out. Should they? I don't know yet."

"No, no, of course you're right. But to *know* and not be able to tell! Are you coming to New York?"

"Yes."

"Where will you be? I'll get in touch."

He gave him the Farbs' number.

"Phil says you have a list."

Liebermann blinked. "How does he know?"

"You told him."

"I *did*? When?"

"At the house there. Do you?"

"Yes. I sit and stare at it. It's a problem, Rabbi."

"You're telling *me*. Just hold on to it. I'll see you soon. Shalom."

"Shalom."

He talked with a few reporters and high-school kids. Crutched himself up and down the corridor, getting the hang of it.

One afternoon a stout brown-haired woman in a red coat, with a briefcase, came up to him and said, "Mr. Liebermann?"

"Yes?"

She smiled at him: dimples, fine white teeth. "May I speak to you for a minute, please? I'm Mrs. Wheelock. Mrs. Hank Wheelock."

He looked at her. "Yes," he said. "Certainly."

They went into his room. She sat in one of the chairs with her briefcase on her lap, and he leaned the crutches against the bed and lowered himself into the other chair.

"I'm so sorry," he said.

She nodded, looking at her briefcase, rubbing at it with a red-nailed thumb. She looked at him. "The police told me," she said, "that that man came to trap *you*, not to kill Hank. He had no interest in Hank, or in us; he was only interested in you."

Liebermann nodded.

"But while he waited," she said, "he looked at our picture album. It was on the floor there, where he—" She stirred a shoulder, looked at Liebermann.

"Maybe," he said, "your husband was looking at it. Before the man came."

She shook her head; the corners of her mouth turned down. "*He* never looked at it," she said. "*I* took those pictures. *I'm* the one that mounted them in there and composed the inscriptions. It was the man looking."

Liebermann said, "Maybe he just wanted to pass the time."

Mrs. Wheelock sat silently, looking about the room, her hands folded on her briefcase. "Our son is adopted," she said. "*My* son. He doesn't know it. It was in the agreement that we weren't to tell him. The night before last he asked me if he was. The first time he ever mentioned the subject." She looked at Liebermann. "Did you say anything to him that day that could have put the idea into his head?"

"Me?" Liebermann shook his head. "No. How could I know about it?"

"I thought there might be a connection," Mrs. Wheelock said. "The woman who arranged the adoption was German. 'Aschheim' is a German name. A man with a German accent called and asked about Bobby. And I know you're . . . against Germans."

"Against Nazis," Liebermann said. "No, Mrs. Wheelock, I had no idea he was adopted, and I wasn't talking at all when he came in. I'm not talking so good now; you can hear. Maybe because he lost his father he thinks this way."

She sighed, and nodded. "Maybe," she said. She made a smile at him. "I'm sorry I disturbed you. It was worrying me that . . . it might involve *him* somehow."

"That's all right," he said. "I'm glad we met. I was going to call you before I left and express my sympathy."

"Did you see the film?" she asked. "No, I suppose you couldn't. It's funny the way things work out, isn't it? Good coming out of bad? All that misery: Hank dead, you hurt so badly, that man—and the dogs too. We had to put them to sleep, you know. And Bobby gets his break out of it."

Liebermann said, "His break?"

Mrs. Wheelock nodded. "WGAL bought the film he took that day, and showed some of it—you being carried into the ambulance, the dogs with blood on them, that man and Hank when they were carried out—and CBS, that's the network, all the different stations over the whole country, they picked it up and showed it on 'The Morning News with Hughes Rudd' the next morning. Just you being carried into the ambulance. A break like that can be tremendously important for a boy Bobby's age. Not just for the contacts, but for his own self-confidence. He wants to be a movie director."

Liebermann looked at her, and said, "I hope he makes it."

"I think he stands a good chance," she said, getting up with a faint proud smile. "He's very talented."

The Farbs came down on Friday, February 28th, and packed Liebermann and his crutches and his suitcase and briefcase into their dazzling new Lincoln. Marvin Farb gave him a copy of the hospital bill.

He looked at it, stared at Farb.

"And this is cheap," Farb said. "In New York it would have been twice this."

"*Gott im Himmel!*"

Sandy, the girl from the Y.J.D. office, called with a lunch invitation for Tuesday the 11th, at noon. "It's a farewell."

He was leaving on the 13th. For him? "For who?" he asked.

"For the Rabbi. Didn't you hear?"

"The appeal was turned down?"

"He dropped it. He wants to get it over with."

"Oh my! I'm sorry to hear that. Yes, of course I'll be there."

She gave him the address: Smilkstein's, a restaurant on Canal Street.

The *Times* had the story in a single column that he had missed, in by the fold. Rather than contest the new conspiracy charge, Gorin had decided to accept the judge's decision revoking his probation. He would enter a federal penitentiary in Pennsylvania on March 16th. "Mm." Liebermann shook his head.

On Tuesday the 11th, at a little after noon, he caned himself slowly up the stairs at Smilkstein's. A step at a time, hauling with his right hand at the banister. Murder.

At the top of the stairs, panting and sweating, he found one big room, a hall, with a greenery wedding canopy on a bandstand, lots of uncovered tables and gilt folding chairs, and in the center, on the dance floor, men at a table reading menus, a crooked-backed waiter writing. Gorin, at the head of the table, saw him, put down his menu and napkin, rose and came hurrying. As cheerful-looking as if he'd fought the decision and won. "Yakov! It's good to see you!" He shook Liebermann's hand, gripped his arm. "You look fine! Damn it, I forgot the stairs!"

"It's all right," Liebermann said, catching his breath.

"It's *not* all right; it was *stupid* of me. I should have picked someplace else." They walked toward the table, Gorin leading, Liebermann caning. "My chapter heads," Gorin said. "And Phil and Paul. When are you leaving, Yakov?"

"The day after tomorrow. I'm sorry you—"

"Forget it, forget it, I'll be in good company down there—Nixon's whole brain trust. It's the 'in' place for conspirators. Gentlemen, Yakov. This is Dan, Stig, Arnie . . ."

There were five or six of them, and Phil Greenspan, Paul Stern.

"You look a hundred percent better than last time I saw you," Greenspan said, breaking a roll, smiling.

Liebermann, sitting down on the chair across from him, said, "Do you know, I don't even remember *seeing you* that day."

"I can believe it," Greenspan said. "You were slate-gray."

"Marvelous doctors down there," Liebermann said. "I was really surprised." He pulled his chair in, with a hand from the man on his right; leaned his cane against the table edge, picked up his menu.

Gorin, at his left, said, "The waiter says not the pot roast. Do you like duck? It's terrific here."

It was a gloomy farewell. While they ate, Gorin talked about lines of command, and arrangements he and Greenspan were making to maintain contact while he was in prison. Retaliatory actions were proposed; bitter jokes made. Liebermann tried to lighten the mood with a Kissinger story, supposedly true, that Marvin Farb had told him. It didn't help much.

When the waiter had cleared the table and gone downstairs, leaving them with their cake and tea, Gorin leaned his forearms on the table, folded his hands, and looked at everyone gravely. "Our present problems are the least of our problems," he said, and looked at Liebermann. "Right, Yakov?"

Liebermann, looking at him, nodded.

Gorin looked at Greenspan and Stern, at each of the five chapter heads. "There are ninety-four boys," he said, "thirteen years old, some of them twelve and eleven, who have to be killed before they get much older. No," he said, "I'm not kidding. I wish to God I were. Some of them are in England, Rafe; some in Scandinavia, Stig; some of them are here and in Canada; some in Germany. I don't know how we'll get *them*, but we will; we have to. Yakov'll explain who they are and how they . . . came to be." He sat back and gestured toward Liebermann. "In essence," he said. "You don't have to spell out all the details." And to the others: "I vouch for every word he's going to say, and Phil and Paul will vouch too; they've *seen* one of them. Go ahead, Yakov."

Liebermann sat looking at the spoon in his tea.

"You're on," Gorin said.

Liebermann looked at him and said hoarsely, "Could we talk in private for a minute?" He cleared his throat.

Gorin looked questioningly at him, and then not questioningly. He took breath in his nostrils, smiled. "Sure," he said, and stood up.

Liebermann took his cane, grasped the table edge, and got up from his chair. He caned a step, and Gorin put a hand on his back and walked with him, saying softly, "I know what you're going to say." They walked away together toward the bandstand with its wedding canopy.

"I know what you're going to say, Yakov."

"*I* don't yet; I'm glad *you* do."

"All right, I'll say it *for* you. 'We shouldn't do it. We should give them a chance. Even the ones who lost their fathers could turn out to be ordinary people.'"

"Not ordinary, I don't think, no. But not Hitlers."

"'So we should be nice warm-hearted old-fashioned Jews and respect their civil rights. And when some of them *do* become Hitlers, why, we'll just let our *children* worry about it. On the way to the gas chambers.'"

Liebermann stopped at the bandstand, turned to Gorin. "Rabbi," he said, "nobody knows what the chances are. Mengele thought they were good, but it was *his project, his ambition.* It could be that *none* will be Hitler, not even if there was a thousand of them. They're boys. No matter what their genes are. Children. How can we kill them? This was *Mengele's* business, killing children. Should it be ours? I don't even—"

"You really astound me."

"Let me finish, please. I don't even think we should have them be watched by their governments, because this will leak out, you can bet your life it will, and bring attention to them, draw to them exactly the kind of meshuganahs who'll *make* them be Hitlers, encourage them. Or even from *inside* a government the meshuganahs could come. The fewer who know, the better."

"Yakov, if *one* becomes Hitler, just *one*—my God, *you* know what we've got!"

"No," Liebermann said. "No. I've been thinking about this for weeks. I say in my talks it takes two things to make it happen again, a new Hitler and social conditions like in the thirties. But that's not true. It takes *three* things: the Hitler, the conditions . . . and the people to *follow* the Hitler."

"*And don't you think he'd find them?*"

"No, not enough of them. I really think people are better and smarter now, not so much thinking their leaders are God. The television makes a big difference. And history, knowing . . . Some he'd find, yes; but no more, I think—I hope—than the pretend-Hitlers we have now, in Germany and South America."

"Well, you've got a hell of a lot more faith in human nature than I do," Gorin said. "Look, Yakov, you can stand here talking till you're blue in the face, you're not going to change my mind on this. We not only have the right to kill them, we have the duty. God didn't make them, Mengele did."

Liebermann stood looking at him, and nodded. "All right," he said. "I thought I'd raise the question."

"You raised it," Gorin said, and gestured toward the table. "Will you explain to them now? We've got a lot of things to work out before we leave."

"My voice is used up for today," Liebermann said. "*You* better explain."

They walked back together toward the table.

"While I'm up," Liebermann said, "is there a men's room?"

"Over there."

Liebermann caned away toward the stairs. Gorin went on to the table and sat down.

Liebermann caned into the men's room—a small one—and into the booth; swung down its doorbolt. He hung his cane on his right wrist, got out his passport case, and took the folded-small list from it. He put the case back in his jacket, unfolded the list to half sheets, and tore them across; put them together and tore again; put them together and—tore again. He dropped the thickness of small pieces into the toilet, and when the typed-on pieces had separated and settled onto the water, turned down the black handle on the tank. The paper and water swirled and funneled down, gurgling. Pieces of paper stuck to the side of the bowl, pieces came back in the rising water.

He waited for the tank to refill.

As long as he was there, unzipped.

When he came out, he caught the eye of one of the men at the far side of the table and pointed at Gorin. The man spoke to Gorin, and Gorin turned and looked at him. He beckoned. Gorin sat for a moment, and got up and came toward him, looking annoyed.

"What now?"

"You should brace yourself."

"For what?"

"I flushed the list down the toilet."

Gorin looked at him.

He nodded. "It's the right thing to do," he said. "Believe me."

Gorin stared at him, white-faced.

"I feel funny telling a Rabbi what's—"

"*It wasn't your list,*" Gorin said. "It was . . . everybody's! The Jewish People's!"

Liebermann said, "Could I take a vote? It was only me in there." He shook his head. "Killing children, *any* children—it's wrong."

Gorin's face reddened; his nostrils flared, his brown eyes burned, dark-ringed. "Don't you tell me what's right and wrong," he said. "You asshole. You stupid ignorant old *fart!*"

Liebermann stared at him.

"I ought to throw you down these stairs!"

"Touch me and I'll break your neck," Liebermann said.

Gorin pulled in breath; his fists clenched at his sides. "*It's Jews like you,*" he said, "*that let it happen last time.*"

Liebermann looked at him. "Jews didn't 'let' it happen," he said. "Nazis *made* it happen. People who would even kill children to get what they wanted."

Gorin's reddened jaw clenched. "Get out of here," he said. And wheeled and stalked away.

Liebermann watched him go, drew a breath, and turned to the stairs. He took hold of the banister and started caning himself slowly downward, a step at a time.

Through the cab window, coming into Kennedy Airport, he saw Howard Johnson's Motor Lodge. Where Frieda Maloney had given the babies to the U.S. and Canadian couples. He watched it swing past, its ten or twelve stories floodlighted in the dusk . . .

After he had checked in at Pan Am, he called Mr. Goldwasser at the lecture bureau.

"Hello! How are you? Where are you?"

"At Kennedy, going home. And not so bad. I only have to take it easy a few months. Did you get my note?"

"Yes."

"Thanks again. Beautiful flowers. That was some publicity, yes? Front page of the *Times;* CBS, the whole network . . ."

"I hope you never get such publicity again."

"Still, it was publicity. Listen, if I give you my solemn word of honor I wouldn't cancel out, would you want to try booking me in the late spring, early fall? My voice will be back to normal; the doctor swears."

"Well . . ."

"Come on; so many flowers, you're interested."

"All right, I'll sound out a few groups."

"Good. And listen, Mr. Goldwasser—"

"Will you call me Ben, for God's sake! How many years has it *been* already?"

"Ben—not the temples and Hadassahs. The colleges and kids. High schools even."

"They don't pay bupkes."

"Colleges, then. Y.M.C.A.'s. Wherever they're young."

"I'll try to lay out a balanced tour, all right?"

"All right. Fill the holes with high schools. Let me hear. Be well."

He hung up and put his finger in the coin-return; picked up his briefcase and caned himself toward the boarding gate.

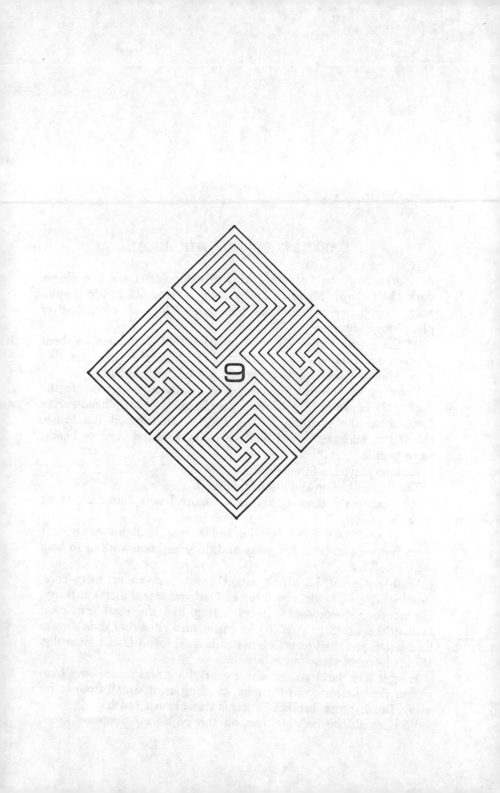

DARKNESS RINGED THE ROOM.

A doorknob glinted, a mirror, tips of ski poles. Dark bed shape, dark chair shape. Metal rim of a cage; a treadmill inside it spinning, stopping, spinning. Rocket models. Wings of a small silver plane slowly turning.

At the room's center, flat whiteness lay tabled under a low-bent lamp. A hand dipped a brush, thinned it, black-inked over penciled lines. Making a stadium: vast, transparent-domed, circular.

The boy worked carefully, bending his sharp nose close to the paper. He began putting in some people, rows of little head-curves focused on the platform in the middle. He dipped the brush, thinned it, backhanded his forelock aside, brushed in more heads, more people.

A piano played: a Strauss waltz.

The boy looked up and listened. Smiled.

He bent to the drawing and made more heads, humming along with the melody.

Great with Dad gone. Just he and Mom. No fighting, no door thrown open and "Put that away and do your homework or so help me God—"

Well, not *great*, he hadn't meant *great;* just—easier, more comfortable. Even Grandma used to say Dad was a real dictator. Bossy, big-mouthed, prejudiced; always acting like the most important man in the world . . . So it was easier now. But that didn't mean he'd hated him, had *wanted* him dead. He'd loved Dad a lot really. Hadn't he cried at the funeral?

He got into the drawing, where everything was nicer. Gave himself to the platform, and the man standing on it. Small from so far away. Brush, brush, brush. Lift up his arms: brush, brush.

Who would he be, this man on the platform? Someone great,

G

that's for sure, with all these people coming to see him. Not just a singer or comedian; someone fantastic, a *really good* person that they loved and respected. They paid fortunes to get in, and if they couldn't pay, he let them in free. Someone that nice . . .

He put a little television camera up at the top of the dome; aimed a few more spotlights at the man.

He thinned the brush to a real fine point and gave little dot-mouths to the nearer bigger people, so they were cheering, telling him—the man, that is—how good he was, how much they loved him.

He bent his sharp nose closer to the paper and gave dot-mouths to the smaller people. His forelock fell. He bit his lip, squinted his deep blue eyes. Dot, dot, dot. He could hear the people cheering, roaring; a beautiful growing love-thunder that built and built, and then pounded, pounded, pounded, pounded.

Sort of like in those old Hitler movies.